BETTER THAN BULLETS:
THE COMPLETE ADVENTURES OF
THIBAUT CORDAY AND THE
FOREIGN LEGION, VOLUME 1

BETTER THAN BULLETS:
The Complete Adventures of Thibaut Corday and the
FOREIGN LEGION
VOLUME I

BY
THEODORE ROSCOE

INTRODUCTION BY
GERD PIRCHER

ALTUS PRESS

BOSTON · 2012

EDITED AND DESIGNED BY

Matthew Moring

PUBLISHING HISTORY

"Introduction" appears here for the first time. Copyright © 2012 by Gerd Pircher. All Rights Reserved.

"Better Than Bullets" originally appeared in the September 14, 1929 issue of *Argosy All-Story Weekly* (Volume 206, Number 4). Copyright © 1929 by The Frank A. Munsey Company. Copyright renewed © 1956 and assigned to Argosy Communications, Inc. All Rights Reserved.

"The Dance of the Seven Veils" originally appeared in the October 19, 1929 issue of *Argosy* (Volume 207, Number 3). Copyright © 1929 by The Frank A. Munsey Company. Copyright renewed © 1956 and assigned to Argosy Communications, Inc. All Rights Reserved.

"An Eye for an Eye" originally appeared in the January 18, 1930 issue of *Argosy* (Volume 209, Number 4). Copyright © 1930 by The Frank A. Munsey Company. Copyright renewed © 1957 and assigned to Argosy Communications, Inc. All Rights Reserved.

"The Death Watch" originally appeared in the May 3, 1930 issue of *Argosy* (Volume 212, Number 1). Copyright © 1930 by The Frank A. Munsey Company. Copyright renewed © 1957 and assigned to Argosy Communications, Inc. All Rights Reserved.

"The Bearded Slayer" originally appeared in the April 11 & 18, 1931 issues of *Argosy* (Volume 220, Numbers 2 & 3). Copyright © 1931 by The Frank A. Munsey Company. Copyright renewed © 1958 and assigned to Argosy Communications, Inc. All Rights Reserved.

"The Mutineer" originally appeared in the September 3, 1932 issue of *Argosy* (Volume 232, Number 3). Copyright © 1932 by The Frank A. Munsey Company. Copyright renewed © 1959 and assigned to Argosy Communications, Inc. All Rights Reserved.

"The Men Who Make the Argosy" originally appeared in the January 18, 1930 issue of *Argosy* (Volume 209, Number 4). Copyright © 1930 by The Frank A. Munsey Company. Copyright renewed © 1957 and assigned to Argosy Communications, Inc. All Rights Reserved.

Published by arrangement with Argosy Communications, Inc.

THANKS TO

Joel Frieman, Walker Martin, Audrey Parente, Gerd Pircher, Rick Ollerman & John Wagner

TABLE OF CONTENTS

GERD PIRCHER

Ah la la la, that beautiful story,
Up on the walls of the bastion,
In the sun glides glory
In the wind flutters a flag,
The beautiful flag of the legion!

Ah la la la, that beautiful story,
Fluttering in the wind on the bastion
And riddled with holes like a skimmer,
The flag still stands,
The beautiful flag of the legion!

(Raymond Asso, *La fanion de la légion*, 1936)

BLAZING SUN... burning sands... march or die... a relief column of legionnaires arrives at a remote desert fort—a square gray block of high, thick mud walls, flat castellated roof, flanking towers, and lofty look-out platform, each embrasure of the parapet manned by a soldier, looking out with leveled rifle... silent, motionless... "not one of them saluted, not one of them answered, not one of them stirred...."

With this well-known scene opens *Beau Geste,* the classic story of the French Foreign Legion. Written by Percival Christopher Wren in 1924, the tale about three orphaned brothers, a missing sapphire, a sadistic sergeant and the desperate struggle in a besieged fort wasn't the first book on this subject—Wren's own *The Wages of Virtue* and *Stepsons of France, A Soldier of the Legion* by C.N. and A.M. Williamson and others predate it by a few years—but the success of this exotic and romantic adventure marked the breakthrough of Foreign Legion fiction in popular culture of the 20th century's twenties and thirties.

Obviously, the audience was attracted by the idea that men who were either wrongly accused of a crime, lost their honor or fled the memory of an unhappy love affair find refuge in this "Army of the Damned" amidst filthy scoundrels, petty thieves, escaped murderers and brutal mercenaries to prove themselves under the most extreme conditions.

P.C. Wren went on to write more books on the Legion, maintaining this romantic view he continued with further stories about the Geste brothers and their friends in *Beau Sabreur, Beau Ideal, Good Gestes* and *Spanish Maine* and created characters like the naive, but stubbornly and courageous Otho Bellême (*Soldiers of Misfortune, Valiant Dust*) or Sinclair Noel Brodie Dysart who after several adventures at sea (*Action and Passion*), in North Africa and Arabia (*Sinbad the Soldier*) ends up in the Foreign Legion on a dangerous assignment in Indochina (*The Fort in the Jungle*).

It was not long before the movies picked up this topic, well known examples being the first two versions of *Beau Geste*—the silent film of 1926 with Ronald Colman and the 1939 picture with Gary Cooper—and Josef von Sternberg's *Morocco* (1930), starring Gary Cooper and Marlene Dietrich. The 1933 movie serial *The Three Musketeers,* featuring a young John Wayne, transferred the story by Alexandre Dumas very loosely to the deserts of a contemporary North Africa. And Stan Laurel and Oliver Hardy joined—out of unrequited love—the Legion twice, in *Beau Hunks* (1931) and *The Flying Deuces* (1939), as did Charley Chase in *Arabian Tights* (1933) and The Three Stooges in *Wee Wee Monsieur* (1939), all playing it for laughs.

Even comic strip and animated cartoon characters put on the famous white *képi* in these years—Warner Brothers' Buddy (*Buddy of the Legion,* 1935) and Porky Pig (*Ali-Baba Bound,* 1940); Ham Fisher's Joe Palooka in the dailies from March 18 to July 28, 1938; above all Walt Disney's Mickey Mouse, on a secret mission in French Northern Africa from March 21 to August 8, 1936, beautifully drawn by Floyd Gottfredson.

But the real playground for Foreign Legion stories was to be found in the pages of the pulp magazines from the mid-twenties to the early forties. Countless Legion novellas, novelettes and short stories were published in the likes of *Adventure, Argosy, Blue Book, Short Stories, Action Stories* and *Frontier Stories*. Prolific pulp writers who specialized on the Foreign Legion were John D. Newsom and Georges Surdez, the latter's works include the novel *The Demon Caravan* which was later filmed as *The Desert Legion*. Robert Carse and F.V.W. Mason were other talented pulp hacks who turned out some Legion fiction. In the early thirties Mason tried to establish a Foreign Legion serial character in *Argosy* with his Sergeant Lemuel Frost, but only about three stories were published.

It was Theodore Roscoe, one of the best writers at *Argosy,* who succeeded in this aim—his Legion veteran Old Thibaut Corday ran for twenty-one stories and ten years from 1929 to 1939. The popularity of Thibaut Corday can be seen from the fact that nine out of approximately thirty-five *Argosy* covers which show a Legion scene depict one of his yarns.

Theodore "Ted" Roscoe was born in Rochester, New York, on February 20, 1906. After high school he worked in several jobs and attended some creative writing courses before he was able to sell his first two western pieces to *North-West Stories* and *Action Stories* in late 1926. His first regularly published series about the adventurer Peter Scarlet appeared in *Action Stories* in 1927. From 1928 on Roscoe added more and more pulp magazines to his clientele—*Air Stories, Fight Stories, Wings, Adventure, Far East Adventure Stories, Danger Trail, Weird Tales* and last, but not least, *Argosy.*

In 1928/29 Roscoe traveled to the Caribbean, Europe and North Africa—there he visited Casablanca, Algiers and Biskra in the Sahara Desert, encountered Legion officers and veterans "with magnificent whiskers and medals," and brought back a *képi* which he kept "near the inkwell" while writing (as he, many years later, stated in a letter)—and in the following years to Central and South America. These travels undoubtedly inspired him to his writings, in particular the voodoo tales and his numerous Foreign Legion stories.

Other noteworthy pulp series by Roscoe are the "East of Suez" adventures and the little crime stories of the American hometown "Four Corners."

Roscoe eventually left the pulp world in the forties, first writing accounts of unresolved true crimes for William Randolph Hearst's *The American Weekly* and then turning to non-fiction about dramatic moments in American history and navy operations in World War II.

Theodore Roscoe died in 1992 in Florida, aged 86.

Roscoe's pulp work—the "Old Thibaut Corday" series ranking among his best—usually consists of bizarre adventures and mysteries in a very unique style, with more turns and twists than a roller coaster and done in a rich and colorful vocabulary. Once, reading an ordinary pulp story was compared to "reading in black and white," reading a story by Roscoe however as to "reading in technicolor."

And all this is particularly true for Old Thibaut Corday—you will not only read about the glistening, shimmering heat of the Moroccan and Tunisian deserts, the stinking, steaming jungles of Dahomey and Senegal, the crowded troopships in the Red Sea, the fierce fighting with howling hordes of black savages and fanatical Muslim warriors, you will see, hear, smell and feel it!

But this doesn't mean at all that Roscoe's descriptions of life in the Legion are accurate and truthful—a good storyteller always succeeds in giving the *appearance* of reality.

So expect neither classic straight forward action stories nor serious narratives, because Old Thibaut Corday, an eighty plus year old veteran of France's most famous colonial unit, bald-headed and cinnamon-bearded, is a born yarn-spinner, an exaggerating Munchausen or, as the people at *Argosy* christened him, the "Bearded Sheherezade of the Legion."

The old legionnaire usually resides in a café on the Boulevard Sidi Carnot in Algiers when suddenly an offhand remark, a newspaper article, a poster on the wall or something similar triggers his memory and he starts to tell a strange tale—a very strange tale—from his past days before, during and after the Great War.

But no matter how fantastic and sensational these "tall tales" may be, at the end Old Thibaut Corday always amazes his astonished listeners with a rational explanation.

In his Corday yarns, Theodore Roscoe often and deliberately reverts to classic motifs and themes—more or less instantly recognizable are parodies of fairy tales, ancient myths and even biblical stories including "the greatest story in the world." A certain scene from *Beau Geste* should not be missed too which the writer recycles at the core of one of his tales.

Naturally not all of the twenty-one stories are on the same level of quality but a few of them surely compete with other masterpieces of pulp fiction—issuing a judgment in this regard is always a question of subjective taste, though.

In "The Bearded Slayer," a claustrophobic hunt for an unseen murderer who spreads fear and terror in an ancient fort goes on with increasing tension. The riotous absurdity of "Monkey See, Monkey Do," Roscoe's own favorite story among the Cordays, is hard to beat. "Red-Headed Dancing Girl" provides a murder story and exciting courtroom drama, set in the deepest African jungle. Both "The Devil Who Played God" and "Jacques the Giantess Killer" show the power of love although presented in a very different fashion, one tragically, the other humorously. "The Man Who Lost His Head" features men getting more and more lunatic up to a murderous final showdown—an intense, almost frightening read, but funny too! The same goes for "The Heads of Sergeant Baptiste" when a Legion company on the march in Senegal—land of the headhunters—is haunted by a murdered sergeant. And there's the incredibly gripping "Snake-Head" with its superb solution. Or "Corday and the Seven League Boots"—a hilarious psychedelic *tour de force* of surreal madness!

But now it's time for you to turn the page and meet *le légionnaire ancienne* Thibaut Corday and his *copains* Yankee Bill the Elephant and Christianity Jensen the Dane....

Gerd Pircher
April 2012

BETTER THAN BULLETS

THIBAUT CORDAY, PRIDE OF THE FOREIGN LEGION, HAD BEEN IN TIGHT PLACES; BUT NEVER DID HE FIGHT A STRANGER OR GRIMMER BATTLE THAN THAT DAY IN MOROCCO WHEN—

"**B**ULLETS?" **CHUCKLED** old Thibaut Corday, stroking bent fingers down the affluent burst of whiskers that still retained their cinnamon for all his fourscore years. "You say, my American friends, that bullets are the best of weapons? But yes, perhaps. And with bullets I am a man the most familiar. *Dieu,* yes! I know them backward and forward and sidewise, and have had three of them in my hip and one in my throat at the same time. I have fired a million of them; fired them until the butt of my Lebel slammed my shoulder into paralysis and the gun barrel blistered my hands. Yes, I know them. Splendid for the fight. But then—I recall a battle I fought in which I used never a blade or a single bullet. Truly, that was a battle. Two companions and I against a yowling heathen gang that was provided with bullets enough to drill a fortress into sponge. And we—the three of us—we three with not a knife or a bullet among us. And what a battle we gave the enemy! No soldiers ever fought with weapons more strange!"

He jabbed a cigarette—one of those camel's hair infamies smoked only in Algeria, thank heavens—into the bush on his face. His old eyes became merry little blue stones couched in the leather and mahogany cheeks; they blinked behind a purling nimbus of gray and gaseous smoke. We listened, for that was wise when old Thibaut Corday consented to talk.

Bullets! Weapons! Fights! Those subjects he knew, perhaps, better than any living man. A veteran warrior, Thibaut Corday. He had been soldier of fortune for more than half a century. Fought in America with a New Orleans regiment for the Lost Cause. Fought with the armies of Britain, Holland, and Imperial Spain. Fought with the Foreign Legion of his own land, from Tonkin to Madagascar, Kotonu to Haiphong. Weapons and battles? This ancient warrior knew them, all right.

"Truly," he repeated, "no soldiers ever fought with weapons more strange than the ones we used in that battle. I have spent a lifetime soldiering, my friends. A lifetime at wars. And *Sacré Nom!* That one, that battle in Morocco, waged on my side without blade or a single bullet, was the strangest, grimmest battle I ever fought. And the funniest!"

He snorted a laugh, and waved his scarred old hands at the twilight slanting across the quiet bay and enameling red the water and mole of the corsairs and curtaining with soft mauve dusk the café on Boulevard Sidi Carnot, where we sat. There was a Holland-Amerika liner down at the big pier, and a busy crowd moved along the ramp. But we forgot the city of Algiers as we watched the twiglike hands a-gesture, listened to the voice from the cinnamon bush, and saw the strangest, grimmest battle that old warrior had ever fought. And the funniest.

IT was in 1907, he began, and I was in the Foreign Legion in Morocco, down near Casablanca. Uncle of Satan! but the country was one bad place for white faces to be. Abd-el-Aziz, the young Sultan, had let the country fall into the savage fingers of that brigand Bou Hamara, and the whole land was on fire with war. The Legion had pushed down along the coast from Rabat after a world of hard fighting against the Moorish tribes, and we got into Casablanca just after our French gunboats had shelled the town into a rubbish heap.

Our officers camped us on the edge of the town, and we were one glad regiment to drop on our blankets. *Mais oui!* It had been a hard march down there. Bad water, no wine, and food that the devil himself would have not touched. Every Legionnaire was dropping with hunger and fatigue, and for a *bidon* of red wine we would have sold our souls to the devil! We would have given them away. We were one sorry lot.

It was late afternoon when my corps dropped our packs in a dusty field, and the sergeant told the men they could scramble for themselves if they wished; but by no means were the Legionnaires to go into the town. The town was still smoldering from the bombardment. We could see brown smoke clinging over the shattered roof tops of the Moorish houses, and the place looked like a tomb and stank with powder. *Oui!* That town was one ugly scar on the coast, but much of its northern quarter was still standing, and the houses up there looked

The three Legionnaires ducked through the
tall grain like schoolboys playing a game.

white and cool and there were olive trees.

We had no water and not a drop of wine, and there was that clump of abandoned houses up on the slope. And we were hungry! A soldier of the Legion is always hungry, and he thirsts like no other man on earth.

And how we hungered and thirsted by the time we had pitched our camp and policed that field and finished the thrice-damned million odd jobs a Legionnaire must do in the making of camp! Tins of *singe*—"monkey"—which is old boot heels ground into plaster—and canteens of warm water were finally given us, but warm water and ground boot heels make food for no honest men. The stomach was knotting under my belt and my throat had dried to sand when that camp was made, and my companions had all but withered away.

"I ain't fer standin' fer it!" announced my partner as he squatted beside me on our blankets. He was a big Yankee, that fellow, from New York City, and he was an iron one. A giant made of bronze with a great black stack of hair and the brightest blue eyes ever seen and tremendous hands that could have twisted a foot from a leg. Yankee Bill the Elephant, we called him. *Pardieu!* but he was a tough one. He had been once a baseball player and the muscles on his arms kept splitting the sleeve of his *capote*. And his big hands, I say! Uncle of

Satan!

There was a story in Bel Abbes about his bending the barrel of a Spanish Mauser. He had grabbed my wrist in anger once, and I believed that tale! But yes, Yankee Bill the Elephant was never the child to stand for anything unfair. You see, all the time we had been marching to Casablanca we had been planning what a gay party we would have getting into the town. And now the commandant's order keeping us in camp and forbidding us to go near the town was a hard one to swallow. Made doubly hard because a troop of black Tirailleurs had been allowed to forage all afternoon.

"I AIN'T standin' fer it," Yankee Bill the Elephant kept insisting to me. "There's those black devils allowed to go in an' grab all th' food an' drinks they can find, an' here we got to eat this canned willy for the next ten days. By golly, old pard, I'm goin' to do somethin' about it. You bet. Are you with me on a little stunt, pard?"

"Sure, pard," I agreed in the language I had learned while fighting in the States. There I had learned what splendid plans these Americans could devise, for I fought with your South at that time, and there was something happening all the time—some of the most surprising plans. And if my giant partner had a plan that would ease my parched soul and moaning stomach, I was one *salopard* if I would not aid him. "What is your 'stunt,' my Elephant? If it has to do with food I am enlisted at once."

Yankee Bill laughed, told me to wait a moment, and ducked from the tent. A few minutes later he returned with Christian Jensen at his heels. This Dane, Christian Jensen, was one little package of sin and dynamite. Little and made of copper wire he was, with eyes that blinked from a too-constant staring at infamy, a bright grin that fairly glowed when he was mad, and at head of the reddest hair out of hell. My partner could have chosen no better a companion for any scheme and in two seconds the three of us had our heads together while Yankee Bill the Elephant hatched an idea.

After all, it was the simplest of plans. The easiest project in the world. We would stroll over to a wheat field that bordered the camp on its eastern edge, crawl off through the grain, circle the smashed Moorish quarter of the town, and end up in that cluster of little white houses and olive trees and shade. Assuredly we would find something worth eating, drinking, and taking away in those abandoned houses. We could scuttle back before the bugle blew for the roll-call, and nobody but the Angel Gabriel could be the wiser.

"Why," exclaimed Yankee Bill the Elephant, "it's so easy it's foolish. We just promises that sentry over there a good whack o' food when we gets back, an' he lets us off into the grain. Once we get among them olive groves we're safe as canaries in a nest, see? We runs up to them houses, loads our pockets an' dashes back. We got just three hours. Are you hyenas with me?"

He pointed at the whispering yellow wheat that lay like a moving sea between our camping ground and the olive trees hedging the town. "We ducks off in there. Of course we got to go unarmed. It'd look suspicious for us to go get our Lebels from the stack. Besides, we don't need no arms. From the looks of it they ain't a livin' soul in that quarter of the town. Are you *salopards* coming?"

Christian Jensen and I were coming. We clasped the plan of Yankee Bill to our dry bosoms as if we had never heard of the guard house where we were sure to groan if we were caught. Hitching into our *capotes*, the three of us strolled from the tent over to the wheat. As the Yankee had declared, it was so easy it was foolish. A whispered word to the poor devil mounting guard and we had his mouth hanging open for the choice morsels we promised him on our return. Then we were ducking away through the tall grain like schoolboys playing a game.

It did not take us long to reach the olive groves and the abandoned white houses. We chuckled like children as we crept through the trees and strolled into an open garden bright with colorful Moroccan flowers. *Mon Dieu!* We were a thousand miles away from the war when we stepped into that garden among the olive trees. There was a quaint, box-square house with a flat roof sitting across the garden, and the blank-faced plaster walls were cool and nice as music in the dusk. Yankee Bill, the Dane and I—three ragged, starving Legionnaires in dusty *capotes*—stared at that house and chuckled. Yankee Bill set his *képi* at a swashbuckling angle on his head. Christian Jensen's Danish face split in a joyous grin. Like three merry pirates we crossed the garden and pushed through the arched Moorish doorway.

THE house was of typical Moorish design. The outer door opened on a hall leading to a little square patio around which the house was built. A little courtyard that dreamed with the scent of orange trees. *Sacré Nom!* Was like stepping through the golden gates into Paradise. We stood there grinning like monkeys and panting out cheerful oaths.

That court was a lovely place, and if the other houses we intended to forage were going to be as pleasant our trip was going to be a happy one.

Across the court a flight of stone steps led to a balcony where we were delighted to see a door opening into the house. The three of us were about to dart up the steps when a sound beneath them halted our intent. Stooping, the Yankee opened a little door beneath the stairway. And a pair of swart little pigs darted out between our legs, escaping from their pen.

Only the Yankee could have caught them. The little animals ran fast as rats. But they could not elude Yankee Bill the Elephant. Not that prize. He trapped them in a corner of the court; came gasping back to us with a pig squeaking under each arm. No more starving, now. The Dane, the Yankee and I went up those steps with a will— Yankee Bill carrying his pigs and telling what juicy chops they would make. We went up those steps and plunged into a cool, dusky room hung with Arab rugs and Spanish shawls and European pictures.

"Every man for himself," laughed Yankee Bill the Elephant. "I reckon they ain't a soul left in this place. Musta cleared out when the shells started to pop. Nice house, this. Europeans livin' here. We'll take a look around. Wait'll I tie up our Sunday dinner." Catching a shawl from the wall, he bound the pigs up and set them near the door. Those poor little pigs! They looked like old ladies at the Opera Comique with their black and white hides wrapped in that shawl. Then Yankee Bill was shouting once more.

"Quick! Look! Am I dreamin', pards, or what do I see in that farthest corner, there? Whoops! How about it, Corday, old *cochon!* How about it, Christianity! Look at that!"

We looked. Aunt of the Devil! how we looked. Yankee Bill's eyes sparkled like tiny fires, and the Dane was staring as if he had found the pot of gold which fools think does not lie at the end of the rainbow. They should have been there in that room with us to see what we saw. Yankee Bill the Elephant was counting in an awed, religious voice: "Six—eight—thirteen—fifteen. Fifteen! Wow, you willy-eating devils of the Legion of the Damned! Fifteen! That makes five apiece! Whoops!" You know how a Yankee can yell "whoops!"

We yelled, too. Fifteen bottles of nice, ruby-red wine. Five bottles for each of us. We laughed. We wept. We grabbed hands and danced around the little pyre of shining glass. The Dane lost control and grabbed the first one. Yankee Bill and I snatched up one. We cracked off the necks with that little gesture executed with so much grace, so much dexterity by Legionnaires. Cross-legged, like Arab tailors, we sat down in the very middle of the floor and honored our long-insulted throats. The Dane got his second bottle. I grabbed mine, and Yankee Bill the Elephant got his.

Christian Jensen then started to croon the excellent chorus of *La Casquette du Père Bugeaud.* Can you see us? Can you see us sitting there, our sunburned faces illuminated, ruby-red bottles waving in our fists, moist voices softly humming that jolly little Legion tune about Father Bugeaud and his silly sun helmet? No party of artists in Montparnasse could have been more exalted. Five bottles apiece!

It was a gay hour for us, and that is never a lie. Only, it was a gay three hours. We did not realize it until our last bottle finished the pyramid of emptied ones; and the Dane suddenly pointed out a big, round yellow moon rolling past our open roof. Yankee Bill the Elephant lurched to his feet with a genial oath, and made for the door that opened on the balcony over the patio.

Spang!

There was a shot, you understand, and the good Yankee's *képi* went sailing from his head.

HAVE you ever looked down on a courtyard yellow under the moon and seen it suddenly fill with a howling, rampant mob of demons bristling with knives and guns and lusting for blood? Have you ever heard those soulless, shrill yells that saw out through a Moslem's black teeth? Yells grimmer and bloodier than the curse of Cain? A sight to see and a sound to hear that will melt the spine of a stone image.

And the three of us in that room up there were not stone images. *Non!* Soldiers of the Foreign Legion may not look it, but they are flesh and blood. And they make splendid toys with which a Moslem gang may be entertained. What entertainment! No white man ever wants to fall in the hands of an Oriental enemy. Ideals are not known to the Oriental. Ideas are. They have a lot of them—such as cutting off a captive's eyelids, snipping off his hands, roasting his bare heels over a slow fire, or tying mad mice on his stomach, and putting a heated bowl over the rodents so they will burrow in. *Dieu!* Those Moslems are not generous captors. They are not! And now they were spilling like a flood of dirty water into the courtyard, torturing the shadows with their savage yells.

The yellow moonlight gleamed on a score of brandished blades;

shone like dull gold on the barrels of twenty rifles; glistened on the brown faces that snarled under their shaggy wigs and bobbing turbans. Yankee Bill the Elephant hopped backward after his *képi*, and let out a curse that heaven must have blushed to hear. Christian Jensen and I bobbed to our feet like jumping-jacks. As the Yankee flung shut that balcony door a rain of bullets knocked for entry on the wood.

The face of Yankee Bill had gone white as newly-milled flour. His big hands fluttered up and down his chest. Christian Jensen was grinning fearfully; and I do not know what I did. One thing was certain. We had been on the edge of a peaceful doze, for while five quarts of wine may mean nothing to a Legionnaire who has a stomach of rhino-hide, it certainly warms his pulse. But right at that instant we were sober and cold-blooded as icicles. *C'est ça!* We were sober. Aunt of the Devil, how sober we were!

"Christmas! Jumping Christmas!" gasped Yankee Bill the Elephant. Only he did not say Christmas. "The whole army o' Bou Hamara must be down below. Listen t' that riot! Wow! An' we ain't got a gun nor a knife between us!" And he went on to exclaim.

I, myself, managed to think up a few passionate remarks; and Christian Jensen, the Dane, howled: "Blessed Saint Boniface! We are unarmed! Rats in a trap! Rats in a trap!"

"We ain't rats in a trap!" bellowed Yankee Bill. "We're three men in a trap. But," he yelled, "we ain't caught yet! We—"

Bullets drummed like a fury of rain against the door. Then the lead stopped beating. We heard a commotion, and knew the Moslem demons were coming up the stairway to the balcony. I fled to a slit of window that looked out on the balcony; and saw those savage, snarling devils moving up the steps. Those stairs were not very wide, and they climbed single file. Came on warily.

From their trappings and beard-dye I recognized them, and went sick to the pit of my soul. I had seen such men before. Moslem dervishes of the Aissaoua sect, one of the most terrible holy orders in Africa. Fanatical demons who yearned from the bottom of their hearts to kill an Unbeliever. If they could finish off their Unbeliever in a slow and painful way, so much the better. And if they died in an attempt to kill or catch the Unbeliever, Mohammed would jerk them into the front seats of Paradise, pin them with medals, and let them dance with the pick of those heavenly ladies who live in hollow pearls up there. So they were brave, those Moroccan Aissaoua dogs, because they could not lose. Fanatical to insanity. Cruel. *Sacré Nom!*

I WENT sadly sick as I saw them mount the stairs. In the meantime, Yankee Bill had ordered the Dane to lean against the bolted door while he dashed around looking for another exit. He bounced into at little dark room behind the one where we stood; came back yelling that it was empty and had no further door. He said there was something or other in there but I did not hear him very well because those Moslem screams for blood were too unhappily loud in my ears. They were almost on the balcony.

I was sweating like sin then, and instinctively got away from that slit of window. Yankee Bill the Elephant was swearing a long, lurid stream. Hunched against the door, Christian Jensen was grinning like a stark fool. I think we were all seeing a picture of ourselves waltzing over a toasting fire; or groaning, up to our necks in hot sand while warrior ants countermarched down our shaved heads. The Aissaoua Moslems were famous for such pleasant parties.

"Wait," shouted Yankee Bill. "Listen, you two *salopards*. We're Legionnaires. Ain't one of us who hasn't been in a worse hole than this!" (That big Yankee Bill the Elephant lied, and he knew it. We had been in terrible holes, but never one more terrible than this. Yet it was nice to hear him lie. That giant partner of mine was a warrior if there ever was one.) "We're gonna get out of here. Fight our way clear. Get away from that door, Christianity. Listen. Fast! Grab a bottle. There's five for each of us. An' there's only twenty of those dogs outside—"

Bottles! Empty wine bottles! *Pardieu!* they were better than nothing. At once the big American became our general. The Dane bobbed over to the bottle-pile, and me after him. Yankee Bill had one in each big fist. Quick as a cat, he threw open the door.

The first Moslem had just gained the top step, I caught a fleet picture of him there. A mere eye-flicker like one might see if a cinema camera suddenly threw a photograph on a screen. The open door was the camera-shutter. The huge, yellow moon, round as a franc, made the screen against which stood a big skinny demon who had just been kicked out of hell for being too wicked.

His hair, ragged as a bird nest, stuck out under a bulbous turban wound with camel's-hair cord. His face was a mask that might have been worn by a devil-dancer in Cambodia. Two wild, wild eyes. Black fangs hanging over drooling lips. And his rotten carcass was hung with a ragged brown *djeelaba* spotted with blood and grime.

I think he was too surprised to croak when the door swung open and he caught sight of Yankee Bill the Elephant's huge frame. I think he was too surprised to lift his long-barreled Arab rifle.

And that Moslem devil was going to be even more surprised. For the big Yankee's arm coiled and uncoiled like a monstrous thick snake. His huge right hand whipped out fast. He had been holding that glass bottle like a grenade. Now he hurled it as they hurl baseballs in America. Like a streak of red light it flashed from his hand, and struck that devil-mask squarely in the nose. There was a fearful shriek! The flung bottle exploded into a trillion pieces like a fragile bomb. Almost knocked that Moslem's rotten head from his neck. His bare heels came up in the air and he flew over backward like a crazy acrobat. Every one on the steps tumbled to the bottom.

Yankee Bill laughed a shout as he slammed shut our door. "Quick! When they start up again, peg a bottle. It's your turn, Christianity. By Gawd, I guess I didn't curve one over the plate—" (I think that was the expression he used) "—that time! That fellow's face won't grin at our torture party. Quick, buddy! Here they come!"

He had the door open, and Christian Jensen threw like a flash. We heard a smart tinkle, a screech, and the clatter of tumbling bodies repeated. The Dane ducked away, and it was my turn.

Baseball is not a game played in France. I could not hurl my bottle as skillfully as Yankee Bill had hurled his. Neither could Christian Jensen. But we had thrown scores of grenades in our day, and the throwing of bottles was not unknown to Legionnaires, either. My giant partner popped open the door. I saw a ducking turban, and let fly. A bullet whistled back at me in return, but did not strike. And my bottle did. There was a smash and another screech.

YANKEE BILL the Elephant began to laugh. His face went red as a new carrot. His shoulders quivered. He had another bottle in his fist, and the Dane opened the door. Two bullets flickered in and the bottle flew out. How it flew! *Dieu!* That giant Yankee had a way of snapping out his arm when he threw things and they went like projectiles from a mounted rifle. Zip and smash and more yells of pain. You see, that big American giant had once been a baseball player, and he knew how to throw.

"I can fast-ball these skunks to a standstill," he chortled. "Quick! More bottles! I'll stop these dogs an' kill the umpire, too. Hey, open the door, Christianity! They're comin' up again. Let's all throw together this time. Watch out for their guns. Here goes!"

He swung the door, and we all threw together. It was a splendid game. Our bottles smashed one-two-three. Bullets sped back at us, and the Dane won a scratch across the ear that trip. Yankee Bill took a ball through the crown of his *képi,* and I got one through the sleeve of my *capote.*

Too close to be really good sportsmanship. The Moslems were bound not to play fair. They were wild, those devils. Like a pack of tigers snapping at the kicking heels of a child in a low tree. We heard them shrieking to Allah as we slapped shut our door. Their guns barked angrily, and furious bullets pelted into the wood.

"We got to keep them at the bottom of the steps," our Yankee yelled. "Don't let 'em get up here. I think we've put three of them pretty well into the hospital tent." He waved his third bottle. "Break their lousy heads for them. Smash 'em in the face, if you can. Throw hard!"

"Saint Stephen, I hope they bleed for years," panted the Dane.

"Quick, my braves," I shouted at the door. "They come up. All together, then. Let them feel our wine-wet glass! But now!"

Once more we sent three bottles whistling down those steps. I think the wine had made us brave as lions. We let in a swarm of bullets when we opened the door that time, and we sent out behind our bottles a Legion yell that resounded loud above the crack of their guns. We could see the Moslems floundering, dodging at the foot of the steps; their rifles flashing like red flowers blooming in the powder-smoke that now filled the little courtyard.

"They can't get up! They can't get up!" bellowed Yankee Bill, dancing from one foot to the other. "And what rotten shots they are. Wow! And they think we're playing with them, too.

"They think we have a card up our sleeves, my *salopards.* They are almost afraid to charge. Ho, ho! More bottles! Let them come with their guns and knives! Ho, ho!"

Christian Jensen cursed fluently, scrubbing his torn ear with a fist. "But, the devil! The bottles are almost gone—"

"Your shoes, you dogs!" laughed the Yankee giant. "We'll heave our shoes. A good *brodequin* across the scalp will split a skull. Quick! Off with 'em! We'll give these hounds a lesson in Legion games! Fast!"

Now a Legionnaire boot is made perhaps of elephant hide and studded with tremendous iron nails. Those *brodequins!* Once I had

taken one across the scalp in a merry little Legionnaire brawl in Bel
Abbes. It had buried me in sleep for hours. And how I had cursed
those leaded boots on a long march. But now? Those giant-soled shoes
were gifts from heaven. Little Easter presents. We blessed them to
the good saints as we stooped to yank them from our feet.

And what a funny picture we made, standing there with a boot
dangling from each hand, peeking out of the door. Do you know what
passed through my mind? Do you know what the picture reminded
me of? Three little children sneaking in their bare feet downstairs to
see the hemlock tree on the eve of Noel, the Christmas Eve. Only we
were not staring into a pretty room twinkling with a hemlock tree
and presents. We stared into a yowling courtyard crammed with a
savage gang, and the lights we saw were shooting guns and the
presents were angry bullets.

AND so we hurled the last of our wine bottles; and then six nail-
studded *brodequins* went hurtling down the steps into that savage
gang. We flung our shoes carefully and with precision. First the Dane
would open the door a crack, and Yankee Bill would fling a shoe. He
had dynamite in that right arm of his, did Yankee Bill the Elephant.
The Aissaoua devotees who were hit by him that evening must certainly have doubted the benevolence of an Allah who could allow
such a disaster.

Then the Dane would hurl his bottle or boot, after which I would
fling mine. *Sier Dieu!* if we did not hold that rioting crew of fiends at
the foot of those steps for fully twenty minutes. We laid some of them
flat, too. We saw four of the devils stretched unconscious on the ground
under the orange trees, and three more who bled like stabbed cattle.
Cut noses and broken heads.

But our ammunition supply had been perilously low, if not lower
than that, at the start of the battle. And Christian Jensen had won a
bullet scrape across the left elbow that had him screaming. Finally
our bottles were gone, and we had one shoe left to throw. It was a bad
moment, that. A moment that sapped much of my ambition and
courage. Three Legionnaires caught in a little room offering no means
of escape save a flight of steps occupied by an Aissaoua gang. One
shoe left to throw.

The Moslem devils started up the steps for the tenth time. They
were howling like maniacs, firing a steady tattoo at our door. Yankee
Bill waited grinning until they almost reached the top. Then he flashed

open our door; whipped our last boot. *Pardieu!* He hurled that *brod-equin* with every ounce of muscle in his hide. I imagine that shoe gathered a crowd of bullets to its heart, for it winged out into a swarm of them. They did not slow it a whit, and it struck the leader on the steps with a *smack!* that did things to his ugly face, and flung him down the stairway. The mob behind him went over like nine-pins, screaming. We slammed our door.

"Held 'em again!" the American exulted. "But not for too long. They may have us figured at last. They may not believe we have a card up our cuffs now. So come on, you devils! The Legion still rides on top!" Racing over to a wall, he yanked down a beautiful Spanish shawl. What was the Yankee doing? The Dane and I glared. Had he gone mad? He was winding that silken mantle over his head and shoulders, tugging up the collar of his *capote*. "Hurry!" he bawled. "Get a shawl over your heads. Like this. Fast, there! Be quick!" Now he was tearing strips from another shawl; wrapping the rags around his fists. "Like this!"

"Name of Saint Andrew!" gasped Christian Jensen. "What is—"

"We're going to charge!" shouted Yankee Bill. "Get your skin covered, you *salopards*. Wind a shawl around your face. We want to get out before they start up again. Hurry! Didn't I tell you? The card up our sleeves. We'll charge at 'em, an' throw them bee-hives I found in this other room. Three of 'em. Each carry a hive. We'll rush 'em with those hornets, see? An' we got to break through! Quick! The bees!"

NOW Aunt of the Devil! That giant Yankee Bill had found three little wooden cones filled with bees sitting in a corner of that other room! The owner of the house had hidden them there during the bombardment of the town. What a find! What a prize! What a weapon! But *Sacré Nom de Dieu,* what a desperate weapon to wield! A gun, I swear, that was going to have a most deliberate and unhappy back-fire, if I knew anything about it. But with the wine and Yankee Bill's shouts and the ugly clamor of the Moslems jamming the patio urging us to action, we twined Spanish shawls about our cheeks and hands; followed the Yankee into the other room.

Carefully the giant Yankee picked up a hive. Never have I picked up anything as carefully. Never had I enjoyed as many chills trickling down my spine. You know how you feel when a bee buzzes around your head while you are picking wild flowers in the woods? You know that drilling, monotone drone? There is only one sound in the world as nasty—that is the yelling of Aissaoua fiends forming to rush a stairway.

We picked up those three hives, and ducked for the door. *Sacré Nom!* At the door, Yankee Bill the Elephant flung around, and made for those two pigs he had found in the courtyard. We had forgotten those pigs, had the Dane and I. But not the Yankee. Do you think he was going to leave the pigs behind? But never! The gang in the patio was crying for blood and murder. The bees were getting angry and thinking of murder, too. Our hives were droning like rising wind whipping through a valley. One or two tiny airplanes of battle had already swooped out into the room, ready to signal the fleets and begin war. But Yankee Bill could remember his pigs. He would not abandon his bacon!

He snatched up the squealing animals; ran to the door; flung it wide. Then with those screaming pigs under one arm, that humming bee-hive under the other, he let a wild, most fiendish bellow boom from his shawl-swaddled face, and charged out onto the balcony.

History overflows with famous charges. The Light Brigade, Gibraltar, Waterloo, Delhi, Rome, Gettysburg—mad, gallant charges. Not one of them could have equaled the charge we made down those steps for sheer recklessness, insanity, color and the bizarre. I do not wonder the devils in the patio stood as if bewitched as we rushed at them down the stairway. We must have been a crazy, impossible sight. I would wager ten thousand francs those Aissaoua fiends thought we were three *jinn* loosed from the Caves of Darkness. Demons popped from the Underworld. We looked like nothing else.

Imagine that giant Yankee, his face swathed in a lustrous silk shawl embroidered with lovely scarlet and purple roses, blue and green fringe tossing before his wild eyes, bounding down the steps with two yelling, shawl-wrapped pigs under one arm and a buzzing hive under the other. Followed by two howling madmen similarly bundled in lace and silk, and bounding like grasshoppers, too.

It is no exaggeration to say the three of us were an absinthe drinker's dream. Nor is it an exaggeration to say we moved our bare feet with a speed. We descended quickly, shouting at the tops of our lungs. For the hives we carried had begun to disgorge their contents. Their occupants poured like brown smoke from the little doors. A smoke that stabbed and knifed and buzzed and burned. Uncle of Satan! but those bees were mad.

YOU know the legend of the Spartan boy who carried a fox under his cloak and never whimpered as the animal gnawed his vitals? Believe me, there was a similarity in carrying those hives. Halfway down the steps Yankee Bill hurled his. Then the Dane sent his hive sailing; and I needed no invitation to throw mine away.

Arching downward, those three spouting cones landed squarely in the midst of the astonished throng in the patio. In half a second it was a milling, squalling broil. Arms shot skyward. Turbans dodged and bobbed like corks on troubled water. Those Moslems sent up an outcry that punched holes in the moon as they churned into a frenzied, scrapping tangle mixed by tiny yellow darts that sped and stung.

And the three of us? We kept right on going down. Our weapons *had* back-fired, and those bees barbing our hides added no small impetus to our charge. In half a second we were in the middle of that boiling, yowling, kicking, biting mass. Fighting like inspired fiends.

Yankee Bill the Elephant went stumbling under a gun butt, and his pigs escaped. The frantic beasts had added their piercing squeals to the uproar; now they raced frantically between our legs, voicing ear-splitting screams. May I sweat green if those Moslem devils did not go wild then. "Pig! Pig!" they shrieked. Pigs, yes! And bees!

Howling, fighting, battling to unwind tangled arms and heads and feet, the Moslems poured out of the patio; carried us with them into the garden bordering the house. Dodging this way and that, the frenzied pigs raced under foot. They seemed like a thousand. The moonlight was alive with bees and desperate wails. I was not seeing a great deal. An accursed knife had peeled away a portion of my forehead, and the blood was leaking into my eyes. But I was hitting out at everything, hard, tearing blows inspired by bee stings on the nape of my neck.

I did glimpse Christian Jensen riding on the back of a hairy devil, pounding fists at the bawling head. I caught a glimpse of Yankee Bill the Elephant snatching a rifle from fighting brown hands. My good partner was a sight to behold, for the shawl had been ripped from his face and his cheeks were stung to puffy dough. And I glimpsed the curse-roaring squad of Legionnaires that came pounding toward us through the olive trees, *képis* ducking, Lebels spitting spiteful jets of fire and smoke in the moonlight. *Sacré Nom du Quatorzième Diable!*

AND that was the story (save for an abundance of involved and vitriolic profanity) told by old Thibaut Corday, whose whiskers still retained their cinnamon for all his fourscore years. The strangest, grimmest battle he ever fought. And the funniest. He ended his yarn with a chuckle; fished for one of his poisonous cigarettes.

"A queer battle, eh?" he grinned out through a smoke haze. "There was a funny little aftermath. Of course when those Aissaoua brigands saw the squad of Legionnaires, they turned on their unholy tails and fled. One of them had given Yankee Bill the Elephant a mean cut on the cheek, and that giant American was raging. So he gave chase around the house. *Oui!* And what do you believe, my friends? He came back with that Moslem villain kicking and yelling under one arm, and those two pigs kicking and yelling under the other.

"The captain with the Legionnaires was so pleased. He took the two pigs and the Moslem from Yankee Bill, and he congratulated us on our capture of the leader of that wicked Aissaoua gang. Because we had fought so bravely he would sentence us to only fifteen days on bread, water and hard work in the guard house. A bee stung him on the leg, and he added an extra day. Those bees were stinging that Moslem from head to foot, but he spat out a lot of bad French at us, later on, and do you know what he said? He cursed us, and said he did not mind the bees. Those bees had not routed his gang. But the pigs! A million curses on us for letting those pigs touch him and his men. Pigs! The greatest taboo in that fanatical Mohammedan world. *Sacré cochon!*"

He blinked merrily at us, and cigarette smoke purled out of the cinnamon bush. "Bullets?" he chuckled. "Bullets the best of weapons? Perhaps. But then, my friends, there are bottles and boots and bees and bacon. As good as bullets? Aunt of the Devil! Better!"

THE DANCE OF THE SEVEN VEILS

YANKEE BILL THE ELEPHANT WAS A MAN OF THE LEGION; AND THE WAY OF THE LEGION IS A DEADLY WAY, IN THE BURNING WASTES OF THE SAHARA.

DUSK WAS making subtle magic over the flat rooftops of Biskra. We sat at the little Arab café, old Thibaut Corday and I, watching the legerdemain of tropic twilight. Our table faced the public triangle where Cardinal Lavigerie loomed, imposing in marble, above the hooded heads of a dusky Moslem crowd. Wrapped in mauve shadow, the statue of the famous *Père Blanc* missionary came to life and stalked with vestments fluttering toward the dark heart of Africa, while the Arabs below turned into a murmurous cordon of wraiths.

As we watched, a yellow moon wheeled from behind a fan of date palms into a sky the color of a Spahi's tunic. Cobalt shadows wandered up Rue Berthe; and the moonbeams and shadows called a faint, queer music from the Rue Sainte hard by. Softly on the wings of the dim night came the echo—the whine of flutes timed to the throb of tamtams. The call of the Ouled Naïl, beckoning to the dance.

Old Thibaut Corday cocked his head to catch the tenuous refrain; pushed aside his Amer-Picon bottle; turned to me with a chuckle in his beard that had retained its rusty cinnamon for all his four-score years.

"Those dancers down on Rue Sainte are getting to work. Always they start with the moonrise, and they are on time to-night." Staring out across the triangle, he chuckled in his beard again. "Look, then."

He pointed a finger that years of trigger-pulling had bent into a hook. For the venerable veteran had a trigger-pulling record. He had pulled triggers with Confederates out of New Orleans in the sixties, with the British in the Boer War, with the legions of Spain, Holland, to say nothing of his own beloved *Légion Étrangère.* Not age, but medals had stooped his shoulders; nothing had dimmed the wink of his twinkly blue eyes; and only triggers had crooked his finger.

Now he pointed the hook at the statue of the cardinal. "Look, then," he repeated. "The Arabs move off in a body and leave the good Lavigerie standing alone. Those Arabs hear the music of the dance and immediately turn for Rue Sainte. But notice: the cardinal is not lured by those dancers. A good man, the cardinal. He ignores the music. He does not even turn his head. No Ouled Naïl is making him deviate from his straight and narrow path. He ignores, and keeps on his straight and narrow path to cure the heathen in the Congo."

THIBAUT CORDAY paused, fixed me with an eye like a little blue stone. Another series of chuckles exploded from his cinnamon whiskers and he plugged them back by ramming a stubby pipe into his teeth. Cramming the pipe with what appeared to be monkey fur, he touched a match and exhaled a gaseous whorl of smoke. I anticipated a story behind this purling fog, and I was not to be disappointed. Eyes reminiscent, the old veteran settled back in his chair and flung a smoke bomb and a hand at the statue deserted in the triangle.

"Cardinal Lavigerie was a noble and splendid saint," he said slowly. "For the glory of Africa and France he held bravely to his hard way, even as now he refuses to turn his head for those dancers down on Rue Sainte. But let me tell you something. I once saw a dancer who could have turned the head of the strongest character in the world. *Ma foi!* I have seen my share of dancers, that is so. But never a dancer to equal the one of whom I tell. Never! Never such a dancer, or such a dance!"

He slammed a fist against the table and the Amer-Picon bottle did a waltz. Thus reminded of the bottle, he promptly refreshed his memory with a lusty swig through his fearful brush before going on:

"Never, I say, have I seen another to equal that dancer or that dance! I was with *le deuxième régiment étranger* at the time, and we were fighting on the lip of the Sahara where the Atlas mountains climbed down to have a look over the edge of the universe. Not too far from here, that place was, but about thirteen million miles from anywhere.

"There was a countryman of yours in the story, so it may be of interest to you. And the dancer of whom I tell—name of a pink pig! What a dancer! That dancer could have turned the head of the sternest Puritan in the world; could have turned the marble head of our marble saint out there. You shall hear about this amazing dancer, and the heads that were turned. What a story! But listen—"

THE fight started down at Ahmed ben Addadud's gin dive in Bab Hadoun. A nice little weasel-coop was Ahmed ben Addadud's, full of dancing girls and games to play and things to drink and smoke. You walked through a little blue door into a room crowded with half-caste Arabs and Tirailleurs and riffraff, and Legionnaires from the barracks at the other end of the town. A scrabbling, sweating, babbling crowd was always jamming the place; and the night Yankee Bill the Elephant, Christianity Jensen the Dane, and I went through the little blue door, the place had the aspect of a station crowded with passengers who waited the first train for hell.

"Don't let this nest of rats bother you," Yankee Bill the Elephant advised me. "There's a couple of Kabyle dancers in here worth seeing. Real artistic stuff, I mean. One of the girls is pretty decent. No rough stuff. Got a nice face, an' she hadn't ought to be in here."

So that was why my partner, my giant American *copain* had been vanishing every evening, and this was where he had been coming. I gave the big ox a smile. Yankee Bill the Elephant was nothing but a great big boy dressed in a Legion uniform, after all. A big grinning child with over-developed muscles, and a friendly pair of brilliant blue eyes under a shock of black hair.

Genial and kindly as a summer day with his friends—and every man was his friend until proved otherwise. Then he was a one-man tempest, and not so childish, either.

"These dancers always did fascinate you, Yankee Bill," the Dane chided. "You were always watching them in Sidi. One would never think to look at your so tough face that you were a patron of the arts. I guess not. However, let us see your Kabyle lady." Christianity chuckled.

The little Dane possessed the biggest pair of ears in the Foreign Legion, and he was pointing them at the dancing platform where three Arab musicians were seating themselves with ostentation and making preparatory discord on their instruments. A girl in poppy-colored bloomers and a scarlet shawl stepped to the platform. I will say in the Yankee's defense that she was extraordinarily good-looking for a Kabyle. "Is that the lady?" asked the Dane.

Yankee Bill's mahogany face had split with a grin from ear to ear. Shoving back his *képi* on his head, he elbowed way to a table near the platform; and we three sat down before he answered. "That's her. That's little Zobeid. How about her, Corday, old *cochon?* How about her, Christianity? Ain't she an ace? Listen, you two jealous Legion hounds. Most of these Arab dames expect a man to give them presents, don't they? Well, last night she come to my table, an' said because she liked me an' I'd never tried to bother her she was going to give me a present.

"You oughta seen what she gave me. To carry for luck. I got her present in my knapsack to always carry on the march, an' remember her by. Some present, too!"

"*Sapristi!*" I exclaimed. "But you are always picking up the queerest of souvenirs, my Yankee. What did your friend give you?"

"I'll tell you if you'll promise," he began, "not to—" And then he was on his feet with a roar, knocking over a bottle of wine into my lap, and bringing the whole room to its feet at the same time. I caught the merest glimpse of what it was all about. The dancing girl had moved to the edge of the platform, and some ruffian standing near had grabbed her by the ankle. Now he had a clutch on her wrist, and she was slapping at his face. I heard him laugh as he swung her to the floor, and when he turned around I got a shock. Somewhere I had seen him before.

THE man was a lousy-looking scoundrel, that is so. His skin looked like greasy brass against his white drill suiting. He was thick and medium height, with a face like a decaying melon. I caught sight of a thin-lipped mouth drawn tight in a grin made cruel by a beautiful set of pearly white teeth. A wig of curly, black hair. A handsome, cleft chin. Eyes like evil little raisins set in cups of blood.

The glittery eyes and the white-toothed grin I recognized as the eyes and grin of a man who would enjoy whipping a rabbit. But I got no chance to study that face right then. The ponderous shoulders of Yankee Bill the Elephant blotted out that face; and the next minute my American *copain* had leaped the table and charged.

Ahmed ben Addadud's gin dive screeched and floundered. Tables went over. Bottles smashed. I heard the Kabyle dancing girl give a soprano scream. At my elbow, Christianity Jensen was cursing the masterful oaths of the Legion. Vaguely I saw the giant fist of the giant Yankee Bill whip out through the smoke; and for the first time in my knowledge of it I saw it miss. The white-toothed, evil-eyed melon ducked aside. A black hand sprang up curled about a wicked trench knife. The blade flashed. The *képi* sailed from the head of Yankee Bill as one of his legs collapsed under him. But he was up in a second, and there was a thin river of red enamel leaking down from his left temple to his chin.

"Pull a knife on me, will you?" he was storming. "Try to knife a Legionnaire, eh? You dog, I'll break your face in two!"

"Salopard!" screamed the white-toothed one. "I should cut out your heart—"

Wham! It was Christianity Jensen's service revolver. *Wham! Wham!* The gun in his fist jerked as it spat flame. My numbed mind cleared and caught the little Dane's idea. I grabbed out my weapon, and fired too.

Bam! Wham! Bam! The thundering echoes almost brought down Ahmed ben Addadud's lousy ceiling.

We did some splendid shooting, the two of us. Oil lamps tumbled from the walls as if thrown down by the hand of *le bon Dieu,* and in thirteen seconds we had shot the place into an inky, squalling midnight.

Then we were battling to escape a whirlpool of clawing bodies. Heaven only knows how the Dane and I managed to reach the little blue door on either elbow of that infuriated American, and yank him into a night-hung street. Ahmed ben Addadud's was boiling like a red-hot caldron with shots and whistly shrieks, and it would all have been funny as the devil if the Yankee had not won that gash down his face, and if I had not ripped the sleeve of my *capote,* which would gain me a future visit to the Legions famous *salle de police.*

Nor was Yankee Bill filled with gratitude. Sweat and blood poured from under his *képi* visor as he raged: "If I hadn't seen Zobeid duck safely out of a back door, I'd dive back in there and find that skunk who tried to annoy her. I'd smash his ugly head. Why'd you stop me? Who told you two devils to shoot out those lights? I'd have broke his face—"

"Name of Saint Adrien!" squealed the Dane, clapping a hand over the American's mouth. "Not so loud. Quick! We must get back to the barracks. Do you know who that man was? Bones of Stavengeren! That man is the greatest roué in Africa—Captain Giacomo Roque of the Legion. Of the Foreign Legion, I tell you. And I saw it posted in the barracks this morning that he has come back from furlough. He is to command our company, and to-morrow he leads a detachment out of Bab Hadoun into the Sahara. We can only pray God we are not in that detachment."

No wonder the ears of the little Dane were sticking out like white butterflies poised for flight. Then what do you suppose our Yankee Bill the Elephant had to say?

"I knew him all along," he growled. "A polecat. Boasts the reputation of a heart smasher all over Algeria. Brags about his conquests and how he wins them with those beautiful teeth of his." The American brought up a fist that looked bigger than a smoked ham in the dusk, and chuckled. Yankee Bill had a way of chuckling that could have brought a grin to the face of the Sphinx at Ghizeh—unless he chuckled the way he did just then. That chuckle would have made the Sphinx sweat.

"It was like him to sneak a knife at me. He won't dare come out in the open about this knife play affair of his, but he may try to make my life unhappy. Because we are in his detachment going into the desert to-morrow, you know. I'm glad. Maybe I'll get a chance to whack those teeth out of his head!"

Now, *Sacré Nom de Dieu!*

JUST that—*Sacré Nom de Dieu!* Because I suddenly remembered this Captain Giacomo Roque, and I also knew where he was going to lead our detachment. Captain Giacomo Roque! The Hand of the Devil, they had called him over in Morocco. Only it had always been my contention he was the devil's younger brother, and Satan had kicked him out of hell for being such a powerful candidate to the throne. In Morocco the Legionnaires told a Legion legend of how Captain Roque had been bitten by three scorpions which had promptly turned up their tails and died. I believed that story.

He was the man who was leading us to the Eblis River. Just the man for the business. You know that Eblis River region southwest of Bab Hadoun? No? You are lucky. Eblis is the Moslem name for the infernal regions, and that country southwest of Bab Hadoun was aptly christened. It was the country of the Beni-M'zab.

Mother France was having the devil of a game in those days trying to tie strings on the region; and those Beni-M'zab tribesmen had made fierce resistance. There were not many of the Mozabites, but they were like an itch, irritating as sin and hard to locate. The Legion had been chasing around after them at the double-quick; and at last had come the order to wipe them out. To this end, the detachment left Bab Hadoun, bound to lance needle bayonets through the first of the Beni-M'zab carbuncles on the hand of France reaching along the Eblis.

Now a devout humpbacked Senussi holy man in El Guerrah once told me that Allah was letting the Eblis River country run to hell as express punishment to the Beni-M'zab. Orthodox Islam despised the Beni-M'zab as heretic because they were not of the four great branches Islamic. Those Mozabites were fanatic to insanity. Puritans of the Moslem world; but they were unorthodox on some point of faith, and so, according to my devout Senussi, Allah was punishing them by letting their country go to hell. But that humpbacked holy man was wrong. Their country had gone to hell for certain, but it seemed not to punish the Beni-M'zab. They loved it. And the Foreign Legion of France won the punishment, as you shall see.

Particularly did Yankee Bill the Elephant, Christianity Jensen the Dane and I win punishment. We marched in the detachment out of Bab Hadoun, westward toward Brezina. And the thought of that march makes my feet burn to this day. *Pardieu!* what a march it was. There never was and never will be a road through that region. Allah would not like it, and *le bon Dieu* would never bother to argue with him about it. Aunt of the devil! What a country. Struggling, coughing, panting, our column tramped a landscape of jagged, sullen hills that at night were cold as the kiss of a courtesan, and hotter than a furnace at the first hue of day. Every red cliff and scarlet crag radiated heat like a stove. Hills that were ugly, grim, petrified by the blasts blowing up from the south. Hills that roasted under a blazing daylight that boiled the eyes in their sockets and made smoke of the breath in the lungs. A terrible land.

BY noon of our first day's march every man was blistered, footsore, covered with white dust from *képi*-crown to *brodequin*-toe. Our water was sour in our canteens; our *capotes* steamed on our backs. Our rations would not have matched the breakfast of a Gascony pig. Our nerves were shattered by the snipers who did such splendid sharpshooting at every unexpected turn.

Bam! would go a Beni-M'zab sniper gun; and the first Legionnaire in our column would be apt to drop with a pretty crimson fountain showering out of his forehead. They left nothing for us to shoot at save a bouquet of blue smoke drifting up from behind a red bowlder. Those Beni-M'zab snipers, you comprehend, were ghosts who vanished on the echo of their gunshots.

But yes, it was hard on the nerves. Most especially on the nerves of Yankee Bill the Elephant, Christianity Jensen the Dane, and I. For we were marching in the lead of that column, you realize, by order of Captain Giacomo Roque and none other. The fight that had started in Ahmed ben Addadud's gin dive was continuous on our march to the picturesque River Eblis. And it was Captain Giacomo Roque who pushed the battle now.

The Corsican officer was a crafty fighter, that is so. Yankee Bill had guessed sagely. Captain Roque did not dare come into the open, because of his inexcusable knife-play of the previous evening. However, his—shall I call it infighting?—was unexcelled. A vicious martinet astride a dripping pony, he pranced along from one end of the column to the other, lashing the men with his sneery white-toothed smile; spouting verbal abuse. Truly, his tongue had been salvaged from an Algiers sewer.

"Hola! you lousy lizards, lift your mulish feet," he would bawl at the staggering Legionnaires. "Sons of camels, do you think you stroll the Rue de Rivoli? March, you devils! And no faces at me, or you will see how an officer of the Legion deals with defaulters. I am a better man than any of you, with the ladies and with the men. Just lift a finger against me and see what happens. I would blow off your pig heads. March, dogs!"

His finest imprecations he saved for Yankee Bill. Spurring his pony until it bled, he would gallop to the big American's side and sneer and curse him and gibe and cast aspersions and dares. The other Legionnaires hated him for a leper, and would have stabbed him in the back quickly enough had we not been on campaign. Squirming inwardly and cursing in their throats, they tramped along with faces black from anger. But the sagacious American knew this was what the Corsican enjoyed. Yankee Bill knew men like Captain Roque loved to corner a victim, torture and watch him twitch. Accordingly, Yankee Bill refused to twitch.

"Now here is a pig for certain," the princely captain would growl through his beautiful dental equipment at the Yankee. "A prize dog. A man who needs taming and would do well in the Penal Battalion quarries at Oujda. What have you to say to that, my American son of a camel? Nothing? I thought not, you *salopard*. You do not dare talk back. You know how quickly I would hurl you into some lovely prison, eh? Ho, ho! A fine gentleman with the ladies, I suppose? Let us say, with Kabyle dancing girls. But a cowardly *salopard* at heart, *oui?* A dog, a pig, a coward!"

And Yankee Bill? All smiles. Grinning cheerfuly from ear to ear he would look up into Captain Roque's face with the calm and happy expression of a man just listed for citations. Maybe you think the good captain liked that? No! He wanted the Yankee to make an overt move, make some insubordinate gesture that would rate a prison sentence.

I thought the Yankee would explode at mention of the Kabyle dancer, but he managed a broader smile than ever. Which made the Corsican's forehead darken, and inspired him to larger infamies, such as washing his foul mouth with fresh wine, the while we groaned of thirst as we watched. (But, yes, those scorpions must have died on the spot!)

"HE wants killing, that one," Christianity Jensen hinted to me, one time when our captain had fallen back to outrage a straggler. "How does our big Yankee keep his peace? Saint Boniface! but that officer has been at him every step of the way."

Yankee Bill overheard, but he said nothing until that night. We had dropped our packs, and stood at ease in the dim dark, waiting for the sudden cold to freeze the marrow of our bones. All day we had led the line of march, expecting a sniper bullet to buzz along and burn one of us through the bowels. But Captain Roque had been doomed to acute disappointment, as our only casualty was holes through our *képis.* I stood fingering the four holes in mine and wondering why God was just, when the Yankee dug an elbow into my ribs and held up that smoked-ham fist of his.

Captain Roque was at the tail of the column; and we could hear his snarly, bullying voice sawing like a file on iron through the cold gloom. My American *copain* shook his fist at the tantalizing, dour sound.

"There's always ways to hurt blowhards like Captain Roque," he said mildly. Too mildly. "He thinks he's so clever with the women an' that toothy grin of his. Killin' is too good for a *salopard* like that. They fail to rate the honor of bullets or steel. They're the kind who die of blood poison from stepping on a tack. And this good Roque needs to have his bombast removed." One of Yankee Bill's fingers touched the scratch on his forehead, then went tapping over his pack; and he chuckled. "Don't worry. I'm carryin' Zobeid's little lucky gift in my pack. Maybe it'll bring me real luck. Maybe I'll get a chance to knock those pearly teeth out of Captain Roque's fine skull."

The voice of Yankee Bill the Elephant was far too mild. I heard the Dane beside him exhale a contented sigh. I smiled. Things might happen to this varlet Corsican captain of ours. It was not well to tease an elephant. Elephants remember.

WE reached the Eblis River and attacked the Beni-M'zab at daybreak. I shall not soon forget my first sight of that place, or the way of our attack. We had marched all night through a land as dead, cold and awful as a man thirteen years in the coffin. No snipers there. Nothing save black hills and a cold silence.

Even Captain Roque was stifled quiet in that Valley of the Shadow. *Ma foi!* but the Legionnaires would have welcomed a gunshot to break that oppressive quietude; and we were almost glad to see the ghost moon retire to permit a sun like a flaming chariot wheel to roll out of the east. Just as the sun wheeled clear we came to that place where the mountains climbed down to have a look at the edge of the world. Our trail twisted out of a ravine; suddenly we stood on a ledge of rock that overlooked eternity.

Without an order, every man of us dropped his pack; our Lebel butts thumped ground in unison, and we stared. And glared. It is not often a man gets a chance to look over the edge of the world.

Here the mountains stopped up short as if they had been hacked off by a giant knife; made a fence to a sweep of flat sand that raced away and away to meet scarlet skies east, south, west. The vast, sweeping plane never stopped when it met the sky, you understand. It kept right on going to the end of the universe. We stood atop those scarlet palisades, and stared up a world-wide, sandy boulevard reaching a million years over the rim of things.

The Walrus and the Carpenter who wept to see such quantities of sand in Lewis Carroll's famous "Through the Looking Glass" would have dropped dead at this sight. I wanted to weep, I tell you. Because there was a tiny thread of mercury leaking out of the cañon below us to die on the rim of that awful desert. The Eblis River. It made a little mirror-like pool before it expired; a little pool surrounded by three date palms and overhanging cliffs which cast real shadows. A half league from this pool, where a peninsula of rock struck timidly into the desert, stood an infinitesimal mud fortress no bigger than an atom.

The green flag of the Prophet waved atop that impossible blob of brown mud; and I knew what it was. A Moslem monastery. A stronghold of those Puritanic Beni-M'zab—the only men in the world who could have locked themselves up in such a place of fearful desolation. What religious exaltation!

It made me sweat to think of the handful of fanatical hermits down there. Wild, forgotten men who ventured from this tiny stronghold only to pillage some unwary traveler or caravan, then buried themselves back in solitary confinement to spend their days growing whiskers and reciting the ninety-nine beautiful names of the Apostle of Islam. *Mon Dieu!*

Staring, Yankee Bill the Elephant got a whisper out of his white mouth. "Look at that place, Corday. That's what we gotta wipe out. An' listen to the stillness. Wow! Sort of gets me by the throat."

But, yes, the silence wound ghost fingers about one's throat, and choked. That silence, that sand, that awful solitude made immense by the puny blob of mud under a green pennant. I swear, the echo of a man's voice could not get twenty feet away without dying of loneliness. It sent prickles down my spine, for it was a place where no man should tread. Only a pig like Captain Roque would have dared interrupt.

Galloping up from the tail of the column, he drew rein in front of Yankee Bill, the Dane and me, and voiced a loud squall. "Dogs! Who gave the order to halt? Up arms, you *salopards*. We charge that rat nest below and smash it to bits before noon. Forward, you yellow dogs."

THE Corsican had no imagination, no subtlety for fine points. At double-quick, the two squads of Legionnaires pounded down the trail, galloped along the twisty bank of the river, cantered past the pool among the quiet rocks, and debouched with fixed bayonets out on the desert. It was silly.

The Corsican spread us in a serried rank, and we thumped along, pointing our needle bayonets at the blob of mud under the green banner. The blob paid us no attention, either. It grew in size as we neared it, and turned into a squat, round tower. But it was adamant. We might as well have been charging an empty tomb.

"Saint Sulpice!" panted the little Dane at my side. (He and the Yankee and I ran elbow to elbow.) "The place is deserted. I knew nobody could live in this little corner of forgotten hell!"

But we were a hundred yards away when eight jets of flame burst from the turret under the flag. Smoke toiled up toward the metal sky. Bullets skipped under our astonished feet. *Tac-tac-tac-tac!* You have heard that deadly, nerve-shaking drone of a machine gun? You should have heard eight of them flinging hot steel across that impossible desert, to break our rank and rip the silence into ribbons!

Can you see this strange picture, then? Can you see that tremendous stretch of Sahara hedged on the north by red cliffs and escaping in three other directions farther than the eye could see? Can you see our little column of Legionnaires legging it out of the cañon where the river wiggled; dashing over the hot, open sand with bayonets pointed at that tiny Moslem tower? Then—*tac-tac-tac-tac-tac!* go eight anti-quated machine guns under the rippling pennant of Mohammed. Fire spits out of the tower turret, as a scorching rain of bullets pour through the blatant sunlight, dig founts of sand, and sends the soldiers of the Legion scampering back to the cañon. It was absurd, impos-sible, fantastic. In the first place the country was unreal, void of life, and no human beings should have been found there. In the second place, the Beni-M'zab tower was smaller than nonsense; and that eight ancient Maxim rapid-firers should defend its walls was past belief.

Le bon Dieu alone knows where those Beni-M'zab hermits obtained eight Maxim guns. But they certainly knew their usage. "Yah! Yah! Yah Allah!" the monks would scream as we attacked, and their guns would rattle like thirteen thousand drums. We charged, and those Beni-M'zab monks sat safe in their tower, laughed like the devil, and drove us back.

Again and again, and from every angle, we assaulted the tower. Time after time the hurricane of bullets, drawing a circle about the tower, fended us off. There could not have been more than a dozen of those Beni-M'zab defenders in that tiny blob of mud; but we might as well have attacked twenty armies.

Captain Giacomo Roque went purple faced from rage. Every device of tactics he knew he tried. We surrounded the tower and closed in. We feinted attack, drawing up fifteen men under shadow of the rocky promontory east of the tower and charging from there, hoping to draw the Beni-M'zab all on one side while our remaining force assaulted the other. Useless. Those monks were not fools. Not so! They stuck to their posts behind their eight machine guns; watched every angle of possible attack. All morning, all afternoon, all evening, the Legion charged and fled. Up to the line of the machine-gun fire, then back to safety. Like a game.

When the moon was up we lay like twenty-one exhausted scarecrows around the pool among the rocks, panting, tired Legionnaires.

We had not lost a man; we Legionnaires had been mighty quick to escape the range of those old Maxims. But there were bullet holes in our *capotes,* and more than one wound among us. We were certain as sin that the Beni-M'zab tower could be captured by nothing less than the entire Foreign Legion with the French navy thrown in.

And what of the personal quarrel between our gentle Corsican captain and my big American *copain,* Yankee Bill the Elephant? There had been little space for hostility between a Legionnaire and his officer that day; but Captain Roque had managed a few sneers and hate-hot glances at the Yankee, and every time the men had fallen back Yankee Bill had smiled a knowing smile at his captain. As if our failure to capture the tower was the Corsican's fault, and the Yankee knew a better way.

Of a certainty it made that Captain Roque furious. Now, as we lay gasping in our retreat, the Corsican brought up the issue. He had been marching up and down in front of the men, waving his fists, cursing, stopping only to swig drinks or liquor from his canteen.

"DOGS! Cowards! If there was a man among you, we could have taken that tower long ago." That sort of thing. Now he planted himself in front of the recumbent Yankee Bill. The Dane and I lay on either side of the Yankee, and we wondered what was going to happen. Flat on his back, hands under his dusty head, Yankee Bill smiled up at the raging officer. Moonlight flickered in Captain Roque's eyes, made his teeth shine, outlined the veins standing out on his blue forehead. He glared down at Yankee Bill, and leered and snarled:

"*Bien,* here is a dog who smiles wisely. Perhaps, my bold fool, you can suggest how that tower can be captured."

It was decidedly irregular for an officer to talk thus. But the Corsican had been swigging at his canteen with automatic regularity, and must have been pretty drunk. The Legionnaires within earshot got up on their elbows to listen; and Yankee Bill stood up to salute.

"*Oui,* my captain," he said in his mildest voice. We all were treated to a real surprise. A jolly smile was on that big Yankee's face, as he declared: "But yes, perhaps I could help win the tower. Listen: Suppose you take the men back to that promontory of rock east of the tower. I wait here." He drew a rusty watch from his *capote* pocket. "Look, then. At the tick of midnight, you attack the tower. While you battle on the east, I will creep alone across the sand, climb the wall and grab a machine gun. I would only need one. Perhaps I could do it alone. May I try the plan?"

I guess that speech took the breath out of those listening Legionnaires and Captain Roque. I felt as if I had been kicked in the lungs. You can wager the captain gave a delighted smile, and replied: "Excellent. We will try the plan. You are a brave man, after all."

"But, name of Heaven!" panted Christianity Jensen, to Yankee Bill when Captain Roque had marched off chuckling. "It is suicide, Yankee Bill. The Corsican knows you will be killed, and loves the idea. This is madness. You can never get into that tower."

"Don't lose no sleep while you wait for midnight," the big Yankee had advised. Once again he touched that scratch on his cheek, and once again he tapped fingers over his pack. "The Legion will win the tower, see if we don't. This moonlight has give me a plan. Nobody will get killed. I'm carryin' Zobeid's little present to bring us luck."

Chuckling merrily, he left the Dane and me, and sauntered down to the pool to get a drink. The moon in the black sky was big and yellow and bright.

"BONES of Stavengeren," groaned Christianity Jensen for the thirteenth time in as many minutes. "But why did Yankee Bill suggest this foolish plan? For him to rush that tower alone is suicidal. Surely those monks will keep a guard on that side of the tower. He will be riddled. Those Beni-M'zab will not be fooled by this ruse. We tried it twice before to-day. Captain Roque is delighted at the Yankee's foolhardy plan. He hauls out his watch and grins like the devil. Midnight cannot be an hour away."

The Dane pointed a finger at the cleft in the cliffs where the pool lay concealed from view. The distant cañon-mouth where Yankee Bill was hidden, awaiting his one-man assault. From where we lay, the cañon-mouth, west of the tower, could hardly be seen. We were lying atop a rock-shelf on the promontory east of the tower.

That tower was not six hundred yards away; quiet as a tomb in the moonlight, but I knew those Beni-M'zab hermits were vigilant as tigers. That handful of Moslem Puritans had not seen the twenty of us sneak out on the promontory, but they must have sighted the gleam of our bayonets as we lay in line up there. Our fire might draw their attention all right, but the Yankee could never cover the distance from the cañon across the open sand in the bright moonlight. Foolishness. I glanced at Captain Roque, sprawled flat near by. The Corsican was grinning evilly. Midnight was scarce sixty minutes away; perhaps it would never come.

A restless tremor passed along the recumbent line of Legionnaires. Every eye was on the tower, every mind counting the minutes. Every tongue whispered of the Yankee's madness. My companions were uneasy, too. If that neck of desert had looked like the end of the world in daylight, you should have seen it under a round yellow moon. The quiet was incredible. It yanked our nerves and wet our cheeks with sweat. It was not of this world. So we waited. and the Moslem monks in the tower below waited behind their machine guns. Once I glimpsed a white turban moving. The green flag whispered.

"Listen," muttered the Dane at my side. "Do you think Yankee Bill is playing a game? Perhaps he does not wait beside the pool behind the rocks. Perhaps this is a trick to give him a chance to get away. Desertion."

Pardieu! I had not thought of that. I glared at the hidden and distant cañon; opened my mouth to reply. And then my mouth clicked shut. A curious sigh ran along the line of Legionnaires. A gasp escaped the Dane. A sibilant curse popped from the teeth of Captain Giacomo Roque. We of that Legionnaire line stared to make the eyes hang out of our buzzing skulls. Were we mad?

Was the moonlight, the atmosphere of that evil spot tricking our minds? Or did we really see a live ghost flit from the mouth of that cañon? A live ghost shrouded in white veils came skipping from the spot where the pool lay hidden, and flickered across the sand toward the Beni-M'zab tower. Aunt of the devil, but it robbed one's heart of blood!

"Look at that!" panted the Dane, clutching my arm. I was looking all right. So was every man of us lying on that ledge. Looking, yes! *Mon Dieu,* how we looked! We did not believe our eyes.

When the ghost whirled nearer, veils blowing in the moonlight, and we saw it was not a wraith but a dancer, we did not believe our eyes a whit more. No! We stared and gasped oaths, and hugged the rock on which we lay, and knew we were insane. That moonlit corner of hell was lucky to be inhabited by Moslem hermits and Legionnaires; never the place to see a dancer shrouded in misty white veils.

WE forgot we were Legionnaires waiting a midnight assault. We forgot the Beni-M'zab tower below us. We forgot everything. Eyes pasted on that whirling figure, we remembered only to breathe; and I, for one, forgot that, and almost suffocated. That dancer came gyrating across the sand. The sand was blue in the pallid moonlight.

The dancer's weaving arms were white as milk save where brass bracelets flashed. Face shrouded by a fluttering veil. Lithe body, sinuous and white, wrapped in the delicate misty raiment that clung and shimmered and fluttered in the moonbeams. Tiny as a nymph against that vast background of Saharan sand and hedging cliff's, that incredible dancer twirled over the flat sand, nearer and nearer to the tower.

Can you picture it? The line of Legionnaires panting and pop-eyed atop that ledge. The desolate Sahara running to the ends of the world. The chill moonlight laying long, blue shadows. And that utterly improbable veiled dancer flitting over the sand. I am a Dutchman if I did not think I was stark, raving mad.

What a dancer, I say! I had seen the Ouled Naïl, the mystic dancers of Cambodia, the Seven Snake Sisters of Rabat, the queer dancers of Dahomey, and some pretty good ladies in Cadiz, Marseilles, Singapore, Mombassa, Bangkok and New Orleans. But never had I seen a dancer like this one who had popped out of the night-hung cliffs fencing the Sahara to charm the moonbeams.

I will wager I was gasping like a steam valve. That dancer and that dance! Uncle of Satan! The *danse du ventre,* the *can-can,* Russian ballet, snake-arm, what you Americans call "shimmie"—that dancer did them all and some new ones in the bargain. We watched from a distance, but we were plenty near enough, that is so.

Once I forced a look at Captain Giacomo Roque. His face was scarlet. His teeth were grinning steam. His eyes were the heads of steel nails driven into a rotting log. *"Dieu,"* the Corsican was panting, *"Sacré nom de Dieu!"* I should say so.

What of the little blob of mud under the green pennant below our promontory? Perhaps you think something was going on down there? But yes. Something was. Now I could not understand that impossible dancing figure, but I could comprehend what was happening in that Beni-M'zab monastery. I could almost see those Moslem monks, crowded together, staring with eyes like coals over the edge of their crenellated turret; staring like the very devil at the dancer on the sand below.

Imagine that handful of Moslem hermits, shut away in that spot of bitter desolation for Heaven knows how many years, suddenly treated to the sight of a dancer wrapped in veils, a dancer with arms white as milk in that moonlight, and graceful feet and a veil-misted torso, doing the *can-can* better than could the very mother of the Ouled Naïl Mountains.

I could fancy how those desert-bitten, forgotten hermits were staring when the dance went on under the very shadow of their prison. Those Beni-M'zab monks were Puritans chiseled out of granite; devout, steel-souled men. That dance looked like the vision of Bacchus to us of the Foreign Legion, but comprehended how it must have looked to men who had not seen a pair of lithe white arms for years and years! And it was going on, so to speak, right under their window. For the dancer was pirouetting on the sand where the shadow of the tower lay.

SUDDENLY the veiled figure stopped, and a white arm beckoned. Beckoned, yes, to those eyes that must have been glaring from the tower turret. It was unfair, I tell you. Like dangling a juicy steak at the mouth of a starved lion. Those Beni-M'zab hermits were the starved lion. It is no wonder they believed this vision in veils a *houri* sent by Allah from paradise to console their sterile souls. No wonder they forgot their machine guns.

Perhaps they believed the Legion had gone away and this houri stepped from the sky was an omen of victory and an award from Allah the Merciful.

At any rate—what do you believe? Every man of us hidden on that ledge east of the tower saw it all. We saw those Beni-M'zab monks swarm over the low tower wall like little, white-turbaned ants. Yes! They clambered out of their impregnable little tower, and started for the beckoning dancer. The veiled figure waved a hand, and those monks—there were twelve of them—legged it over the sand. The dancer turned to run, and those dried-up desert monks gave mad chase. Right then it came over me like a flood of light! *Le bon Dieu* alone knew where Yankee Bill had found her among those desolate cliffs. But somewhere, somehow, the big American had found this dancing genius, and worked out the scheme. Now you could have cut off my head with a paper sword!

The other Legionnaires and Captain Giacomo Roque caught the idea, too. As one man we bounced to our heels, jerked up our Lebels and charged down from the rocks. Those poor, duped monks of the Beni-M'zab never saw us until we had covered the distance to the tower. Even then they wavered between following the houri and trying to get back to their guns. Too late. They turned about squalling like trapped cats, and with one volley we sent them to meet a real bevy of *houris* in the excellent paradise those good fighters deserved.

And the dancer? Aunt of the devil! That veiled figure stood like a statue on the sand some five hundred feet away from us, and we heard a shrill laugh. Somehow that laugh halted the feet of the Legionnaires. We stood with our Lebels smoking in our fists; glaring from the extinguished Mozabites to the dancer who had betrayed them.

We Legionnaires dared not move, but Captain Giacomo Roque did. Uttering a lusty bawl, the Corsican kept right on running. He pounded across the sand like a satyr with evil in its eye. He had lost his *képi* and his greasy curls were flying. The moonlight was not nice on his avid face; no wonder the dancer turned to run.

Straight for the cañon-mouth fled the shrouded figure, with the Corsican ruffian making after. Running like antelopes, they covered a quarter mile in record time, but the Corsican gained. The distance between them closed in—then abruptly the veiled figure turned. We saw our noble captain dart on with grabbing hands outstretched. Then, *sacré Dieu!* A white arm whipped out from the blowing veils. *Whack!* We could almost hear the blow. Down went Captain Roque in the manner of a man hit by a lightning bolt. The astounding dancer spun about, and fled like a white streak to vanish among the cliffs where the Eblis River made a final pool among the hidden rocks.

IT was too much for dog-tired Legionnaire brains to handle. We stood like fools for five minutes that were five centuries, then jumped over the bodies of those poor Beni-M'zab holy men, and cantered up to the unconscious form of our captain. I reached him first, and I want to tell you, I received a jolt. He lay like one dead, face up on the sand where the dancer's mighty blow had dropped him. His face was chalk and he had a scarlet streak for a mouth, and I dropped my rifle when I saw. They lay scattered on the sand like so many dice. You comprehend? His front teeth had been knocked out of that bulldog's head!

He could not speak when we roused him to his feet, and no wonder. He could only lisp oaths and spit blood, for his mouth swelled like a sponge sunk in red ink. He was one dismal sight, that Corsican captain of ours, but we Legionnaires did not expire of sorrow. We did not.

We helped him stagger over the sand toward the mouth of the cañon in the cliffs; and I would have given thirteen million francs to read his thoughts. My thoughts were not worth a franc. And they fell in value to a sou when we rounded the bowlders sheltering the pool under the palm trees—it was where the mountains climbed to look over the edge of the world, you remember—and gained the spot where the dancer had disappeared. There was no dancer there. But no! Only a certain giant Legionnaire called Yankee Bill the Elephant.

His *capote* and shoes were off; he was naked to the waist and looked as if he had been diving. In one hand he held four brass bracelets. He wiped water from his face, and said to us:

"A dancin' girl came runnin' in here like a bat outa hell. Lord knows where she came from. She was fleeing like the devil was after her. I was sittin' here waitin' for midnight to come. She jumped right over me, dived into the pool an' went down like a stone. It's deep, an' she's gone for good, I reckon. I was just gettin' up to go see what that sound of shootin' was for. But I dived after her. She must be down a mile. I found these bracelets. Look."

He pointed sadly at the pool. There, on the moonlit, restless surface floated seven white veils. But I was not staring at those seven veils. No! I was staring at Yankee Bill's right hand, the hand that held the bracelets. It was swollen and blue, and it looked as big as two smoked hams in the eerie dusk.

OLD Thibaut Corday sighed a fog out of his beard, reached for the Amer-Picon bottle. His eyes were twinkling like little blue stones, and he chuckled down his drink.

"The Dane and I wondered," he admitted softly. "The other Legionnaires could not, but we did. There was that present given by the Kabyle to Yankee Bill. Could it have been those veils and bracelets? Perhaps. Then again, that terrific blow in the mouth.

"We wondered. Do not think we could not have been deceived. Captain Roque and those monks, too. The Corsican had been drinking, and those monks had been buried alive for years. Also, a good distance intervened. The place reeked atmosphere. The Yankee's hand had certainly hit something between the time we left and found him.

"But we asked no questions, to be told no more lies. Captain Giacomo Roque said nothing about the affair. How he said nothing! He kept silent perforce for a long time, because his mouth was slow to heal. He was silent when it healed, too. Perhaps it injured his pride, removed his bombast, to have been knocked toothless and unconscious by a dancer in white veils. Besides, his false teeth did not fit well. They used to drop out every time he would start to bawl an order. It was sad. He became a very silent man."

Old Thibaut Corday, veteran Legionnaire, drained the Amer-Picon. "But what a dancer and what a dance!" he sighed, standing to his feet. Then he nodded his head toward the triangle.

"Even Lavigerie has gone," murmured the veteran. "Perhaps to look for the River Eblis. *Bien!* At any rate, my friend, come along. The dancers are still busy down on Rue Sainte. They say there is a man in disguise down there who dances beautifully. Throws off a red wig at the end of his dance and is showered with money. Perchance he is a prize fighter, too. For this is Africa!"

AUTHOR'S NOTE: IT MIGHT INTEREST THE READER TO KNOW THERE WAS SUCH A MAN DANCING WITH THE OULED NAÏL DOWN ON RUE SAINTE IN BISKRA. WE WERE IN BISKRA IN FEBRUARY, '29, AND ENJOYED A VIEW OF THIS UNUSUAL PERFORMANCE. OUR DANCER WORE THE USUAL OULED NAÏL COSTUME AND EXHIBITED A VERY SKILLFUL KNIFE DANCE, SURPRISING HIS AUDIENCE OF ARABS AND FRENCHMEN BY REVEALING HIMSELF IN MUCH THE SAME MANNER AS OUR BROADWAY VAUDEVILLE FEMALE IMPERSONATORS. IMAGINE, HOWEVER, OUR UNMITIGATED SURPRISE ON HEARING THE FELLOW WAS AN AMERICAN FROM—OF ALL PLACES— KENTUCKY.

—THEODORE ROSCOE.

AN EYE FOR AN EYE

WHEN TWO MEN HATE
EACH OTHER AS DID THE
BLACK LADU AND THE
RED-HEADED "CARROT,"
THE FOREIGN LEGION
IS TOO SMALL TO HOLD
THEM BOTH WITHOUT AN
EXPLOSION LOUD ENOUGH
TO SHOCK EVEN WICKED
OLD AFRICA.

THIS IS a true story. The fat American tourist from East Syracuse, New York, did not believe it, but the fat man was a fool. Old Thibaut Corday claimed the story true at the start. The paunchy tourist "had to be shown." He was shown, all right. He didn't know Thibaut Corday the way the rest of us did.

"It is a true tale," the old Frenchman promised us. "But, *nom de Dieu!* it is the most unbelievable story in the world. There were some queer, mad dramas played out in the Foreign Legion of France. This was one of the queerest; one of the maddest."

The veteran Legionnaire, soldier of fortune who had battled under twenty different war-flags, gestured a bony hand at the tourist from East Syracuse. "Monsieur the American just mentioned that he had made his fortune manufacturing glass eyes. His remark recalls to me this story of the Legion. It is a wild, savage, bitter story, I repeat, for no story of the Legion deals with life in a Boston drawing-room. Quaintly enough, this story has to do with a glass eye. And a live eye, too. You know that grim saying from the Bible: 'An eye for an eye'? But yes. This is the story of an eye for an eye. And a grim little story it is."

The old soldier leaned back in his chair, loaded his pipe with what appeared to be dog's hair, and let a brown fog burst from his cinnamon-colored berry-bush of a beard. Behind a nimbus of malodorous smoke his eyes twinkled like little blue stones couched deep in his leathery skull, as he framed the yarn in his mind.

The rest of us waited in silence. The fat tourist who had made glass eyes wiped sweat from his triple chin, and leaned forward with an adipose smile. A shaft of blazing African sunshine speared under the café awning, and I moved my chair into shadow. Boulevard Sadi

Carnot panted in the blatant afternoon heat, and the Bay of Algiers beyond the harbor ramp looked like a sheet of furbished metal. Thibaut Corday, veteran Legionnaire, hung his bald head in smoke, and began:

WHEN two boys love the same girl there is apt to be plenty of trouble. Especially if they already hate each other, as was the case with those two young cadets at St. Cyr. They did not like each other a little bit, those two.

They were cousins, to begin with. And their rich old fool of an uncle, who had been an officer under Montholon at the time of Louis Napoleon, had sent them to the academy to make them into generals. Old uncles were always sending favorite nephews to St. Cyr to make them generals. Bah! And this old uncle did more. He offered money prizes to the boy who gained the highest marks at the school. A splendid way to turn early dislike into a nice little hate.

Now, these two cousins were of about the same build and feature. They might have been brothers, save in disposition and color of hair. One of the boys had red hair; the other had black hair. (This color of hair was going to play a big part in what was to come.)

The name of the black-haired cousin was Hyacinth LaDu. Hyacinth LaDu was not a nice boy. He was not. He was always getting drunk and cheating at class and having nasty little affairs around town. Even in those early St. Cyr days he was what they call in the Legion a *"salopard."* Now, *salopard* is not a nice name. It is not. And Hyacinth LaDu deserved it, as you shall see.

The boy with red hair was no angel from Paradise, but he tried to be a gentleman and live up to the traditions of a noble old family. Because of his red hair his fellow cadets at the academy nicknamed him La Carotte—The Carrot.

I remember him in the academy as a quiet boy with many friends. He was lazy, but a good student. He enjoyed most his classes in horsemanship and gunnery, and planned a career in the artillery.

His only real enemy was his cousin, Hyacinth. Hyacinth hated him. You see, La Carotte kept winning all the prizes given by the old uncle, and it made Hyacinth as jealous and mad as a March hare.

By the end of their second term at St. Cyr, La Carotte had won every prize save one. Hyacinth was a better man with the foils. The Carrot could handle his swords well enough, but that black-haired, black-eyed cousin of his was the best fencer in the military school. This was honor enough for any young man. But Hyacinth LaDu was

Their feet bled in warped boots. Their backs
groaned under soaked, heavy packs.

not a young man. He was a *salopard.*

He raged in his heart because he had not won all the honors. To
show you what a churl he was, one day his cousin, La Carotte, congratulated him on his swordsmanship. Hyacinth spat in La Carotte's
face.

"Pah! Why should you congratulate me, noble cousin of the red
hair? A lot you admire my swordsmanship. You, who have played into
the favor of our uncle with lies and cheating. But yes. I know I am
the best swordsman in St. Cyr. Watch out, then, my Carrot, or I may
slice you down."

NOW, dueling was the most popular sport for cadets in those days,
and the student duels were not the play affairs the law requires them
to be now. There was many a meeting on the field of honor. Occasion-
ally two students would fight to the death. To give a mortal wound,
of course, was considered bad form. The more honorable were content
to cut off an ear or slice the chin or cheek of an opponent. That was
honorable satisfaction.

The dueling clubs had some fanciful rules. Of course, La Carotte
and Hyacinth belonged to dueling fraternities. Hyacinth, fast becom-

ing a master at *escrime*—fencing—was always fighting duels. He was so skilled with his sword that he could well afford to be easily insulted. He was often giving the challenge, and he delighted in butchering the face of an opponent. More than one luckless cadet wore an ugly scar from the agile sword of Hyacinth.

Some of them wore two scars. This was one of the fanciful club rules: If you cut off the ear of an opponent, for example, he could ask a return chance to cut off your ear. If you cut away his lip or gashed his cheek, he could have a return match to try gashing yours. Should he lose both times, he was doubly defeated, the winner had double the honor, and the affair was closed.

Hyacinth LaDu was the first man to cut both ears from the head of an opponent. A generous dueler would not have done so. Hyacinth LaDu was not generous, *c'est ça*. A heartless foe.

La Carotte was not for fighting duels. Every student save his own dear cousin was his friend. Hyacinth tried to juggle up a fight with La Carotte, but such affairs were not managed with honor. Then there came to the town a girl from Paris who was not like other girls. *Sacré!* she was not.

She had skin like Carrara marble and hair of spun gold. Her eyes were fires of blue cobalt. Her laugh was like the tinkle of ice in a slim glass of *crème de menthe* and forty times as intoxicating. She had that figure one sees only in dreams. Aunt of the devil! but she was more beautiful and attractive than Mme. Du Barry, Antoinette Parbonne, and Ninon de Lenclos put together. Two young officers from St. Cyr promptly fell in love with this star-eyed angel, and started violent courtship. Their names were La Carotte and Hyacinth LaDu.

It is easy to guess how such a rivalry would terminate. The whole corps at St. Cyr awaited the duel with bated breath. It was not long in the making. I do not think the beautiful, starry-eyed girl tried to prevent it. *Mais non!* It would be flattering indeed to have a duel fought for her. So she played with the emotions of both young officers as a kitten plays with two dried leaves. That charming angel. What did she care if two boys carved up their faces for her?

The trouble was, only one of those boys would do all the carving. The angel fanned the fires of hatred with coy promises and kisses that made Circe seem a clumsy harridan. And Hyacinth LaDu fed fuel to the flames. That black-haired genius had only wanted a chance to cross swords with his red-haired cousin.

One day in public he started a quarrel over the girl, claimed La Carotte had publicly insulted his honor, demanded a meeting, exchanged calling cards, and asked La Carotte to choose his own blades. Poor Carrot. What could he do but pick his seconds and agree to duel? And he chose light drill sabers.

That red-headed Carrot spent a bad night. He knew he was the victim of a frame-up, as they say in America, and he knew his scoundrelly cousin would make the most of it. As Hyacinth was the best swordsman in St. Cyr, La Carotte knew he stood about as much chance of success as a gelatine chicken trying to swim a creek. His friends begged him to refuse the match.

La Carotte was not the sort to back down. He would not give his lovely cousin a chance to name him a coward. He would go out there and lose his ears, no doubt, but he would go down fighting. Moreover, the girl, on hearing of the proposed duel, promised her hand to the boy who should be the victor. Nice of her, *oui?*

THE duel was held in a little wood. I myself was there, and I recall it well. The sunshine of dawn slanting through the plane trees. The soft mists of early morning rising from the fields like smoke in the chill air. Foliage glistening green with dew. In the distance a rooster crowing. Early morning in France—nowhere else on earth is it quite the same.

There was the crowd of cadets, talking in muted tones. The bearded doctor with his medicinal smile, his long cloak, his case of surgical tools. The four seconds with swords drawn. The judge droning out the final protest, which nobody would heed. It was all as formal and rigidly disciplined as a scene from a stiff play.

La Carotte was white-lipped, but smiling. It could hardly have been pleasant to realize he was matched against the finest sword in the academy, to realize how joyously this sword would try to brand him, to know that in a few minutes he would have an ear sheared from his head or the end sliced from his nose.

His cousin would give him no easy cut on the cheek, he knew very well. There was a sneering smile on the face of Hyacinth LaDu as vicious as the blade in his hand. The glint in his black eyes was as cruel as the gleam of the razor-sharp saber edge.

Now the seconds wound a scarf about the neck of each to protect the jugular vein, then indicated proper positions. The cadaverous doctor wiped their blades with antiseptic solution, and backed away.

Sabers crossed, La Carotte and Hyacinth awaited the signal, tense as cats. The signal was given. *Go!*

And how they went! Uncle of Satan, how they went! The students, huddled in their capes, watched in soundless awe. Here was a duel that was a duel. La Carotte was fighting like a cornered tiger at the start. His only chance was to get in a freak slash at his cousin early in the game, or he was done for. For the moment those watching brother officers could see nothing of the whipping blades. Steel against steel rang loud. The sabers flashed like bands of cold fire. The woods echoed the clangor.

But La Carotte was no match for his nice cousin. Hyacinth only played with him. He could have finished the affair the minute La Carotte began to tire, but Hyacinth was not that way. He wanted to play La Carotte till his saber dropped from fatigue; wanted to make a clown of him. And he wanted a chance to do something else.

The combat raged on. Bare arms labored. Breath whined like steam from gritted teeth. Sweat pasted the cloth of their white shirts to their spines, poured down their cheeks. For a quarter hour Hyacinth parried, stabbed, slashed, cut and thrust at his helpless opponent, making La Carotte dance like a mad toy. It was a refined piece of cruelty.

Then, just when the judge might have interfered, Hyacinth pinned La Carotte's saber against his thigh, spun aside with an agile twist, whipped his saber fast as light, danced in the gleaming point, and jabbed La Carotte in the left eye.

Dropping his blade, La Carotte stumbled back with an agonized cry. Blood poured through the fingers of the hand clapped to his face. The seconds charged the field. You comprehend? Hyacinth LaDu had cut the left eye from his cousin's head. A barbarous slash.

But the nice Hyacinth was claiming satisfaction, shouting through a poisoned leer, "First blood! There was no ruling against it in the club. Let my cousin demand a return match, and I promise you I will blind him!"

La Carotte was fainting in the arms of his seconds, but all could hear his words:

"Make no protest, I beg of you. I demand a return match. I will get the eye of that *salopard!* As God is my witness, I will get his eye if it is the last thing I ever do!"

DO you know about the country of Dahomey? *Non?* Then you are lucky. The less you know about Dahomey the luckier you are. Some people think hell is a place down in the middle of the earth. Others think it is a state of mind, and snap their fingers. Both are mistaken. It lies on the west coast of Africa facing south. A little strip of meanness and pollution jammed in between Togoland and British Nigeria. Only it is not called hell on the map. It is called Dahomey.

The Niger River coils down its northern border like a big fat snake, and into it spews a tributary called the Makkri. That Makkri River is sick, that is so. It breaks out with swamps as black as midnight and jungles as evil as the curse of Cain. It has crocodiles and snakes, poisoned insects, spiders as fat as eggs, fevers, diseases, suffocating heats, bubbling mud.

It is the sort of place where a tropic downpour sets everything steaming, crawling, and growing. Green plants sprout in half an hour. Now you see one snake. *Pouf!* Now you see a million, and three lush vines besides. That is the Makkri River. That is Dahomey. Not a picnic ground by any stretch of imagination.

Why the diplomats in Paris wanted to annex this festering sore to the already infected French hand reaching into Africa is a hard guess. At any rate, the diplomats planted a flag on the coast in 1851, and in 1895 they thought they had better grab up the whole country. These diplomats with their pretty beards did not have to fight the Dahomey king, you comprehend. The clean-up squads of *La Légion Étrangère* did.

About 1896 a column of Legionnaires marched up the Makkri River bottom. Those Legionnaires marched fast. They marched fast, though they did not make a great record of speed. They could make little speed against the muck and heat, the putrid jungles and trackless swamps, the natives waiting for them in ambush. But they made as much speed as they could, for they were trying to relieve a beleaguered garrison trapped in the hinterland.

If they did not get there pretty soon there would be nobody for them to relieve. Moreover, they were being chased by a beautiful mob of Dahomey patriots who wanted nothing more than to burn the Tricolor at the stake.

It would go hard with the Legionnaires who were caught by the natives of Dahomey. Those black men were savages just one jump ahead of animal. They pounded drums and carried poisoned spears and wore necklaces of skulls around their throats. Their idea of a nice time was to tie a Legionnaire to a stake, torture him like the devil for two hours, and burn him to a crisp. The Legionnaires would not have minded the burning, but the torture was something to make them lift their feet with nervous speed. So the column plugged doggedly through the Makkri River jungle, hoping it would get to the outpost in time, if it got there at all.

It was a pretty pathetic little column by the time it came within an hour's trek of the garrison. Thirty men had started out. The sun had dropped six by the trail on the way. Fever had dropped seven more. Nine had fallen squirming with poisoned darts in their throats. The eight remaining were half mad with fatigue and fear. All night long the pulsing, throbbing *boom* of the African drums had twisted through the fetid dark about them.

Dawn had brought a brief cloudburst to bog the path, then furnace-hot, suffocating sunshine. The eight were dripping sweat, torn, muddy, haggard as old rags. Their feet bled in warped boots. Their backs groaned under soaked, heavy packs. The Lebels they carried weighed tons and blistered their shoulders to the bone. But they marched. They were bringing relief to an outpost that had had no food or ammunition supply for thirty days. They marched. They were soldiers of *La Légion!*

THEY made a typical Legion squad. There was a Frenchman in the lead who had signed on the roles as Georges Parselle. There was a Pole, a Dane, a Greek, two Spaniards, a Bavarian, and Captain Henri Cochet, the famous little Belgian who had, you remember, killed his wife and his Flemish general in a hotel at Brussels. But this is the story of the tall Frenchman who marched in the lead and had signed on the Legion roster as Georges Parselle, which was not his name.

As he marched he sang a song he had learned in America. He carried his gun lightly, for he was tough, that one. The sweat stole out of the long red hair tangled on his forehead, washed down his face and melted in his matted red beard. The fingers tapping gayly on the butt of the heavy Lebel were made of leather. His face was made of rawhide. He was very tough.

He had just come out of the Zephyrs—the brutal *Bataillon d'Afrique*, the hardest disciplinary battalion in the world. He had spent six years with the Zephyrs to make him learn how to be a good Legionnaire. Six years in the Zephyrs would make a giant out of a baby. Georges Parselle was able to sing after a terrible night march through Dahomey jungle. He had a sense of humor, and sang in time to the throb of the savage drums.

"You, Georges Parselle," Captain Cochet finally bawled. "Stop that singing, you big red-headed son of a pink camel. Your voice is worse than the torture we will get if the blacks catch us. You are the bad one just out of the Zephyrs, eh? A bad dog. Quiet, then. March, the rest of you."

The man with red hair smiled, setting faster pace. So he had gained the reputation in the Legion of a bad dog? It made him grin. The blue eyes in his leather head glistened when he grinned. The bad dog of the Legion, was he? But he knew of another Legionnaire who was worse.

It had been fifteen years since that red-headed one had last seen Hyacinth LaDu. But he had hunted. Everywhere. Until he had located him in the Foreign Legion. Now, if he ever ran across Hyacinth, Hyacinth would have to pay. He would see to that. Had he not spent four years training his sword under some of the best masters in France and Italy? Had he not spent five years tracking his cousin down? Once he found him, there would be a duel that was a duel. It would be only fair. An eye for an eye.

THE jungle came to a stop because it was tired, and hedged a grassy plain. Some three hundred yards from the edge of a jungle, a tiny blockhouse stood atop a knoll. A half mile beyond the outpost, where the grassy field encountered jungle again stood the preposterous beehive-shaped huts of a native town. The outpost of France standing atop that Godforsaken slope had been erected to protect the native town. But those black jungle savages had turned against the outpost of France, and tried to annihilate the garrison.

Obviously they had done rather well. The Tricolor hanging listless on the stockade staff was shredded. Four soldiers hung in four different attitudes on the stockade wall. By the looks of them they had hung there a long time. They would rattle when somebody picked them up to bury them.

Captain Henri Cochet cursed when he led his column to the edge of the clearing, and saw the figlike guard mounted on the stockade.

"Dead. Four dead. And where are the others? There were only two squads. The devil! Have those African pigs killed them all? Not a living native in sight either—"

The Legionnaires stared and turned gray in the face. Then they turned white. A shrill, ghastly yell trilled up into the blazing morning sky, and they saw a lone man standing on the rim of the stockade. He looked more a ghost than a man as he stood there screaming at them to come on. Then his voice was lost under a squalling sound that came from the direction of the beehive town.

The figure on the stockade vanished. A moment later a solitary machine gun opened fire from the barricade. And the appalled Legionnaires glared in cold fear at the flood of bobbing, woolly heads, the mass of waving spears, the spreading sea of inky bodies that came storming forward from the distant town.

"Holy St. Adrian!" the Belgian captain gasped. "Those blacks. They come by the million!"

They seemed to come by the two million to those eight frayed Legionnaires. The black drums boomed like angry seas. The natives came loping across the grass like boiling ebony surf. They were wary of the machine gun in the tiny fort; ran in a screaming crescent at the soldiers on the jungle's rim. Colored plumes waved from their topknots. Their elephant hide shields gleamed with paint. Brass trinkets glinted weirdly on their oiled bodies. Their barbaric screams, their pounding drums, their rattling *juju* gourds, the jangling of their brass anklets made an uproar that could have frozen the soul of a stone image. *Sapristi!*

"Heaven above!" Captain Cochet moaned. "Our scouts reported a small force concentrating in that town, not the whole Dahomey army. They must have been gathering there under cover for weeks. Quick! Attention, men—listen. Four of you will dash for the outpost. A chance one of you may get there! You must run like the devil; take water, ammunition and food. I will take the rest of us back down the river. We will bring back the whole battalion. It will take us two days. Who will try a dash for the fort? Georges Parselle, you are a tough dog—will you lead?"

Now, the outpost, you understand, was between the charging army of natives and the Legionnaires. But the natives were running like antelopes. And they threw spears like bullets. The four who would try to gain the fort would practically commit suicide. But our Georges Parselle was tough.

"I will go, *mon capitaine,*" he agreed, managing to chuckle in his red beard. Whereupon the other Legionnaires volunteered as a man. The captain chose the Pole, the Bavarian, and the Greek.

UNCLE of Satan, how those four devils of the Legion raced to gain the stockade! The other four fled back into the jungle to start their heart-breaking race for help, and the red-haired Frenchman, the little Pole, the fat Bavarian, and the thin Greek sprinted like Olympian racers to get to the outpost before the black horde did. They ran across open ground, up hill, weighted with full equipment. How they ran! They made speed now.

The Greek was first to go. A spear came sailing out of the sky and shafted through his chest like an arrow. The fat Bavarian went down next with a dart in his stomach. He did not die, and as the little Pole jumped over him, the Pole shrieked: "Kill yourself, fat one." It was sage advice, and the fat one put his Lebel under his chin. The sound of the muffled shot sent the two remaining sons of *La Légion* running like mad.

They were almost at the stockade when the Pole stumbled. Our Frenchman stopped to give aid. A spear whizzed through the sunshine and nailed the Pole to earth. Last of the four, Georges Parselle reached the gate. He shrieked, and the gate swung inward. Spears burrowed into the wood as he slammed the gate behind him and the massive bar fell.

The lucky Georges—and never believe that was not luck—found himself in a small, square inclosure occupied by one living man. There was no time to say hello. The lone defender screamed and jumped to the smoking Hotchkiss gun mounted on the stockade. Our lucky Legionnaire sprang to his side. The Hotchkiss rattled and Georges worked his rifle.

It was queer. The savages paid little attention to the two soldiers on the stockade. Those wild blacks were mortally afraid of the rapid-fire gun. And they knew they could get the two white men whenever they felt like it. But they wanted to catch the four who had fled away for help. So they tossed a few spears at the fort, and swarmed on down the slope.

Cursing the glorious oaths of the Legion, the two on the wall harried them with a withering fire until they were out of range and gone. Then the man at the Hotchkiss gun swung on his companion with a crackling cry.

"Water! Give me water and food, for the love of God! Never mind the blacks. They will not attack until noon. St. Anthony! They fear this machine gun. But I just now fired its last cartridge. Give me water!"

The red-haired Legionnaire tossed a full canteen, a bar of chocolate and a can of dried beef. The other sprang at the offerings. He was a wild man. Under his *képi* his face was black with grime. His black hair dripped sweat. His black beard was a bird's nest. He was skin and bone in a dirty uniform. Swigging water and wolfing food, he gasped out his story in a hoarse chant:

"I am the last of the garrison. My last two companions were killed yesterday noon when the natives charged. I could have escaped from this hole of hell, but I was out of rifle ammunition. I was starving. My only weapon left was that damned Hotchkiss—too heavy to carry. You—you have saved my life, *mon soldat.*" His piercing eyes were on Georges Parselle.

The red-haired Legionnaire was nodding and smiling, staring down the slope toward the jungle, where the black savages had been absorbed in the lush undergrowth. He did not see the queer glare that came to the other man's eye.

Suddenly that other man sprang, snatched the rifle from the knee of Legionnaire Georges Parselle. *"Holà!"* he cackled. "I thought I knew you. Hands up, you dog! One false move and I blow your red head from your lousy neck. So. You failed to see in me your charming cousin, eh? But I know you! Ha-ha! La Carotte—surely you remember Hyacinth LaDu!"

Taken by surprise, the Legionnaire who had been La Carotte at St. Cyr and Georges Parselle in the Army of the Damned, reached skyward with a grin.

"So! I failed to recognize you at first, my Hyacinth. But I know you now. I knew you were in the Legion. Went half around the world trying to find you, too. But I never expected to meet you thus. A long time since we dueled last, my Hyacinth. But when we get out of this mess and get back to camp I will challenge you to a return match with sabers, and cut out *your* left eye as nicely as you could wish. But—"

La Carotte said no more. Without warning his amiable cousin brought down the rifle barrel against his skull with a bone-splitting smash. La Carotte fell. The laugh of Hyacinth LaDu echoed evilly in that fort of death. That Hyacinth LaDu was a born *salopard.*

SWEAT bubbled out on the forehead of La Carotte when he woke to consciousness, found himself naked and bound, flat on his back with Hyacinth standing over him. His feet were lashed at the ankles.

His hands, brown knots on his chest, were lashed at the wrist. So tightly were the cords drawn that his fingers throbbed with a pain to match the ache in his head. Groaning, he glared at his chuckling cousin.

"So, my Carrot," explained Hyacinth LaDu. "I was hoping you would wake up before I left. My dear red-head, I never hoped to have this luck. You have been a curse to me. I heard how you were study-ing the sword, swearing vengeance, swearing to get my left eye. Ha-ha! But I did not think you would follow me into this infernal Foreign Legion. Do you know? I saw you the day you arrived with the recruits at Sidi-bel-Abbes. It was I who bribed my corporal to report you as a defaulter and have you flung into the Zephyrs. I had hoped the Zephyrs would kill you."

The brains churned in La Carotte's throbbing head. Squirming on the ground, fighting his bonds, he strove to rise.

"You—you cowardly dog!" he snarled. "So it was you who had me sent into the penal battalion? *Nom de Dieu!* If I ever get my hands on you, my Hyacinth—"

That Hyacinth LaDu laughed so gay a laugh. "But you never will, little Carrot. You see, in a few hours you will be quite, quite dead." He leaned over La Carotte, sneering. His eyes were venomous, twin-kling with hatred. "You cur! Always have I hated you. Perhaps you could win our uncle to your favor. Perhaps you won honors at St. Cyr. And you ruined me, too. I gave you fair duel, and you had me flung out of the school!"

"You lie! My friends did that. I begged them to make no report. And did not the authorities fling me out, too? Did I not lose my commission, and the good favor of our uncle? He disinherited both of us. Untie me, you lying pig. This is no time to jest!"

"This is no jest, my Carrot. Never a jest. You have been chasing me. I have caught you, instead. You followed my wife and me as far as America. That damned girl. How I wish you had won her! She would have been nice for you. She ran off with an American sailor and took my money. *Sacré!* I think you planned with her to do that."

"You are mad!" La Carotte gasped. "I heard she had made a fool of you, dear Hyacinth. And how I laughed. I laugh again. And you had best untie these thongs, or—"

"They are tied very tightly. They are strong bits of rope, *oui!* Do you think you could have me thrown out of St. Cyr and have me love you? You son of a camel! You had your friends say that I had cut out your eye. I, myself, hoped I had done so. So you lied about it, eh? Faked the wound. Now I find you with two perfectly good eyes, you pig, and—"

"Let me up, Hyacinth!" La Carotte snarled. "Stop this madness!"

Again Hyacinth LaDu laughed. With a brutal kick he flung his helpless cousin against the stockade wall; propped him to a sitting posture.

"Now," he growled, "I am going to say farewell. Because I think you will enjoy it. I will tell you what I am going to do. I am going to flee from this outpost. There is a path in the jungle. On my belly I creep into the jungle; gain this path to the river. There is a boat hidden there. Our scouts were supposed to use it. I will take this boat and go down river to the coast."

He screamed a laugh. "One man alone can do it. I have your rifle, your food, your ammunition. Let me tell you: I have also a bag of gold that was owned by our captain who now lies buried below the ground with eleven others of this garrison. I have that bag of gold. Ho-ho! A nice little plan, eh? I escape from this hole of death, and I escape from this accursed Foreign Legion. You, dear Carrot, have given me the chance. I thank you."

The cold sweat was pouring from the red hair of La Carotte. "You fool," he gasped. "By to-morrow afternoon the whole Legion battalion from up river will be here to smash that native town to hell. They will find you have deserted the Legion. They will catch you and riddle you with bullets!"

ONCE more that merry Hyacinth LaDu could laugh. *"Non!* That is where you suit the plan. It is wonderful." He pointed at a heap of dusty garments lying at his cousin's lashed feet. "See? Those are my things. That is my uniform. That *képi* and *capote*, those breeches are mine. They wear my insignia. In a pocket is my name-tag. You see? While you slept a moment ago, I stripped you, and changed uniforms. Listen. Now I am clad in your outfit, you comprehend? What then? Well, at noon, the savages, following their custom, will attack the fort. They will find no machine gunnery to scare them off. They take the outpost and find you. They will take you and my uniform back to their town. This afternoon they will burn you at the stake. It is very nice.

"When the Legionnaires come from up river they will find your body. But you will be a piece of charcoal, eh? And finding my uniform scattered among the blacks, they will think it was I who was burned at the stake. Finding no trace of you, they will think it was you who deserted with the gold. What then? Why, they will be looking for this dog who had just come out of the Zephyrs. They will send out orders to capture you, a man with *red hair.* Ho-ho! By that time I will be on the coast. I will have cast off and hidden your uniform. I will be disguised as an Arab or a trader. I have black hair. It is all very perfect."

Now it was all very perfect, that is so. You can imagine how perfect La Carotte thought it was. The heart in his chest became a chunk of ice. "Hyacinth! You cannot mean it. Think! They will torture me. Cannot you save me from their knives? A bullet! Shoot me in the head. Kill me—"

But Hyacinth LaDu had moved to the gate in the stockade wall. Then he turned a pleasant smile at La Carotte. "I am sorry. The blacks would not burn a corpse. And you must burn, you see. Now I must go. The drums are sounding again. They will soon be back. And so, farewell."

Slipping through the gate, Hyacinth LaDu was gone. La Carotte struggled, cursed, battled to gain his feet. Strive as he would, he could not loosen his bonds. His fingernails bled. He bit and wrenched and tore. The sun rode to its zenith, a blazing ball in a brass sky. The wind brought the echo of nearing drums, and the evil breath of the dried corpses on the wall.

La Carotte glared about him. If he could only find a bayonet, a chunk of metal, anything to pry free his hands. He could see nothing. His cousin had planned well. Groaning, he inched his body across the dirt. Perhaps he could reach the empty Hotchkiss gun on the stockade. He rolled.

He was almost at the wall. The four cadavers mounting guard paid him no attention. They were alone up there. Suddenly La Carotte realized they were not alone. He looked up in terror. Where there had been four black heads on the wall, now there were ten. The six fresh heads had woolly topknots stuck with plumes, and bright white eyes. They opened big red mouths and showed rows of grinning, filed teeth. They yelled.

AN absinthe drinker's nightmare would have been an angel's placid dream compared to that triumphal march into town. La Carotte was carried at the head of the bizarre procession by two giant blacks who stank with paint and grease and infamy.

Next came the Dahomey witch doctor, a gorgeous little fellow, livid with yellow stain, his head decorated with antelope horns and parrot feathers, his face barbarously tattooed, spikes thrust through his nostrils and lips. Brass rings jangled on his arms and legs, ropes of human skulls rattled around his skinny neck and bulbous stomach. If he was not Satan himself, he was Satan's twin brother.

Behind came the warriors, leaping, bounding, dancing, waving spears, rattling gourds, beating drums. *Sapristi!* The hot afternoon rang with their jubilant cries. But the Legionnaire in the lead sweated ice water.

Soon they were among their grass huts. Black village women and children rushed out to greet them. The white man was extended no sympathy. None at all. The good black ladies threw stones and curses and filth. The black brats hurled mud and screamed with delight. The village chanted and boomed, brayed and danced. There would be what you call a hot time in the old town to-night. That was the heart of Africa! Uncle of Satan!

They carried La Carotte across an open marketplace. In the middle of the square stood three stone *juju* idols as tall as the statue of Venus in the Louvre, but scarcely as beautiful. In front of the biggest idol, and the best, stood a big wooden stake. La Carotte closed his eyes.

But he was carried across the square, down a stinking lane and into an old grass hut at the end of the lane. The hut stood almost at the edge of the jungle. Its roof had fallen in. It was not a Boston drawing-room, you comprehend, for it had been used as a corral for goats. *Parbleu!* They carried the naked Legionnaire into the middle of the hut and stood him up against a little stake and tied him, standing, with a thong about his middle. The yellow witch doctor came in and tossed that uniform of Hyacinth LaDu's in a corner. Then the crowd went away. La Carotte was alone.

Outside the drums boomed and boomed. The early afternoon sun overhead poured a savage ray into the unshaded, foul-walled hut. La Carotte fought and fought. Sweat poured down his face. His wrists bled. The sunlight scorched his skull. The breath whistled from his lungs. If he could only break the rope lashing his hands. The muscles stood in bunches on his naked arms as he strained at the cord. It would not break.

Now and then a warrior or an old woman would go past the hut door carrying a bundle of sticks. Maybe you believe La Carotte enjoyed that little sight. He did not. It was not nice to see those sticks going by and think of the fire they would make. He tried not to think of it.

He spent his time thinking of the things he would do to that treacherous *salopard* of a cousin if he ever got free. Those thoughts made him smile. And he wrestled in a frenzy of rage and terror to get the rope from his hands. Aunt of the Devil! That was the very strongest cord in the whole wide world.

At length the witch doctor came sneaking through the door. In one hand he carried a paint brush. In the other he carried what appeared to be a lady's hat-pin. When he came close to La Carotte, the Legionnaire flung up a knee and knocked that wicked bundle of bad smells a thwack in the tummy that doubled him up howling. It made the devil pretty mad. He had intended to paint a *juju* picture on the stomach of La Carotte. Now he thought better of his intended artistry, and simply flung a splash of yellow on La Carotte's heaving chest.

Then he danced forward with a beastly yowl, avoiding the writhing elbows of his victim, and raised his long hat-pin. The sun shimmered on the pin. La Carotte went stiff with horror. Before he could apprehend the witch doctor's next move, that master of infamy stabbed out with the pin and jabbed La Carotte squarely in the left eye.

Now there was a funny thing. That needle went smack into the left eye of the Legionnaire—and the point bent into a hook! La Carotte moved no muscle. He did not bleed. He did not even scream. You can bet it gave that African horror something to think about. It gave him a first-class shock. He stared at his bent hat-pin; stared at the cold, uninjured eye of his victim. Never before had he stabbed at the eye of a captive and seen it left so calm and smiling. He opened his mouth and no sound came out, and he fled from the hut.

To say that La Carotte was in no way startled, too, would be a lie. That pin-jab had set him thinking, too. That good left eye of his! That splendid left eye! He had completely forgotten about his left eye—but he remembered it now. That eye. It had cost him nine hundred francs and it had come all the way from Switzerland. He thought about it with every bit of brain matter left in his cranium.

The sun beat fiercely on his bowed head. Outside his hut the drums were booming their crazy, cadent rant. More naked natives were hurrying past his door carrying bundles of sticks. It would take a huge pile of wood, indeed, to burn a white man whose left eye could bend a hat-pin.

And La Carotte? Well, he had been thinking about that eye, himself. He had been studying the rope lashing together his wrists, and the blazing sunlight had been burning on his bare head and body, and he had been thinking about his left eye. And suddenly he smiled. If only they would give him time.

HYACINTH LADU had been sleeping on a knoll at the edge of the wide, green river. He had been sleeping the sleep of the just, a genial smile on his bearded lips. And why not? In his *musette*—rather, the pack was his fool cousin's—there was a bag of gold. On the bank of the river lay a nice canoe, ready and provisioned for the trip. Beyond the bend of the green river lay freedom. Everything was gay for that Hyacinth LaDu. As he slept he chuckled through his gentle snores, dreaming of Paris and Monte Carlo and Biarritz and beautiful women with ravishing curls.

He awoke feeling cramped. Then he shrieked. He could not seem to get up. The fact was, he could not get up. He was bound hand and foot and tied to the ground. The sunshine of dawn, slanting through the jungle trees, made the sweat-beads glitter on his face. He stared at the awful figure standing over him, and the blood congealed in his excellent veins.

"Good morning, my Hyacinth," said La Carotte in a kindly, tired voice. La Carotte smiled, and his blue eyes were merry. He made a humorous figure, for he wore only a *képi* and a *capote* and his face was very dirty. "You sleep soundly, Hyacinth," he went on. "That is well. Typical of a brave criminal before he dies. And from the sound of things, you will die quite soon, my Hyacinth. The natives followed hard on my tracks and they are not a half hour away. Look, then. I have mounted your rifle on the knoll beside you. A string runs from the trigger to your little finger. If you do not want the natives to burn you and torture you—and they will be most savage to-day, you comprehend—you had best pull that string. The bullet, Hyacinth, will hit you squarely in the left eye."

La Carotte laughed softly, and added: "Now I will be off down the river in the canoe. I must join my battalion as soon as I can. And speaking of left eyes, Hyacinth, thank you for mine. It is a good left eye, Hyacinth. A splendid left eye. Well matched and of peerless quality. It saved my life. A wonderful eye. And a perfect burning-glass."

And just as La Carotte reached the bend of the river he heard the shot. A soft *bang!* Like that. So La Carotte chuckled in his red beard as he paddled along. It was all very fair. An eye for an eye.

"BUT I thought," declared the fat tourist from East Syracuse, New York, "that you said you'd tell a story that was true. Y'don't expect us to believe *that* yarn? Say! Y'mean to say this here Legionnaire fellow used his glass eye for a burning-glass and burned them ropes between his wrists? That's a hot one, that is. An' how about nobody noticing his glass eye? Y'mean to say he had a glass eye so cleverly made, fitted an' matched that nobody'd know it wasn't fake? Say. I'm in the business an' I never seen one that good, I can tell you. I don't believe there ever was—"

Old Thibaut Corday, the veteran Legionnaire, said nothing. He just chuckled in his cinnamon beard, and winked his left eye; and his left eye dropped with a glassy twinkle into his hand. Catching the optic in his fingers, he held its pupil to the sun. A tiny spot of light shimmered on the table top. The eye seemed to wink as the dry wood began to smoke. None of us enjoyed watching the smoke.

THE DEATH WATCH

QUEER THINGS HAPPEN TO THE FOREIGN LEGION IN AFRICA; BUT THE MADDEST AFFAIR OF ALL WAS THAT NAVAL BATTLE IN THE RED SEA.

PROLOGUE

S OMETHING WAS doing down on the square before the
mosque, Djemma el Djeddid. Boulevard Sadi Carnot lay white-
washed in bright moonlight, and the bay below its ramps was spangled
with tinsel silver. By day Algiers might be pseudo-French; but dark-
fall made it mysterious, Arab-haunted, African.

To-night the square before the mosque might have been lifted
from the "Arabian Nights." From our tables under the Brasserie
Terminus awning, old Thibaut Corday, the veteran Legionnaire, and
MacDowell, of the British consulate, and I could see the serried ranks
of shrouded Arabs, the bobbing turbans, the waving hands. MacDowell had looked up from his wineglass to remark:

"Those beggars seem more excited than the usual evening mob.
Let's stroll down an' see what's interesting 'em."

Arm in arm, the three of us walked toward the mosque. We had
just gained the outer fringe of the crowd when Thibaut Corday snatched
me by the wrist. The gnarly fingers of the old veteran bit into my flesh,
and I jumped in surprise.

A look at his face made me jump again. Torchlights smoked atop
poles raised in the center of the square, and the lambent glow shedding over the heads of the mob found the veteran's face a strange
mouse-gray. Sudden sweat glittered on his leathery forehead. He
looked ill.

"Corday!" I exclaimed. "Are you sick?"

"Sapristi!" The words steamed out of his cinnamon beard. "Sick! I
guess I am. Name of Julian the Apostate! Do you see what this crowd
is staring at? Uncle of Satan! Yes, I am sick."

MacDowell muttered in astonishment. "But I say, Corday, it's
nothing but a beastly marionette show. A pair of blooming Arab

showmen working a Punch and Judy, that's all. Haven't you seen a puppet show before? I'd call it damned amusing—"

"Amusing!" Old Thibaut Corday panted, pointing a trembly finger at the little stage under the flares.

Now, it was nothing to go ill about. There were the tawdry wooden puppets yanking, dancing and fighting on their strings. There was the showman hidden behind the stand, working the dummy figures and clacking out their dialogue in shrill Arabic. Just such a Punch and Judy performance as delights street crowds the world over.

But Thibaut Corday was not delighted. His face was waxen.

"Mon Dieu!" he groaned. "I can watch it no longer. Let us get away. Back to my room in the hotel. I have there a bottle of *cointreau.* I want a drink, for by the bones of St. Pierro of Pisa, this sight has made me sick!"

Back in the veteran's little room, MacDowell and I drank in silence, mystified. Certainly the old Frenchman had become vastly distraught. He drank his liqueur at one gulp. And Frenchman usually do not drink in a hurry.

FINISHING his *cointreau,* old Corday bustled to a cupboard in one corner of his room. I knew that cupboard of Thibaut Corday's. Pandora's Box was never more interesting.

There was history in that cupboard, for it was crammed with relics of the old man's warrior days. Legionnaire *képis* and *capotes.* Weird knives and guns. Canteens, cartridge boxes, *brodequins,* bayonets. A cupboard that echoed with the clack of gunnery; sheltered gear that was stamped with the insignia of twenty armies. For Corday's *brodequins* had marched him from Asunción to Shiloh, Loango to Hanoi. And the cupboard told the tale.

Now he took from that cupboard a little book. Dust smoked from the arid bindings as he turned the volume over in this hands. Here was a bizarre relic from the wars. I could not suppress an oath of surprise as he dropped into a chair facing us, the volume clutched between his palms.

"That book," I questioned; "what has that to do with—"

"It tells the story," he muttered. "You can read it between these leaves. Look, then."

A shaft of moonlight slanted through the open window. Keeping a thumb over the title, the old man held the book to face the moonbeams. MacDowell and I could see a tiny hole drilled through the pages, from cover to cover.

"A bullet hole," the veteran Legionnaire confessed. "And this little book tells the story. It is a story of the French Foreign Legion. That racket in the square below recalled it to my mind; for it is also the story of a puppet show, played by Legionnaires, you comprehend. And in the cast was the queerest and the bravest man who ever signed the roster of that Army of the Damned.

"But before you stay to hear the tale, I will warn you. My story sings of bravery and courage to a high note seldom attained. It sings of self-denial, valor, heroism that must have warmed the heart of *le bon Dieu*. But there is no sugar-coated fiction-pill to sweeten its end, save the memory of that glorious hero. And if you do not want to dream to-night, you had better go."

We stayed.

"Bien. This book tells the story. But I will start it for you."

And, later, we dreamed.

CHAPTER I.

THE LITTLE YANKEE.

QUEER CHARACTERS there were in the Foreign Legion, but *he* was the queerest of them all. He had little deft hands and dainty feet. His hands were the hands of an artist. His feet were those of a dancing master. He might well have been either. He was not. He was the strangest character one could hope to meet.

Can you picture his face? It was small and pointed under a flourish of hair blacker than the wing of a raven. Slim, like he was. The chin was sharpened by a stiff goatee. His lips were thin, and smiled to show perfect china teeth. His eyes were the eyes of a bird.

With those robin eyes and that pointed face, and those slim, agile hands the hue of wax, he resembled nothing more than a window model one could see in the store of a Paris merchant. You comprehend?

He looked like a wax doll.

Now, there are few recruits in the Foreign Legion who look like wax dolls. *Jamais de la vie!* Not on your life. The most of them resemble ruffians hacked out of canned beef, with hands tough as horn

and feet that know nothing of polkas but can kick like the hoof of an army mule.

This recruit, then, made a novel figure in the barracks at Sidi bel Abbes. Perhaps the strangest thing about him was his nationality. You would never have guessed it. He was, of course, an American.

He gave his name as John Smith. But every Yankee who joined the Legion called himself, you see, John Smith. To distinguish him—though Heaven knows he could easily have been distinguished—the company nicknamed him Jacques le Bouc. Jack the Goat. Because of the tuft on his chin.

The men did not like Jack the Goat. He did not get along well in Company Thirteen. He kept to himself, learned fast, worked like a Trojan to become a soldier. He was different, because his lips were sealed. Soldiers of the Legion are supposed never to tell their past histories. But they invariably get drunk and tell. They boast, for the most of them have pasts worth boasting about. Jack never told a word about who he had been or what he had done or why he had joined that Hell Battalion. All Company Thirteen could learn was that he was a Yankee. That was enough for me. I had met these Yankees before, and I knew they were men.

Those Poles and Greeks and Germans and Gascons in the outfit disliked Jack because he was reserved and silent; and the under-offi-

He was cut off from his fellow
Legionnaires by the charging tribesmen.

cers set out to make life miserable for him. He was bullied, brow-beaten, teased, abused, tripped up on all manner of evil detail.

In the barracks the men tortured him with brutish tricks. On the drill field the sergeants worked him like a quarry slave. He looked like a gentleman, and Legion drill sergeants do not like soldiers who are nicer than they. The drill they gave him must have disjointed his spine. The bullying he won in the barracks must have shredded his soul.

Sometimes he fought back. But he was a foot smaller than his kindly companions, and his little, thin hands were sore as boils from the unaccustomed work. Jack the Goat took a good many beatings, and he never had a moment of peace. You know the American expression of "being the goat." But yes. That little, frail Yankee was the "goat" of his company in every sense of the word.

From the first I liked the odd little Yankee; though I could not help him to conquer his unkindly comrades, save by giving advice. In the Legion a man must fight his own battles. And in the Legion, where the weapons of inner conflict are big fists and big boots, a small, quiet man such as Jack the Goat found life a misery.

Things went badly for Jack the Goat until the day when the regiment marched down into the Ouled Naïl mountains to attack an Arab stronghold there. *Sacré!* Something happened during that battle! Something that won the American the respect of the men and made them leave him alone. It was all very strange. One of the strangest things I had ever witnessed.

THE Arabs were gathered atop the crest of a hill, and the Legion-naires debouched from a ravine below, to attack.

Save for the queer, mad incident at its end, it was the usual mountain engagement. Company Thirteen moved up the hill with needle-bayonets fixed and flashing sunshine, guns spouting flame, *képis* dodging a hail of return fire. Dust rose in clouds under our pounding heels. Smoke from the steady gunnery rolled up into the clear sky.

Every crag and cliff tossed the echo of rattling rifles punctuated by the screams of smitten men, the squalls of officers, the chilling wail of Arab tribesmen waiting the shock of our arrival.

"Yah! Yah! Yah Allah!"

The Legion can sweat when it hears that battle cry.

It made a gorgeous picture for that clement afternoon. The Legion moved up in a long, plunging, blue line. The Arabs were gray phantoms flitting from bowlder to bowlder, sharpshooting with friendless accuracy. A Legionnaire would drop out of parade with a bullet in his hide, and the blue line would close in.

It took us twenty minutes of marching in the face of a scalding fire to climb that slope, and when we had covered half the distance most of my squad had fallen and I found myself elbow to elbow with the Yankee.

On the other side of John Smith the Goat marched three tall Poles. As they stalked onward, pumping their Lebels, they found time to hurl taunts at the little Yankee. But Jack the Goat, I found, was deserving of no taunt. I watched him from the corner of my eye in certain admiration.

This must have been his baptism of fire; yet he closed in like a veteran, unafraid. His eyes flashed gayly, his thin lips smiled no smile of fear, his jaw stuck out with courage, and his goatee fairly bristled. He could shoot like an automaton, too, and before we knew it he was all but leading our column. Napoleon was a small man. So was Jack.

"Good for you, my Jack!" I shouted to him. "You do well for a recruit. Shoot low, and mind your footing on the loose rocks up ahead." It was the first time he had marched in mountain country where the trails were treacherous as a witch's kiss. "And watch out for their attack."

He flashed me a friendly grin and yelled:

"I like it!"

But the Arabs liked it, too. All this time they had been concentrating a force among a mount of rocks to the left of our advance. Suddenly, in typical, fanatic Moslem recklessness, the whole body of wild men charged down from the rocks!

I can see those Ouled Naïl devils coming at us, to this day. I can see their spitting rifles, their bobbing hoods, their dodging beards. Like antelopes they came, hurling a wicked fusillade into our serried rank.

But we knew what their wild charge meant. They were running low on ammunition. This was their shock-blow to shatter our line. True enough. After two volleys, they were dropping their long-barreled guns, and knives as grim as Turkish scimitars were sprouting in their hands.

Now, it was one thing to walk into gunfire where the bullets were invisible; it was quite another sensation to face a horde of scimitars that flashed like crescents of silver fire in the sunlight. That taxed the nerve of the Legionnaire if anything did. But not a man of our blue line faltered.

"*Yah! Yah Allah!*" screeched the oncoming horde.

"*En avant!*" shrilled our bugler.

Meet the charge with a charge! And with a whooping, whipping smash, the blue line rushed to meet the rushing gray.

You have seen cats fighting on a roof? The bodies seem suspended in the air in a sort of squalling whirl. Our fight was somewhat similar. Hand to hand it was, with bayonet-stab for knife-slash, fist for fist, boot for boot, teeth for teeth.

I swear that for half a minute I could see nothing but the whirl. Dust rose in a choking cyclone. The ground shook underfoot. The screams of the combatants—the Moslems called to Allah, while the Legionnaires called to Heaven in a dozen tongues—and the clang of steel on steel must have deafened the ears of *le bon Dieu.*

Then abruptly it was over. The smoke and dust had thinned, the blue of the Legion had drowned most of the gray. Uncle of Satan! I swear we had smashed those sons of the Ouled Naïl flatter than the Seven Cats of Assasta. With expert Legion care we had, it seemed, finished the Moslems to a man.

If an Arab scimitar was a moon of death, those needle-bayonets of ours were swords of doom. A good many of our stout veterans lay slumbering on the stones with never a guard detail to torture them again; but the Arabs cluttered the ground like piles of soiled laundry.

I STOOD wiping my bayonet on an Arab's burnoose, meanwhile watching the blood drip from a gash on my hand and saying to myself: "Now we have killed them to the last man."

Then I heard the Legionnaires around me yelling like maniacs, pointing, and cursing with surprise.

We had not killed the Arabs to a man. There were five of them left; and the whole five were racing like mad back up the hill. They were not retreating, however. Those Ouled Naïls were warriors who did not retreat. They were charging.

And when I saw whom they charged, I let out a cry, I can tell you that. They were charging with knives upraised at the strange little Yankee with the wax hands and the stiff goatee. Jack the Goat. You comprehend?

He was two hundred yards away.

Angels only knew how he got up there alive and alone, but there he was. Arabs marked the path of his advance like chickens would mark the trail of a speeding Renault car down a country lane.

He stood alone, I say, backed against a bowlder. An Arab lay dead at his feet. His bayonet gleamed with crimson in his hand. He watched the five attacking demons with a grin that matched the glint of their waving scimitars. He had lost his *képi*, his raven hair fell in a sheaf down his forehead, and with a smile he watched death bound at him. Aunt of the Devil, what a sight!

"To his aid!" I shrieked, finding my wits. "Help him. That is the Yankee. Jack the Goat—"

We went to his rescue, a crowd of us. But the Arabs were closing in, running faster than rabbits. Guns spitting, we fired as we ran; but in our excitement we sent wild bullets. Those five Arabs would be at him in a second. They would cut him to monkey meat. I ran with fear in my heart, and six comrades came hard on my heels. Then, *sacré nom de Dieu,* if I did not stumble and bring the whole six down on top of me like a football game!

We got to our feet, screaming curses, expecting to see the Yankee cut to pieces. We saw no such thing. While we had sprawled on our faces, that little Jack the Goat had done something. He had reached down and picked up the dead Arab that had spraddled before him. Now the dead one he held propped at his side.

It was not an unknown method for a soldier to protect himself with the body of a dead one. But Uncle of Satan! Those five Arabs were not attacking. They were not dancing in to slash out with those fearful knives. No. What do you think? Just as I regained my feet I saw it all, or I never would have believed.

Those five Arabs threw down their knives as if they had been snakes of Gehenna. Then, by the bones of St. Mitrophane of Voronesh, they went down on their knees, bowed their backs and flung out their arms as they bobbed their foreheads against the ground. You understand? They salaamed!

I do not know how we Legionnaires recovered from astonishment enough to capture those prayerful five. But we got up there, rammed our bayonets into their ribs, and stood them up against the bowlder. Whereat the amazing Yankee let drop the body of the dead tribesman and saluted us with a grin.

"Thank you very much," he said, dusting off his knees. "It was a close call for a little old man, eh? All right, friends. Let us drive the captives into camp. They won't make trouble."

Nor did they. Do you know what they said? *Parbleu!* They marched off meek as lambs, but before they went they pointed at the body of the Arab our Jack the Goat had held beside him. They pointed politely, saying the dead Arab was their chief.

Furthermore, they said, just as they had been about to cut down our Jack the Goat, this dead chief had spoken. They were frightened about it, for dead chiefs seldom spoke to living Arabs. But this chief had talked out aloud, telling them to throw down their knives and let the white soldier live, for such was the will of Allah.

Queer? I should say it was queer. Jack the Goat, himself, offered no explanation; leisurely he strolled off to pick up his lost *képi*. I? I examined that dead Arab. The body was cold with three bullets in the skull. Arab superstitions, eh?

Somehow, the little Yankee got along well in the company after that. The Legionnaires were mighty civil to Jack the Goat; left him to his own devices. Behind his back, though, there were strange whisperings, furtive glances. I did a lot of wondering, too, you may well believe. Jack the Goat kept to himself, learned his soldiering well, and because he had, somehow or other, caused the capture of five live Arabs, he was made a soldier of the first class.

I was his only friend. Even so, he would seldom talk to me about himself. Looking back, it seems portentous and queer that the only time he spoke to me of himself was that first night our transport ship nosed down the Mediterranean. We stood aboard that rotting vessel, the *Fleur de France,* which was steaming to the aid of a Legion outpost beleaguered in French Somaliland. It was on that ship of Satan that this strangest story of the Foreign Legion played to its mad end.

CHAPTER II.

THE FLOWER
OF FRANCE.

THE *FLEUR DE FRANCE,* please know, was not a boat. She was the ghost of a boat. All rusty, clanking bones and wheezes and uncanny groans and smoke. The Flower of France. Bah!

They sent her down from Marseilles to load her with army supplies and ammunition at Bizerta. Then they crammed her lousy main deck with black Tirailleurs, sharpshooters. Then they sent to Sidi bel Abbes for a squad of Legionnaires to look after the Tirailleurs.

I was among the eight Legionnaires who boarded the *Fleur de France* to look after the Tirailleurs. I have every good reason to re-member my companions. There was the German, Schneider; De Nogales the Venezuelan; Fuertes the Spaniard; a French *apache* named Le Canif because his face was like a knife. There was Kalnikoff, a former Russian general of Cossacks. There was Lieutenant Gentilet, who had once been a major at St. Cyr and was now to command our detachment. Lastly, there was the little Yankee, Jack the Goat.

When we knew our job, the eight of us went pretty sick. There we were aboard a transport older than Noah's Ark, stuffed with a company of African colonials to keep an eye on, bound for Somaliland to relieve an outpost and kick the devil out of a Somali rebellion.

You know French Somaliland? It is a mean little strip of Africa lying on the coast where the Red Sea spills into the Gulf of Aden through the Strait of Bab el Mandeb. It is bounded on the west by Abyssinia, on the north by Eritrea, on the south by a British protec-torate.

It was going to be a long voyage down there on a rotten hulk like the *Fleur de France.* We Legionnaires did not like the idea. We did not like the company of black Tirailleurs crowded on the main deck below us. They looked like a lot of black gorillas just out of Congo. They were commanded by a giant negro named Ahmed.

Pacing the deck below, they would turn their white eyes on the bridge where our cabin was. They carried light carbines across their massive shoulders and monstrous *coupe-coupe* knives in the sashes that belted their white uniforms. They were a bad lot to be fighting under the flag of France.

"They are villains every one," Lieutenant Gentilet assured us with a grim smile.

It was our first night at sea. The *Fleur de France* was staggering down the Mediterranean toward the Suez Canal. We Legionnaires were standing on the high forward bridge where we were quartered, looking down on the Tirailleurs decked below.

"They glare at us who stand up here," the officer went on, "with evil in the eye. Already I have had a quarrel with that Ahmed who is their captain. He is angry about the food and thinks we Legionnaires are favored with better quarters. Pah! Fancy good cabins on this lousy craft."

Such a thing could not be fancied. You should have seen the boat. She had that high forward bridge where we Legionnaires were jammed in a cabin. Aft she was a canal barge. A skinny funnel stuck up amidships. Every wave that hit her boarded the forecastle under the bow where her luckless sailors lived. And every inch of her hulk was a vermin-nest.

"A lousy craft," our lieutenant snarled again. "Look at her. Her engines just about move her. Two life-boats." He indicated the dory slung over the stern. "There is that dory, and there is that rowboat over the bow. I hope to high heaven a storm does not hit us on this trip."

"And so do I," agreed Jack the Goat, after the officer and the others had gone to their cabins.

The little American and I were alone on the bridge. Wind was rising and stars were scattering down the sky. The squeak of the boat's hull, the low throb of her struggling engines, the tramping boots of the Tirailleurs on the deck below made an undertone to the chant of the sweeping sea.

In the air was the smell of salt and boat-tar and coal-smoke. Now and then we could get a whiff of the black men on the main deck; catch the echo of their thick voices.

THE little Yankee laid a hand on my sleeve. "Lieutenant Gentilet expects trouble, eh? Trouble from the boat and from those Tirailleurs. It is a long, long way down to Somaliland."

"Too damned long," I suggested. "I do not love the idea, my friend. Here we are, eight Legionnaires on a boat filled with blacks. The Tirailleurs can be handled on land. But at sea it may be something else. And I think we'll have a stiff fight with the Somalis when we do get there."

He turned his face to me. I could see his eyes shining in the darkness, and I knew he was smiling. He put a small hand over mine.

"Look here," he explained. "You've been a friend to me, Thibaut Corday. The others do not like me. In the barracks at Sidi they made hell for me. After that battle with the Ouled Naïl they left me alone, but they are not my friends. Just now they went to the cabin for a go at cards and didn't ask me to join. They think I am something strange. But you have stuck by me. I reckon you've wondered about me, eh?"

I was surprised at this speech. "But yes," I admitted. "You are not exactly like the common Legionnaire. You have not confided in them, you see, and then that fight in the mountains—"

He laughed. "But I *am* like the others. Look here, Corday. Why did you join the Legion, anyway? Will you tell?"

"A woman," I growled confession. "And that is why most of them have joined. A woman has driven them to hell."

"I am like the rest," he said softly. "A woman. I will confide in you, Corday. You have been a friend. Yes, a woman drove me into the Legion. She was my wife—in America. She was younger than I. We worked together for years. I loved her better than anything on earth. I love her still, even though she ran away. We were in New York City. I was just at the pinnacle of success. She left a note. She was going to another man. She had met him in Europe, I believe. She said she no longer loved me, and was going to this man. It sort of finished me, Corday."

He did not cry, but his voice cried. Some men can love like that. I felt like the very devil for him, and patted his shoulder. That untrue wife of his meant something to the little man. No wonder he had not spouted his story around the Legion.

"I could not stand the old life," he went on, "so I joined this army. I have enjoyed the work and care little whether I die in Africa or in hell. At all events I'm away from America—the old haunts, the echoes, the memories. Listen, Corday. Listen, carefully. I carry in the pocket—this breast pocket of my tunic—a little package. Wrapped in brown paper. If—if anything ever happens to me, somehow, I'd like you to have it. Will you remember? Will you remember the little packet? It will tell a story."

"I will remember," I promised him. "You want me—"

"To keep it as a souvenir. Something to remember me by. I'd like to be remembered by somebody, Corday. And somehow, I've a queer feeling that something may happen on this voyage. It's in the air. This rotten boat. This trip into the tropics. Down that weird Suez Canal. Through the ancient Red Sea. Like a dream. And those black colonials below. There may be trouble."

We were silent then. The boat sneaked under the stars. Black water, slipping by abeam, glistened like ebony in the gloom. I thought of the strangeness of the world, of the little man beside me, of the wife who had snapped brutal fingers at his stout heart. I thought of that queer incident in the Ouled Naïl Mountains. I thought of the little Yankee's premonition.

I thought of the black Tirailleurs on the deck below. You could not see their charcoal faces in the darkness. You could just see the white uniform. Bodies moving without heads. Trouble. Somehow I became a little ill.

That very same night Lieutenant Gentilet was stabbed in the back. We found him lying on the bridge next morning, quite, quite dead. *Pardieu!*

PERHAPS you believe there was the very devil to pay, then. There was, indeed. One grand uproar shook the steamer from stern to stem. The lieutenant of the Legion had been murdered. The head of the detachment lay dead with a knife-thrust in his spine. Trouble a-plenty.

The *Fleur de France* put in to shore at Monastir and staged a royal investigation. Who had killed Lieutenant Gentilet? The Legionnaires accused the Tirailleurs. The Tirailleurs accused the Legionnaires and the sailors. The ship's crew accused everybody else.

Finally the suspects were boiled down to Ahmed, the Tirailleur captain, to three sailors who had been on watch, to the French Legionnaire known as Le Canif because his face was like a knife, and to Jack the Goat and me.

The little Yankee and I had been on deck later than the others. Ahmed was under suspicion because he had quarreled with the lieutenant. The three sailors had been somewhere at hand. And Le Canif had been a criminal and looked capable of stabbing his dying mother.

All very sad. Nothing could be proved in so short a time, and the rumpus did not restore life to Lieutenant Gentilet.

Then telegrams were dispatched. The new wires along the North African coast trembled with commands. Brigade headquarters at Sidi raged in its spade beard. There were messages. A wild cry for help had come up from Somaliland. Jibuti Port, Obok and the town of Tajura had been attacked, and the Somali coast was in flames. There were women and children in those helpless towns. The Legion outposts there were out of supplies and wanted reserves badly. A handful of guns and men might save the day.

Brigade headquarters sent a raging message to the *Fleur de France*. We were to go on full speed ahead. At Port Said we would stop and pick up Captain Dieudonné Daudet, who would take the detachment down. If any one could handle the job it was Dieudonné Daudet. Off we steamed with smoke boiling from our funnel and the engines straining in our middle; fast for Port Said and to the rescue.

You can imagine things were not too pleasant aboard that rotten transport ship. You bet they were not. Everybody had called everybody else a murderer. The ship and the rations were bad. The Tirailleurs, standing in a solid black mass behind their giant Congo-god of a captain, were complaining. We soldiers of the Legion staged a bitter quarrel with the captain of the good ship Flower of France.

Just off the coast of Egypt a storm lashed out of the East, kicked the boat in the stomach, bent her spine, tore the lifeboat from her stern, and gave her engines the rheumatism. Now the *Fleur de France* could stagger along about six miles an hour. A state of affairs calculated not to enhance a feeling of good-fellowship among its passengers.

I, myself, assumed command of the Legion squad, being older in rank than the rest. If things were bad among the black colonials on the main deck, it was no Sabbath school up there in our cabin on the bridge, where the German, the Russian, the Venezuelan and the Spaniard—ruffians all—were seasick.

Le Canif, the French *apache*, sneaked around with hate in his crooked eyes and a sneer on his lips, pretending his feelings had been wounded because of the unjust accusation that he had killed our officer. Pah! His angular, bony face was the face of a rascal; and I was not too sure the accusation was unjust.

I fail to know what I could have done without the little Yankee at my side. Jack the Goat was a prince. He smiled all the time. He never complained. He was a strange one to see in his Legion uniform, so small and gentlemanly and bird-like. But his heart was of solid gold, that is so. And more, as you shall see.

So I was mighty grateful when we dropped anchor in the harbor at Port Said to pick up Captain Dieudonné Daudet. We lay in close to shore, and I was going off in a small boat to meet the officer.

"I am glad my command is finished," I told the little Yankee. "This boat is dynamite waiting to be exploded. If any one can put out the fuse it is Captain Daudet. He has been here in Port Said on some manner of special government duty. He is the giant of the Legion. The sternest officer in the army."

That was so. Captain Dieudonné Daudet was one terror of a man, feared in the service of French armies from East to West. I had been under his command before, and I knew him.

A big Corsican he was, with a fierce red beard, fierce blue eyes, terrific shoulders and hands. His chest was a keg of muscles and glittered with forty medals. He had been in the Legion for years and his middle name was Discipline. One whispered when one saw him coming, and instinctively snapped to attention. I was glad he was going to take us down to Somaliland.

But when I found him waiting on the pier with his wife, and learned he was going to take *her* with him aboard the ship, my heart sank. A woman aboard that lousy old lugger of a transport. And such a beautiful woman. Uncle of Satan! Here was a match to touch off any dynamite.

AMORETTE was her name. I had heard of this wife of Captain Daudet before. She had been with him in Algiers on recent date. Gossip spoke of her as the most beautiful woman in the colonies. The moment I set eyes on her, waiting on the pier with her giant husband, I knew gossip was right.

I picked up the captain's duffel, and I stared. *Dieu!* She was a wonder. Any woman who could look beautiful on a pier at Port Said would be wonderful.

I remember her yet as I saw her then. I remember her small and stately figure, her burst of gorgeous mahogany-colored hair trapped by a little white sun-hat, her face that was like finest Carrara marble. Her sea-blue eyes would have made a saint break his promises. Her smiling scarlet mouth would have caused an artist to sell his soul. The *houris* whom Del Castillo had painted in the Castle of Yakub el Mansur were not half so beautiful as she.

"For the sake of Heaven, Captain Daudet," I whispered to the officer. "But you are not going to take your wife aboard ship? That boat is a weasel-coop loaded with spawn of the devil."

He withered me with a glance and an oath to remind me of my rank.

"Attend to your business," he snarled. "I am commander now. My wife goes with me to Somaliland. I am to be governor there. And I understand there has been trouble on the transport. The Tirailleurs have raised the devil, eh? Your Lieutenant Gentilet was murdered. So! By the bones of Anthony Carpetsi, things will be different from now on. Pick up my duffel, you *salopard!* Make for my wife a comfortable place in the small boat. What are you standing idle for?"

That was the good Captain Dieudonné Daudet. Nothing for it, but I must make way to the small boat. The beautiful Amorette seated herself in the bow. Captain Daudet and I stood in the stern, and the sailors from the *Fleur de France* pulled seaward.

While we rocked toward our transport, which squatted among the clutter of boats near the canal mouth like some ugly amphibian, Captain Daudet questioned me about the murder and flung oaths and orders.

So a Legion officer had been stabbed in the back, eh? The devil! And the transport was in bad shape? Another devil! Well, those aboard the boat were going to step lively from now on.

"Your Brigade headquarters must be insane," Captain Daudet thundered, "to send only one squad of Legionnaires with a whole company of those damned colonials. But I presume they could spare no more of the Legion because of the fighting in Morocco, eh? The Paris War Department has gone mad, anyway. There are those poor devils trapped in Somaliland—"

He bit off his words in his scarlet whiskers, evidently realizing he was talking to an inferior. Folding his arms across his medal-hung chest, he watched us bear down on the *Fleur de France* with a bitter sneer on his lips.

His girlish wife in the bow was smiling like a lady going for a brief row in the lakes of the Bois de Boulogne. Moreover, she was casting her smiles at me; something I sincerely wished she would not do, for her husband was famed for quick temper and shooting first before he asked. However, she was a woman. What do women know of war?

It made me pessimistic to think of that lovely creature being on the *Fleur de France* with its cargo of scoundrels. Every one of those black Tirailleurs was lined up at the main deck rail when our small boat came alongside.

On the bridge above, I could see the heads of the Legionnaires. Sailors coiling hawsers on the forecastle head stopped work to stare. All eyes were turned on the lady. It made me sweat. I caught a steely glint in the eye of Captain Daudet, which made me sweat the more. Trouble. Always more trouble.

A gangway came down from the deck; the captain, his wife and I swung aboard ship. Pompous as a rooster, the skipper marched forward to meet the famous Legion officer. Captain Daudet ignored his flamboyant gestures of greeting.

"Move this boat!" he roared. "I am Captain Dieudonné Daudet, now in command of this expedition. Do not stand gaping, fool. I have here papers from the War Department giving me full command. Start the engines in this damned barge. Have you your clearing papers? Good! Get us on our way and through the canal. Perhaps you know we are going to fight a war? Splendid! Be on!"

"But the lady, *mon capitaine?* Does she go with us?"

"In the very best cabin you can provide on this stinking craft. She goes with us, yes. You comprehend? She is my wife."

I THINK the skipper of the *Fleur de France* wanted to talk back. It was irregular for ship captains to take commands from expeditionary officers. However, the captain of the *Fleur de France* did not talk back. There was a something in the fierce blue eyes of the giant Legion officer which stifled opposition. The captain of the *Fleur de France* swallowed thrice, managed an almost humble bow, and danced off.

A moment later we could hear bells tinkling in the belly of the boat, sailors shouting, winches squealing. Water churned under the steamer's blunt stern and the anchor rattled up into her prow, showering mud.

Then what do you suppose? Captain Daudet took his wife by the arm and marched her straight across the main deck through that mob of black Tirailleurs. Straight across the deck he marched her, and the African colonials did not stand in his way, you may well believe. Ahmed, their commander, sighted the red beard and the chevrons of the newcomer, and Ahmed snapped to attention with speed.

"Clear your black devils off this deck!" Captain Daudet screamed into the Tirailleur officer's face. "I will stand them on parade to-morrow afternoon. You know who I am? Splendid! I am given to understand that you and your detachment of men have been making a rumpus. This is the end of it. You will report to me later."

Then onward marched Captain Daudet with his wife. On to the skinny ladder leading up to the high bridge; on up the ladder. The Legionnaires on the bridge had sense enough to fall into line and stand at attention. I sprang into line, myself; and the seven of us waited in a stiff row.

Captain Daudet planted himself before us, his wife beside him. Fists on hips, the captain stood, feet spread apart, head thrust forward, eyes traveling from face to face. A moment he said nothing. Then a stream of burning oaths crackled and snapped from his red beard.

"So this is the picked squad of men sent to fight the Somalis, eh? A likely bunch of ragamuffins. Of all the Legionnaires I have ever seen, you seven are the worst. Now, my merry *salopards,* I will tell you who I am. I am Dieudonné Daudet, the toughest commissioned officer in the service. That means something. It means that things are going to click on this transport from now on. It means that the first word of trouble starts me shooting. It means that those Tirailleurs are going to shut their black mouths. It means that we are making record time to Somaliland. That is what it means. And the first man among you to start anything with me will find himself in scalding water, that is so.

"Now, then, scum," Captain Daudet snarled, *"this is my wife!"* He bowed to the lady. "She is going with us. A beautiful person for such foul company. Make no mistake, you dogs. She is to be treated with every respect. The least disrespect will mean a death among you."

Stepping forward suddenly, Captain Daudet shot out a heavy fist. Now we had been standing in line thus: Schneider, the German; De Nogales, the Venezuelan; Le Canif from Paris; Fuertes the Spaniard; Kalnikoff of Russia; the little Yankee, and myself. Lined up against the rail, you understand. So the fist of Captain Daudet smashed like a flung hammer into the jaw of the fat German named Schneider.

Legionnaire Schneider dropped to his face.

"That for you, you dog!" Captain Daudet shouted at the crumpled figure. "Instead of listening to me, you were staring at my wife. Learn not to do so!"

His fist swept out again. *Smack!* Squarely on the chin of the tall Venezuelan. De Nogales fell like a sack of old clothing.

"You," bellowed Captain Daudet, "stared, too. Learn the lesson!"

Le Canif, the *apache,* was next.

"I do not like your face," Captain Daudet smiled, hitting him suddenly with his left fist. "You, too, stared at my wife. Beware from now on!"

And down went that lousy Parisian. Yes. And down went Fuertes from Spain; and down went Kalnikoff of Russia. Down they went. It was like a game of nine-pins. It was Captain Dieudonné Daudet's gentle way of establishing discipline in *La Légion.* Those men had dared to stare at his wife.

IT was a merry little scene. Captain Daudet striking out that bludgeon fist of his. The stricken Legionnaires dropping like emptied sacks. The wife of Captain Daudet standing there with a scared smile. (Perhaps this was a lesson for her, too.) And all around us the harbor of Port Said hooting and tooting in the blazing sunshine of Africa. It was a merry scene, saddened only by the fact that I was in line for a punch on the jaw, having stared like the others.

But our Yankee had *not* stared at the woman. From the corner of my eye I had watched my little friend. Throughout the whole performance he had not moved a muscle. Eyes front, he waited at attention stiff as a ramrod. The thought suddenly came over me: why should the little Yankee stare at any woman? He had learned a lesson on that score.

"Do not hit him," I said impulsively, stepping forward a pace. "Do not hit the American, Captain Daudet. He has been the only soldier of the lot who has—"

"I will hit him!" the officer roared. "Not because he stared at my wife. *Non!* He did not look at her. But I shall hit him because my wife made eyes at him. It will be a lesson—"

And *crack!* He sent the frail Yankee spinning. I must have raised a hand against him, for he hit me twice. Once in the stomach. Again on the jaw. Then I was flat on my back with the others. *Dieu!*

When I came to consciousness it was to stare through a headache at a sky sprinkled with early stars. The horizon was blue as the tunic of a Spahi. I could hear the throbbing of ship engines, smell a desert breeze, feel the tremble of the ship beneath me.

The little Yankee squatted beside me, calmly smoking a cigarette. On his lips there waited a sardonic smile.

"I was commanded to let you sleep," he said quietly. "Now I am to tell you to report for a guard detail."

I groaned a curse and got up on sore elbows.

The Yankee gingerly touched a finger to his jaw.

"That Captain Daudet is a good soldier, at least. His wife is—one of the loveliest women I have ever seen. But in spite of her husband, I think she will make much trouble."

His voice trailed off, and his cigarette became a crimson eye in the gloom. Then he said: "We are sailing southward down the Suez Canal, Corday. We are sailing straight into hell."

CHAPTER III.

INTO HELL!

IN THOSE days the ordinary passenger boat went down the canal in eighteen hours. Since she was only rushing to the rescue of women and children and Legionnaires in Somaliland, the *Fleur de France* took twenty-four hours.

She plodded through the Bitter Lake region with marsh birds wheeling over her taffrail, hooting like lost souls. She halted at Suez for coal, and received another urgent wail for help from the outposts of Somaliland. Then she staggered with a fouled rudderpost into the Gulf of Suez, and it was blazing noon when she sighted Mount Sinai off her port beam. No one on board had much time for sightseeing and thinking about this barren mountain where Moses received the Law. We were receiving a little law of our own from good Captain Daudet. All morning he drilled the Tirailleurs on the main deck. All afternoon he drilled his seven Legionnaires. He made us overhaul our gear, wash down our cabin, police the bridge deck, and unlimber a Chaut-chaut automatic rifle. All evening he raged, stamped and tramped around the cabin of the ship captain, howling for more speed.

His presence aboard ship had made the Tirailleurs quiet as mice. You could see them mumbling to themselves, rolling their big white eyes up at the bridge where Daudet commanded. Were they thinking of him? Or were their minds on the beautiful white woman quartered up there in a forward cabin? During the ensuing three days I wondered. Sometimes it seemed to me those big black African colonials were too quiet.

But all things considered, the *Fleur de France* was plowing down the Red Sea in orderly fashion. Captain Daudet had established an iron discipline over the craft and even urged a few knots extra speed out of its antediluvian engines.

Five days down the Red Sea we sighted the coast of Eritrea off our starboard bow. A junky Arab boat came scooting out from the shore, bringing the news that a platoon of Legionnaires, stationed at Taklai, was going to start a forced march down the coast and would reach our port in Somaliland a few days after we did. We lined the bridge rail, and could almost see that platoon of Legion devils footing it down the mountainous shore.

"*Dios!*" snarled Fuertes, the Spaniard. "It gives me a feeling of companionship to know there are Legionnaires on that coast. It has been lonely on this rat-nest lost in the Red Sea."

"*Himmel!*" grunted the fat German. "I am glad this cursed voyage draws to a close. Every night I have expected those Tirailleurs to mutiny and cut us by the throat. *Ja!* Captain Daudet has held them down, but I think they hate us. And with that woman quartered up here with us—"

"I am glad," muttered the tall Russian, "that our trip ends soon, myself. We sail to-night without mishap to our engine, and to-morrow late we should be near the Strait of Bab el Mandeb."

De Nogales, the Venezuelan, was in his cabin furbishing gear, so he could offer no comment. Le Canif, the Paris *apache*, simply spat in the dark water. The little Yankee, Jack the Goat, only shrugged.

EVENING with ragged clouds in a green sky, a low moon shedding silvery streamers across the calm water, and the coast of Eritrea lying a line of red mountain peaks off our starboard beam.

I was standing on the bow of the ship with Jack the Goat. Three crazy native *dhows* had scuttled under the shadow of our prow and now were lost in the direction of Arabia. In that same easterly direction the smoke of three passenger boats from the Orient hung feathers on the horizon.

Those three tiny *dhows*, those three distant feathers of smoke, that low rim of mountain peaks had made the only break in a monotony of shifting water that was the loneliest sea in all the world just then.

The moon climbed higher in the sky and sneaked into a nest of gray clouds. The *Fleur de France* waddled along creaking, smoking and shivery. The only sound was the occasional bell-tinkle in the pilot house on our bridge, the burble of the cutwater boiling past our bows, the clatter of the sabots worn by the sailor who stood lookout near us.

The little Yankee leaned on the rail and pointed south. "By the chart in the cabin we should soon be passing the Dahlak Archipelago. Right now we are not far from that African coast. Corday, I never expected we would get this far in this bilious old ship."

"Nor I," was my confession. "There has been an undercurrent of disaster ever since we left Port Said. You have felt it, too. I know. A handful of white men on a boat jammed with unreliable blacks. I—"

Jack the Goat caught the sleeve of my tunic. I felt it at the same time. So did the sailor on lookout. He swung around with an oath and peered at the pilot house.

"Parbleu!" he called. "Did you two soldiers of the damned feel that jar? Our engines have completely stopped."

"Did either of you," snarled the Yankee, "think you heard a scream? There! There, by Heaven—there it is again!"

I should say we did hear the scream. It coiled up into the tropic dusk and lost itself in echoes against the metal sky. A shrill soprano scream such as a woman might give.

The next instant all hell broke loose on the bridge. Voices barked and bawled. Gunfire crashed out. Boot heels pounded up ladders and across deck beams. From the forecastle head, where we stood paralyzed, the Yankee and I caught the flash of spitting automatics, brief glimpses of men running through shadows. A sailor came tumbling down from the wheelhouse, wailing in terror.

"The Tirailleurs!" he screamed. "They mutiny. They have smashed into the engine room. That wife of the Legion captain has started it. She walked down from the bridge, a Tirailleur smiled at her, and that captain shot the black man dead. Now they will murder us all! Holy

St. Adrian!"

"Aux armes!" It was the voice of Captain Daudet somewhere amidships. "Legionnaires! Help!"

"Quick!" screeched Jack the Goat, bounding past me. "To the bridge, Corday. We must hold the bridge and the pilot house."

I was after him in a trice, and we went shin-banging up to our cabin like a pair of maniacs. All was confusion on the bridge. Powder smoke hung thick in the air with another odor—blood. Somehow or other the oil lamps had been smashed out, and it was darker than sin in the alleyways.

Amidships the vessel was a howling Gehenna. Gunfire flashed like the flame of lightning down there on the main deck. I could hear bullets thumping into wood and tearing through canvas. I could hear Captain Daudet shrieking oaths. I could hear those black Tirailleurs squalling like a den of raging tigers. I could hear a woman sobbing.

We came across her huddled at the door of her cabin.

"They are dead!" she was sobbing, her voice high with hysteria. "They are dead. And I am lost!"

We did not stop to find out what she meant. Jack the Goat yanked her to her feet.

"Get into your cabin!" he shouted. "Quick! Give me the key. I will lock you in. They cannot get up here on the bridge."

She started to say something, but he clapped a hand over her mouth and flung her into the cabin, slamming and locking the door after her.

We darted on, down the infernal alley; dashed into our own cabin. A lamp was glimmering in there, and I wish it had not been. For the little Yankee stumbled over one body, and I sprawled over another. You understand? Schneider and Fuertes lay there on the floor. Dead! With their own bayonets rammed into their necks.

"The devil!" Jack the Goat panted. "Some one stabbed them while they sat there at table. Look. Playing cards scattered around. Their backs were to the door. Some one yanked the bayonets from their sheaths and murdered them."

"Look!" I shouted, pointing at a bunk. "There lies the Russian. Murdered, too. *Sacré nom de Dieu!* Foul play!"

But we had no time to gossip. We snatched our Lebels from our own bunks and fled into the alley again. You realize how the after deck of the bridge looked down on the main deck amidships? You know about the skinny ladder leading up to the bridge deck from that main deck below? That was where we found the foul play.

Uncle of Satan! I will not forget the picture I found there, as long as I live. No. Nor after I die.

SLIDING from behind a cloud, the moon cruised open sky and shed a spectral ray that made the face of Captain Dieudonné Daudet a devil-mask. His eyes were wild, his cheeks the color of banana meat. His *képi* was gone, and his red hair tossed in the salty wind. A bullet-scrape across his forehead poured crimson streams down either side of his jaw. Curse after curse was crackling from his beard.

A wild sight he made, crouching there at the top of the ladder, swinging the Chaut-chaut rifle to spray a blaze of steel at the deck below.

Can you see that raging jam of Africans on the main deck? Can you see that plunging knot of white uniforms, headless in the dark save where sudden gun-flame picked out an ebony face for a second-tick? Can you see the spiteful jets of fire squirting from their carbines, and the baleful ragged flash of those long *coupe-coupe* knives waving aloft?

Those fiendish knives gleamed like flashes of water. Those charging white uniforms made a boiling surf on the dark deck. And their savage, demoniac outcry rose like the smash of breaking seas. In a body they would rush the ladder. *Rrrrrrrrrt!* would roar Captain Daudet's gun. In a body they would retreat. Like waves.

Jack the Goat and I sprang out of the alleyway, and for a second could do nothing but stare as if smitten. Behind the gun that wove a brocade of white fire down those steps Captain Daudet was magnificent. Magnificent! Do you know what he made me think of? He made me think of that gallant Dutch boy with his thumb on the dike, stemming the torrential flood.

Just as I was thinking that (with no honest time for thinking anything) I saw something else. Jack the Goat saw it, too, and caught my arm.

The ladder defended by Captain Daudet fell from the starboard end of our bridge. At the *port* end of the bridge—right out on the wing—two men were fighting. Silently, almost secretly, they struggled in and out of shadow, bodies locked, arms trapped by arms, faces rammed together.

I could have yelled when I saw them there. De Nogales, the Venezuelan, and Le Canif, the Paris *apache*. Legionnaire against Legionnaire. Fighting like the very devil!

Busy at the ladder, Captain Daudet failed to see them. But the little Yankee and I saw them, that is so. We saw the evil, hate-twisted face of Le Canif, the stricken, knotted countenance of De Nogales. We saw ruby drops scattered from De Nogales's cheek. We saw a short, wet dirk lashing in the fist of the foul Frenchman.

Before the Yankee or I could move a foot, the Venezuelan sighted us.

"Aqui!" he screamed. "Shoot him! He murdered the others. He started the mutiny. Kill him! *Por Dios,* I am—"

Too late! Le Canif wrenched like a tiger. Out came that short, wet knife. Into shadow and out of shadow. De Nogales pirouetted like a dancer, and crashed to his face. It was all so quick.

Jack the Goat fired and I fired. But the *apache* made a flying leap. Like a catamount he went past us. Like a catamount he landed on the back of Captain Daudet, who was bent, unsuspecting, over his shouting Chaut-chaut gun. In and out went that devil's knife. Captain Daudet spraddled flat beside the gun.

The Yankee and I hurled ourselves at that traitorous Legionnaire. Our clawing hands snatched shadows. Le Canif had thrown himself down the ladder to join the Tirailleurs at its base.

DIEU! but the little Yankee moved fast. Springing on the Chaut-chaut gun, he had it hammering in no time. Tirailleur bullets were hissing up to the bridge in a deadly rain. They did not touch Jack the Goat. He was swinging the gun, weaving a network of bullets across the main deck.

His first burst of fire caught that Paris *apache,* Le Canif, smack in the chest, and all but knocked him to pieces. That was good. We saw Le Canif drop into a pile of white uniforms cluttering the ladder base. Then the Tirailleur charge was scattering back and away.

I had swung my Lebel into action, and was raking the shadows clinging to the engine-room house amidships where the funnel jutted skyward. The deck between that house amidships and the bridge where we hung was now clear, save for white lumps scattered here and there, and that piece of garbage in Legion uniform sprawled at the foot of our ladder.

The Yankee with his automatic gun and I with my Lebel drew a line of fire from rail to rail across that deck. Bullets whistled out of the shadows aft, winging over our bridge deck. But Jack the Goat was sheltered by the body of Captain Daudet, and I was behind the canvas fence of the bridge-rail. Thus protected, they could not spot us readily.

"Quick, then," the Yankee howled at me. "Get the sailors, Corday! Where in the name of Heaven have they been hiding? Run forward and find them. Bring guns and another drum of ammunition for the Chaut-chaut. I can hold them back. I can keep them from the ladder. They dare not cross that open deck, and they cannot go under this bridge to get forward. Tell the sailors to come up here. If once those blacks should gain the pilot house—"

The sailors! I had forgotten them. I saw the Yankee could hold those African mutineers for the moment, so I raced back into the alleyway.

As I passed the cabin door behind which Captain Daudet's wife was locked I heard her sobbing in hysteria. The sound lent wings to my feet.

Bawling for aid, I rushed to the captain's cabin. That captain was not there. I banged into the little chart room. Empty! I scrambled into the pilot house. Not a soul to be seen; and the wheel turning idly as if maneuvered by ghostly hands.

Suspicion came suddenly. Sick with fear, I rushed down to the fore deck. Not a sailor to be seen. Now I was sweating and terrified, in all honest truth. Like a maniac I went galloping to the forecastle and screamed into the forecastle companion. No answer save a scurry of rats.

By the bones of King Michael, it got me like a hand on the stomach. I flung around from the hatch, and saw! Empty boat-davits. Yes! With a shriek I sprang to the bow rail.

Overside the water was lost in shade. The moon above had gone, leaving the Red Sea a sweep of muttering gloom. Far away I could hear the sound of squeaking oar-locks and muted voices. *Sapristi!* That thrice-damned crew of sailors, that craven mariner captain had robbed the *Fleur de France* of her only accessible lifeboat, and fled.

CURSE? If I ever cursed any one in my life, I cursed those sailors of the *Fleur de France*. But I had little time to do them justice. I hailed twice and got no answer save the slop of waves against our prow. Then I screamed my names for them. Names that should have made vinegar of the milk in their veins. And then the sound of the Chaut-chaut gun chattering on the bridge flung me into my senses, and I raced back to that upper deck once more.

I was sweating blood as I pounded aft through the gloomy alley of the bridge. What a gay situation was this. In my mind I could see it all. That black hulk of a steamboat lolling idly down a lost ocean. Those raging black troopers charging again and again from the after deck. Charging to rip apart two measly white men, lone defenders of the honor of France. Charging to capture the transport. Charging to gain a cabin where a woman hid weeping—a white girl whose slim beauty they had watched and marked with their bulbous, baleful eyes.

I gained the Yankee's side just in time to fend off another charge. The Tirailleurs were learning respect for that fast-shooting Chaut-chaut gun, and they did not press the attack too far. Carbines spitting, they came forward with a wariness, like so many gorillas clad in white.

They moved down the port and starboard sides of the well-deck, intent on getting under the bridge. Not a devil of them got across the deck. The Yankee and I drew the line with withering steel slugs.

In the old days the sailors of British merchantmen would keep idle passengers off the fore deck where they worked by drawing a chalk line from rail to rail. They called this "chalking their toes." So the little American and I chalked the toes of those howling demon Tirailleurs with a line of bullets that must have sawed a strip out of that deck.

Jack the Goat ripped back and across with his rapid-firer. I sharp-shot into the shadows. They retreated aft of the engine-room house once more. Our gunfire, not needed further, faded to an echo.

The Yankee whirled on me. "Those sailors?"

"Gone!" I panted. "But fast. Here is another drum of bullets for the Chaut-chaut. There are two more drums in our cabin. Then—"

"You mean," he panted in a strained voice, "that the sailors have deserted? They took the boat on the bow?"

Suddenly he was grabbing at me.

"Corday! We're alone with that girl in the cabin. Those blacks will attack again and again and again. How can we run this boat? No doubt they have slaughtered the men of the engine-room."

He seemed stunned. *C'est ça!* So did I. Our silence was one of horror. We were both thinking the same thought—the girl in the cabin.

Overhead the stars smiled. The boat rolled gently on a swell, and the stars walked in a brilliant arc across the sky. Amidships all was still, but aft we could hear the murmuring of angry men. Once or twice a tongue of fire spat from the shadows there and bullets whistled over our heads. Jack the Goat was panting.

Then suddenly he seized my hand in a crushing clasp. "Corday! There's a way out of this! We've got to save that girl. We've got to save this ship, too. Think, man. Down in Somaliland they're waiting. Waiting for this cargo. Food and ammunition."

"Parbleu!" I moaned. "The boat is crippled. To hell with it. But you and I and the girl. Like three mice waiting for the tigers."

I believe I started to cry. The Yankee and I could have gotten along, you comprehend. But there was the wife of poor Daudet.

DO you know what the little Yankee did? He kicked me in the shin.

"Corday!" he gasped. "Listen to me. Listen, I say! Off there is the coast of Africa—Eritrea. You remember the Legion platoon starting from Taklai? They are somewhere along that coast. You must find them!"

I swore a bitter oath. Those mountain peaks were miles away. A haze under the stars.

Jack the Goat twisted my wrist. "You've got to swim for it. Look! Get a plank, a cabin bench, anything. Drop overside. Swim. You can make it. Then find those Legionnaires. Find a boat, a *dhow,* any craft at all. And bring them back. Our boat will not move from this position. First you must run to the pilot house and lash the wheel. You hear? You understand?" His words came in a vibrant rush.

"Sacré nom de Dieu!" I swore. "Do you think I would leave you alone in this trap? Do you think I would desert you on this sink of hell to face alone those black wolves? Do you think I would leave you and that white girl—"

The little Yankee's clasp tore into my flesh. "Corday! Do as I say. It's our one chance. I can hold them from the bridge. Listen! I want to save that girl more than anything else on earth."

Sweat was wiggling down his face. His eyes sparkled like burnished points of metal.

"I want to save her, I tell you," the Yankee insisted. "If we could make shore with you it would be good. But she could never swim it. I cannot swim a stroke. You must go—"

"I cannot!"

"You *will!* First lash the wheel. Then jump and swim like all hell. I will hold the bridge until you return."

"You will never hold it," I snarled. "When daylight comes and those savages see only one man up here—"

But his eyes commanded. If you could have seen his face you would have understood. A stern cord stood down his jaw, and his teeth grinned.

"Get on, Corday, I'll hold out. I'll hold out for days. Just bring me some grub and leave it to me—"

The *spang* of carbines snapped short his words. He trained the sights of his Chaut-chaut ready to answer the fire that had burned up from amidships. The Chaut-chaut rattled. The Africans stopped their shooting. Jack the Goat flung around at me again.

"Will you go?"

I could do nothing but nod. He clasped my hand. "You will save us all, Corday, and prove the hero I know you are. And listen, my friend. If—if anything has happened to me when you return, will you take that little packet from my breast pocket? It will explain. You will take it?"

I promised. He thumped me bravely on the chest and I fled to the pilot house. There I lashed the wheel. After that I foraged for rations and a canteen or two of water, which I placed within easy reach of Horatius-at-the-bridge. Then I dashed to my cabin. The sight of the dead German, the dead Russian, the dead Spaniard in there all but broke my resolution. But I caught up a bench, raced up the alley, dropped to the fore deck.

Down there the *Fleur de France* (a gorgeous flower, was she not?) was silent as a tomb. The high bridge lifted like a ghostly square castle against the stars. I thought of the girl locked in the cabin. I thought of the little man on the after deck of the bridge, crouching behind the Chaut-chaut gun.

I thought of the black swarm waiting to charge from behind the engine-room house. I wondered about the packet in his pocket.

Those thoughts raced through my numbed mind. Then I said a little prayer for the Yankee and that girl—the first prayer I had asked in years; and I said a little prayer for me. And I dropped the wooden bench overboard, stripped off from my uniform, and plunged after.

Chill water struck at my face as I pushed away. The bench bobbed before me to give me courage. Just that wooden bench and I, against the miles that reached to the coast. Just the bench and I and the memory of what lay behind.

Turning my head, I could see the dark, silent hulk of the *Fleur de France* drifting soundlessly into a water mist.

CHAPTER IV.

TO THE RESCUE!

THERE WERE times when I thought I was going to die. My arms were pulling from their sockets. My legs were knotting with cramp. My spine and skull were frozen and the stomach in me burned with the sea water.

Then I would think of a little Yankee guarding the bridge of a skulking hell-ship. I would visualize the white woman locked in the cabin, the gorillas rushing across slippery decks. And I would swim.

There were times when I wanted to die. Those times were the worst. And then *le bon Dieu* would lend me power from unknown sources of the little dynamo that drives all men through a hard, harsh world. *Le bon Dieu* would float that paralyzed, stone body of mine; would move my legs and thrash my arms and hang my leaden chin on the edge of the wooden bench.

And the force which had parted the waters of that very same sea to allow an ancient people to march through, turned the wind and the waves to my aid; sent the currents toward the shore.

A blazing copper sun rolled up behind me and made of the water a blistering, metal element that strove to fight me under. I could no longer see the *Fleur de France*. I could barely watch the mountains of Eritrea; and they grew no larger in size, despite my efforts to near them.

Sacré! Of that terrible, terrible swim I can remember nothing more. I only know that eternities and eternities of time crawled by, that the heart shriveled inside of me, that my bones expired, that the sun finally got into my eyes, and that two coal-black, ugly fishermen who looked like angels dragged me out of the water and raced me shoreward in a crazy fishing smack.

I spent a night in a hut that smelled like a sewer and looked like one, battling for sanity, battling against fever, shrieking and fighting and all but killing the homely devils who had saved me from the sea.

They tied me in a net and rushed away, to return hours later with a tall, thin white man wearing a thin, white beard. The thin old fellow gave me something to drink. I woke with sunshine on my face, and met the thin and bearded old man.

He told me I was sane, living, and a miracle under the sky to be doing so. He told me he was Doctor Augustin Jacques Edouard d'Etiennes, a medical missionary.

Was this Eritrea? Yes, it was. Had he heard of a Legionnaire platoon in the vicinity? But yes, a platoon had been on its way to the Somali coast; they had marched through the town only four hours ago.

Was that his horse waiting in the lane before the hut? It was.

Two hours later, half naked and a third mad, I galloped like a wild man into a knot of marching Legionnaires. They were dusty, footsore, weary and ragged as the ears of a hound. But their *képis* were set at a jaunty angle and the barrels of their Lebel rifles shimmered in the noonday sun. They had been singing lusty discords at the top of lusty lungs. That famous marching song of the Foreign Legion of France:

> "Soldats de la Légion—de la Légion Étrangère—
> N'ayant pas de nation—La France est votre mère!"

From a distance, above the clatter of my lathering mount, I had caught the drumming of their *brodequins,* and the echo of that chorus lingering against the scarlet Eritrean cliffs. It was the most beautiful song in all the universe.

MUBAREK, I think the town was called. It was nothing of a town, at that. But in those days Eritrea was a sort of unclaimed territory. Perhaps Italy should own it. Perhaps France. Neither country was certain. The Eritreans were too black and lazy and genial to care. Certainly in Mubarek nobody cared.

There was a regiment of sick Italian troopers in the town waiting to march over and try a few shots at the fuzzy-wuzzies of Abyssinia, and the only thing they cared about was finding decent drinking water.

That afternoon when our platoon of Legionnaires darted into Mubarek the Italians were away looking for drinking water. The point is, they had a bumboat waiting in an inlet near their camp. A dried-up Venetian lieutenant with furious black mustaches, and two faded soldiers from Verona, by the looks of them, guarded the big bumboat and reeled spaghetti into their unshaved faces.

The lieutenant of our Legion platoon hit the Italian officer with the black mustaches and knocked him into a pot of spaghetti. The two faded soldiers from Verona promptly bolted. Others of our Legion men scoured Mubarek and came back with three terrified ebony fishermen who could navigate the Red Sea.

All of which was not funny. It was not. We of the Legion were in a ghastly hurry to get out there across the water and locate a black scar of a boat fouled with mutiny. A boat that would be creeping down the sea with engines dead, with its main deck running crimson, with (I prayed to Heaven) a little Legionnaire defending its bridge behind a pounding, white-hot Chaut-chaut gun. A little Legionnaire with the heart of Yankee-land to keep him going and a key to a certain cabin door fast in his pocket to keep him from dying.

Soldiers of the French Foreign Legion are not seamen. But no sailors on earth ever manned the oars of a bumboat with stronger arms and stouter wills to win. The oar-blades flashed silver in the blatant tropic sunlight. Spume and salted spray spurted from the bumboat's bow. A Mubarek native stood up there on lookout, warned to strain his eyes.

The young lieutenant of the Legionnaires and I stood behind the native. An automatic waited in the young lieutenant's fist. I clutched a hair-triggered Lebel. In the stern of the boat we carried a little Maxim rapid-fire gun.

Sixty and more hours had gone since I had left the *Fleur de France*. *Dieu*, what a lying name. And I hoped with every inch of my being for the native on lookout to sight her. Yet I feared in the pit of my soul to sight her at all.

THE scarlet sun clambered down behind the bumboat's stern, enameling the water in our wake. The Legionnaires hauled madly at the oars. Eastward. Eastward where the *Fleur de France* might lie.

A few rakish *dhows* and fishermen bobbed past. They had not sighted the transport. The Red Sea was immense. Arab and Eritrean sailors stared in wonderment as our bumboat scuttled away. Eastward. Where the night was toiling in sweepy, greenish shadows down the skies.

"Parbleu!" sobbed the Legionnaire lieutenant.

He was a boy from St. Cyr, with light blond hair and a grim, mannish jaw. A Croix de Guerre was on his breast and a scarlet *fourragère* on his shoulder. He must have been a hard one, to win those citations and a Legion commission in his youth. Never before, though, had he embarked on such an expedition. You could see it had him by the nerves.

"*Parbleu!* I hope we get there on time. Tell me, my old one, did you hoist a distress signal?"

Miserably I shook my head. What would a soldier know of marine signals! The lieutenant cursed, fingering his automatic. The men drove their shoulders to the oars. The native in our bow scanned the horizon. Directly ahead we were raising an island. One of the Dahlak Islands. Few ships cruised this portion of the Red Sea. If our transport lay out there we should sight it soon. We did not.

Night came swiftly. On high the tropic stars flashed like lanterns set in a vast dome of indigo. The island drifted near. The boats of the fishermen and the Arab *dhows* dropped into the sunset. A Japanese moon, the color of a hamadryad's eye, struggled up through the clouds crouching on the island.

The elliptical moon shed a pallid silver light across the restless water, and raised a fog. What a fog! At first there were ragged wisps that smelled of salt. The wisps merged into long tatters of gray haze that rolled like battle-smoke.

Finally our bumboat was plowing through a tumbling vapor, wet, sticky, and white. A vapor that swirled and coiled about us, touched ghostly fingers to our hot cheeks, deadened the sound of thrashing oars and scattered water. Now we were engulfed.

Fog and night on the Red Sea, and a skinny Eritrean native to guide our rudder on this impossible, awful hunt. Fog and night. Never would we find that *Flower of France*. Never would we sight her sinister hull. But the young lieutenant cursed in gallant French. The Legionnaires pulled away. The fog whispered around us and wrapped us in an evil cerement.

At intervals the bumboat cruised fast through a "fog dog." You know the term? A hole in the vapor, it is. A rent in the pouring mist. A pocket of cleared water where the black waves glittered, stabbed by moonbeams shafting from the patch of sky above.

It was mighty weird to bob into one of those open spaces, rock across a moonlit patch of ink-like water and lunge into sceneless mist again. It was hopeless to be blinded so. Terrible.

It was weirder still when the little African cramped in our bow suddenly shot a black hand heavenward and shouted: *"Bwana!* Listen!"

Did we listen? *Sacré!* Our ear drums exploded, bursting with the effort. How we listened. The men stopped their oars. The boat chopped through a gentle swell. When we heard it we raised a yell. You bet we did. There! There it was again. The short, smart sound of rifle-fire.

"Quick!" screamed our lieutenant.

The men drove their oars into water. Spray flew. We scudded from the fog into an open area of glimmering sea a mile broad. There, hemmed in by the weaving shroud of mists, lolled the *Flower of France!*

SHE sneaked along, her gaunt funnel poked up against that oval-shaped moon, water burbling gently under her high bows and flat stern. She sneaked across the water slowly; inching through the wan moonshine that filled the fogless area and made the black water to glint. She sneaked like a thief; her prow pointed toward that spot where the island hung hidden in the fog.

Rags of white vapor clung, coiling, about her high bridge, her deck amidships, her taffrail. Her black hull glistened as if perspiring. On her fore deck a loading-boom swung and softly groaned. In her bowels loose chain was clanking.

"Aunt of the Devil!" whispered the lieutenant. (One whispers when one sees a specter.) "There is your transport, my old one. But, *nom de Dieu!* Is there life aboard her?"

A volley of rifle shots answered his words. We were bearing down on the ship's starboard quarter, you understand. *Rat-tat-tat-tat!* came the sound. Like hammer-taps. Like a brief flurry of hail pounding a tin roof.

The mists that wreathed the *Fleur de France* amidships were split by slim, sporadic tongues of red flame. Those were the carbines of the Tirailleurs. *Spang! Spang!* came the reply. Bursts of fire flickered out of the vapor that hung the bridge. Shots from a Lebel rifle!

I could have screeched with joy. That was the little Yankee! By all the gods, he had held out! He had held the bridge.

For two days and two nights and a third evening he had held the bridge alone. That little Yankee who looked like a wax doll. That little Yankee called Jack the Goat. *Mon Dieu!* I could have wept with the grandeur of it.

"Do you hear?" I panted at the lieutenant. "See? Lebel-fire on that bridge up there. It is the American!"

Tears were crawling down the young officer's face.

"Grand!" he muttered. "Grand!"

Jerking his head, he snapped an order to his Legionnaires. The carbines were snapping on the main deck of the *Fleur de France* again. The Legionnaires hauled like madmen on their oars. Our bumboat sped, rocketing forward.

"Softly," growled the lieutenant. "We must not be seen. We will board her after deck. A squad of us. We will trap those mutineers."

He turned to me. "They must be gathered before that engine-room house, eh? They will not see us under their stern? Look! Could we plant our machine gun up there by the funnel? Good! We will mow them down like flies."

Our steersman, one of the Eritreans from Mubarek, did well. We scudded closer and closer to the ship. Now we could see her after deck was deserted. Those black mutineers were busy amidships.

Dieu! How had that lone Yankee held out so long? It suddenly occurred to me that the mutineers were making this furious assault because the transport had drifted close on the island. Ah, what a Yankee!

Then our boat was under her taffrail. The men shipped their oars. The little black lookout on our bow—though terrified to death, I wager—had valiantly grabbed a hawser dragging from the deck above. The taffrail was not six inches above our heads.

I went up first. The after deck behind that engine-room house was deserted. I motioned the others to come. The lieutenant swung up from the bumboat. Five others came, Lebels hung on their backs. The fifth man dragged up the Maxim gun.

The lieutenant gave low-voiced orders. The men remaining in the boat were to pull away, bear down on the port beam and board her there. Shoot from the water, if needs must. *Bien!* The bumboat slid away.

I was leader now. Silently, rifles unlimbered, the men followed me. In frantic haste we climbed a ladder to the roof of the engine-room house. From this point of vantage, we could shoot down on the main deck.

We spread in a stooping line, scuttled up the low roof past the cold black funnel. The mist-hung bridge up forward we could scarcely see.

We could see the flame of a Lebel up there, but that was all.

But the Tirailleurs we could see, all right. We looked right down on their heads. Their *tarbooshes* were bobbing. Their carbines gleamed and spouted flame.

The giant, Ahmed, moved among them bawling hoarsely, knife in hand. He was urging them to charge, but they did not charge. Why? Certainly they had not sighted us on the roof behind them. Certainly they were not afraid of one lone soldier on the bridge up there.

Our young officer growled. We planted our Maxim gun. We aimed the Maxim at the row of shoulders below; aimed our rifles. The lieutenant raised his hand to give the order to fire. His hand never fell. As if by signal a sudden breeze whipped across the *Fleur de France* and swept away the fog. Like that. And we *saw!*

CHAPTER V.

THE DEATH WATCH!

IF I live through thirteen incarnations, being reborn after thirteen deaths, I will not forget that sight. Perhaps at the thirteenth death I will forget it. If so, thirteen is a lucky number. *Sapristi!*

You comprehend how a breeze had abruptly dissolved the fog; lifted the curtain? Lifted the curtain, yes. Like a curtain lifting to show a stage. But yes. A stage!

There were the five Legionnaires, the young lieutenant, me—on the roof of the engine-room house. Gallery seats.

Directly below us on the main deck crowded the black Tirailleurs. They were wanting like anything to rush the bridge, those Tirailleurs. They wanted to capture the wheel house up there. They wanted to get at a white woman in a cabin up there. They wanted to do it before the ship moved alongside an island they knew was not far away. But they never dared charge the bridge. For that bridge was the *stage!*

Uncle of Satan, how can I tell it? Who would believe? There were men on the bridge up there. *Men,* I say. They stood in a row at the rail, looking down at the deck below. But they never were men. *Non!* No men had eyes like those. No man ever held a rifle slung under the arm, with the stock caught under the armpit—*and fired the gun without finger on trigger!*

The devil! They stood in a row, you understand, on the after deck of that high bridge. Side by side. Their chests leaning against the rail. Their rifles poked over the rail. Their *képis* hung over their ears, jauntily. Their chins on their chests, not so jauntily. But there they were in the line. Schneider, the German, Kalnikoff, the Russian. Fuertes, the Spaniard. De Nogales, of Venezuela. And all dead! Every one!

Yet, they were alive. The German fired his gun. The Russian fired his gun. The Spaniard fired his gun. De Nogales fired his gun. One, two, three, four—like that. The bullets went awry, but those Tirailleurs all screamed as if they had been hit.

"Name of fourteen saints!" groaned the lieutenant at my side. "Look at that! Look at that! Those Legionnaires on the bridge—"

How I looked! Their arms moved. Their heads nodded clumsily. Their guns fired again.

The Tirailleurs sent up a moan. We on the engine-room house sent up a moan. We did not want to believe those four on the bridge were dead. But I knew they were. My companions knew it. The black Tirailleurs knew it. They wore the color of death, those four. It is hot on the Red Sea, no matter the chill of the moon. You would know, had you seen us sweat. *Sacré!* Ice water from our veins.

And while we stared the play went on. Two men strolled out of the alleyway up there. Arm in arm they came. Step by step. They stalked out on that deck and they moved to the top of the ladder. Captain Dieudonné Daudet and the little Yankee.

The American looked like a wax doll. The captain looked like the devil. He carried his sword under his arm and held his head high. The Yankee held an automatic and was smiling.

At the ladder top they halted. And then—by the name of Boniface!—Captain Daudet let out a yell! He yelled, I say, and the Legionnaire last in the row at the rail yelled back.

Back and forth they yelled, and in half a split minute-tick those Tirailleurs below were yelling, too. Down on their faces they went. They bobbed their heads, flattened their bodies and clawed at the slippery deck. And right then—as if unable to restrain its nerve longer—the Maxim gun beside me let go; and flung reality to the scene. Our machine gun roared and roared.

It seemed to snap a thread. Captain Daudet and the little Yankee came tumbling down the ladder.

AH, that Flower of France! The little Yankee was dead, but he told the secret. Or part of it. For his left leg had been lashed to the right leg of his captain. The four on the bridge had been tied standing against that rail. Ropes from their gun-triggers led to the alleyway where the living had hidden. Ropes from their arms. Ropes from their collars. What a show!

And the gallant Yankee who had planned it all? The gallant little American who had told me he would hold out somehow? Because he had finally been shot, he could not explain.

But I remembered the packet in his breast pocket, and sought it out with quavering fingers. The little package told the story. I read it to myself. I read it to the young lieutenant. I read it to the white girl safe in her cabin. We wept. Think of the bravery of it all! Think of the jest!

And so before the curtain came down for the last time, the young lieutenant stooped and pinned his Croix de Guerre on the Yankee's breast and hung the scarlet cord across the Yankee's shoulder.

And the *Fleur de France*, drifting into the fog bank, wrapped him in a kindly, cool mist.

EPILOGUE

OLD **THIBAUT CORDAY,** veteran of Legionnaires, poured himself a drink with shaking hands; and gulped it down the way no Frenchman should. MacDowell and I drank, too. The mat of moonlight had moved across the floor. Now the pale light played on the old man's face, and the eyes in his leathery head were burnished blue stones.

"Nom de Dieu!" he breathed. "But there was a puppet show for you. Think of that little Jack the Goat holding off those tigers by lining up those soldiers who had died. The Tirailleurs could perhaps brave a corpse that shot a gun. But they could not face a corpse who *yelled.* No more than could those tribesmen of the Ouled Naïl. And thus did the strange little American hold the *Fleur de France*, on her way to Somaliland. Thus did he save the transport and the wife of Captain Daudet."

"But," muttered MacDowell, "how about those dead Legionnaires—"

"Yelling?" Old Thibaut Corday smiled. "Look, then."

He held out the thin little book that had come from his cupboard of memories; the little book with the hole drilled through its leaves from cover to cover.

"This," said the veteran with a wry smile, "was the packet in the Yankee's breast. You see that bullet-hole? Sardonic, is it not? Our Legion had lost its head and killed one of the bravest men who ever honored its ranks. That bullet-hole, my friends, was made by our Maxim gun. A wild, terror-driven shot. See, too—the title of the book."

We read the title, MacDowell and I. The Britisher made a noise in his throat. I spoke it out to make sure.

MY FORTY YEARS AS A SHOWMAN
By Professor John Smith
Famous Maker of Marionettes, and America's
Greatest Ventriloquist

MacDowell got to his feet. "An astonishing story, Corday," he acknowledged. "And you were right—a story to make one dream. But I don't like your yarn, old top. I don't like to have the Yankee shot down at the end."

"The only way for it to have been," murmured the old Frenchman, getting to his feet with a sigh. "Look here."

He opened the book to the title page. Moonbeams slanted across the yellowed paper. MacDowell and I saw a photograph printed on the leaf. A picture of a doll-like little man wearing a stiff goatee and a high hat and a cutaway. Posed beside him, in the rigid manner of those "family-album" times was a girl.

Despite the fading of the print, despite the outlandish costume of the day, we could see the girl was of marked beauty. And here was a strange thing:

The bullet which had sped through the book had clipped through that picture on its fly leaf, making a hole through that lady's heart. Below the photograph ran the legend: "Professor John Smith and His Wife."

Old Thibaut Corday spoke softly. "You remember he told me of that wife? She had left him on the very night of his triumph in New York. That was why he had joined *La Légion*. So. But listen, my friends: That printed picture cannot affect you the way it affected me when first I saw it that dreadful night aboard the *Fleur de France*. For then I knew. The little Yankee had purposely thrown himself down that ladder to stop our Maxim bullets. *Le bon Dieu* knows how to exact justice. Think of the punishment it would give that false wife of his to learn of that heroism, that sacrifice. And she did learn of it, most certainly. *C'est ça!* For that Amorette—that beautiful woman of Captain Daudet's—that lovely lady who had waited in the cabin while a lone, brave Yankee Legionnaire defended the bridge with the greatest courage I have ever known—but yes! *She* was the girl of this photograph! She was the American's wife."

Old Thibaut Corday's voice went silent in his beard. Outside, the moonlit city of Algiers was a city of the "Arabian Nights." Down on the square before the mosque the crowd of Arabs was dispersing, murmurous in the perfumed dark. We could catch a note of laughter. The puppet show was done.

THE BEARDED SLAYER

INTO A GRIM DESERT
OUTPOST THAT DATED
FROM THE DAYS OF
CARTHAGE MARCHED
THIBAUT CORDAY AND
HIS FOREIGN LEGION
COMRADES—TO UNDERGO
A REIGN OF TERROR AT
THE HANDS OF AN UNSEEN
MURDERER.

STRANGE TALES had come from the lips of old Thibaut Corday, champion soldier of fortune and veteran Legionnaire extraordinary. Of clement evenings when the Bay of Algiers was silvery, the moon a scimitar in a star-powdered sky, the stench of the Algiers *Kasbah* behind us had dimmed a bit and the tom-toms were starting in, you would find us there beneath the Brasserie Terminus awning.

Old Thibaut Corday would be there first; ghostly in a chair that faced the bay and so looked across the Mediterranean where France lay beyond the horizon. Then the young British consulate attaché and I would arrive; and finally the lad from the American Express would stroll up Boulevard Sadi Carnot to take the last place at our table.

A story, then, was inevitable. A bottle would go the rounds. Then the old man would crowd his pipe with terrific tobacco, and weave us yarns out of the smoke. Strange tales; for he told of Africa—last outpost of the strange; and he told of the Foreign Legion of France— the army which mans that outpost. There was the story of the phantom that danced on the desert, the tale of the Legionnaire's eye which was glass and saved his life in Dahomey and proved to be the story-teller's own optic, and the story of the dead men who guarded a transport's deck.

Strange tales; and the old man could tell them. In his face of burned leather the live eye would twinkle like a star and the glass eye would glow like a planet as he marched with the Tricolor and fought his Legion battles once again.

His four score years of life sat as lightly and proudly as the faded *képi* on his post-bald head. And his bushy beard, that should have bleached snow-color in the blasting suns of Tonkin, Congo and the

The knife had nailed him to
the side of the doorway.

Atlas, was still the bright, gay hue of cinnamon.

Now it was this same beard of old Thibaut Corday's that started things going one night.

"A jolly good set of whiskers, those," the young British consulate agent happened to admire with a chuckle. "Quite rare in this age of razors."

The ancient Legionnaire was seen to smile. His hands went seeking for his pipe; and the rest of us went quiet. Soon a cloud of dour smoke burst from the topic of our regard; and the old soldier grunted.

"This beard," he grunted. "Once it *was* a beard. There wasn't a better in the Foreign Legion of France. *Sacré!* I was thirty years old and lying in a regimental hospital with a Bedouin's bullet in my hip when I decided to raise it. I was a long time getting well, and my beard grew with one grand vigor because I didn't have anything else to do. When I went back to the barracks I marched behind the finest and longest and reddest beard of the Army of the Damned. Now, bah! I am old and my beard is a faded and weedy tangle—" (It was not!) "But then, when I was thirty, it was, indeed, a master beard. It fell almost to my midriff and was red as a new-baked brick, and I was proud of my beard as a peacock is proud of his tail." The old veteran snarled through his smoking whiskers.

"But just listen to me, *mes amis*. This pride is one foolish emotion. The beard which was such a joy to me was soon to prove one fierce curse. At a certain garrison named Bab Eschmoun, way down in a desert just a fast jump this side of hell, my noble long red beard proved a thing to tear out by the roots.

"For it got me into one trap of trouble. Aunt of the devil, how it did! This fine beard of mine lost its prestige in a most shocking way, and *mon Dieu!*

"If it did not almost lose me my life. There's a murderous story behind this beard of mine, my friends—"

Strange tales old Thibaut Corday had told. But the most fantastic of all, I believe, was this story that came from behind his beard.

CHAPTER I.

MURDER!

CONSIDER (BEGAN old Thibaut Corday) Bab Eschmoun. I said it was an outpost on a desert just a fast jump this side of hell. You know how fast a man might jump from Hades, but he wouldn't jump far because his feet would be scorched. *Non*, that desert with Bab Eschmoun in its middle was only a short distance from the Fiery Gates.

You could see those Fiery Gates at dawn and sunset, and you could feel the heat all day and all night. The desert was simply a pool of burned sand, forty kilometers in circumference, lying couched between scarlet mountains, with the outpost marooned in the center. The surrounding cliffs wouldn't allow the heat to escape. They wouldn't allow any man to escape, either.

The War Department in Paris makes some odd decisions. Oddest of all was its decision to make a Foreign Legion outpost of Bab Eschmoun. The place had been a military stronghold in the days of the Carthaginians when they pushed into southern Tunisia. But that, you comprehend, was back in 800 B.C., when Rome was a child and Greece was under way and Christianity and Mohammed had never been heard of. Those soldiers from Carthage built Bab Eschmoun when the world was hardly out of swaddling clothes. They named it Eschmoun after the most savage god of their lot.

When the Moslem Berbers conquered the place thirteen hundred years later it looked so old they were frightened. They called it "Bab" Eschmoun because "Bab" in Arabic means gate, and I presume they thought it looked like a gate to the nether worlds. A Moslem holy man wanted to make a shrine of the place but legend says he was stabbed in the back his first night there. The Arabs buried him and consecrated the place to Allah and got out.

When the Legion conquered the Arabs of Tunisia a few hundred years later it found Bab Eschmoun full of spider webs and scary echoes. The Arabs kept away from the place; they were smart. The Paris War Department was not. It made an outpost of Bab Eschmoun, and sent a company from Sidi-bel-Abbes to garrison the place. I marched south with that company. And I marched behind the longest, bushiest and reddest beard in La Légion.

I HAD seen some queer detachments leave Sidi for the south; but none to equal ours. Four squads of ruffians just out of a Moroccan campaign. Poles and Greeks and Russians, Gascons and Bavarians, the usual Apache-sweepings that are soulless enough to fight like heroes for the Légion of France.

First in command was old Achille Gautier, a fine soldier of the St. Cyr tradition, slated for high office in Tunisia should he control Bab Eschmoun for a while. The soldiers loved this colonel with his head like Moses and his quiet genial voice, his scholarly spectacles and his habit of carrying a book in the crook of his arm as he rode in saddle or strolled across a battleground where man and shells fell thick.

He could pray like a saint and curse like a cannoneer; was not above having a glass of *pinard* with a recruit, and his company would have followed him into a furnace—and often did.

Second in command was a tall Corsican, driven by the disfigurement of smallpox from the opera stage to the Legion headquarters at Sidi. His gimlet black eyes, wig of raven hair and pock-ravaged face loaned him the appearance of a captain of the Camorra. He had been a captain in the *Battalion d'Afrique,* which was worse. And because he had been too severe in that dreaded penal regiment, Headquarters had planted him back in the Legion. Our detachment would march in step, now, and curse this Gepetto Cellini under breath.

I think the two young lieutenants from St. Cyr, the blond whiskered giant Anatole Gers, and fat little Augustin Castelnau, did not like the Corsican, either; and our pig-headed non-coms hated and were hated by everybody. This, of course, was not unusual. A detachment of Legionnaires on the march is not a Sunday School taking a May walk. But this was not the point which made our detachment a strange one. The odd element entered in our midst was the lady.

Now an army community in North Africa is gossipy as a market full of fishmongers' wives; and how La Légion had gossiped when Colonel Gautier, with his saintly glasses and his book, had picked this Nina Blondel from the dance platform of a café on the Cannebière in Marseilles, rushed her up to Nôtre Dame de la Garde, and ended his leave with a bride.

That brave old walrus had done well by himself, that is so. What a wife! Tall and lissom and warmly blond, with the sort of figure that makes a man forget his good intentions, and the sort of eyes that make him remember them again, *Sacré!* she had the most beautiful blue eyes a lucky soldier could ever hope to see.

When that foolish Colonel of ours had brought her back with him to Sidi, his men had fallen on their knees to worship. Some of the officers in Gautier's staff had fallen on their knees before her in private, but the fair Nina had a piercing glance of contempt that would shrivel such a man to a worm. I know very well, for I was his orderly at that time—before the Moroccan campaign we had just ended.

The other wives at Sidi hated her, and the gossip waxed fat. There were stories. She had married Papa Gautier for his money. She was a common dancing girl and had once been in a traveling carnival. She was half Arab. You know how the wives of army officers would talk when a lady fifty times as beautiful as they entered their dull ranks. They predicted she would desert the colonel in one week. She did not. When our detachment left Sidi for Bab Eschmoun, young Mme. Gautier rode at the head of the column with her husband.

CAN you imagine such a lady—a waxen carving by a master artist, I tell you—riding at the head of a detachment of lousy Legionnaires, heading off into a God-forgotten region like southern Tunis? I marched in the front rank and stared at the savage sunlight that bathed her tossing head piled high with golden hair.

And then I regarded the ugly ruffians tramping with me, and the staff officers riding behind the colonel and his lady. The captain with his pitted face and gimlet eyes! I noticed that Corsican. He never lost a chance to spur to Mme. Gautier's elbow. He nodded at her and he smiled. She would arch her fine head and turn up her nose and look away, and I could see Captain Cellini blush with anger.

The two young lieutenants from St. Cyr were different. The massive Anatole Gers, he never took his dull blue eyes from the girl, and fumbled at his saddle bag whenever she glanced his way. The fat and stubby Augustin Castelnau would wink and dimple like a cherub if she turned to ask him a question. It was all very funny for a Legion detachment pounding through red desert dust on its way to garrison an outpost for a year.

Mon Dieu! I was not too certain I wasn't in love with this lady, myself. But this is by no means a love story. Uncle of Satan! Trouble was to begin soon enough, and it was soon to be more than trouble. It was soon to be murder. There was blood soon to run, and plenty of blood, and this slaughter was brewing under our iron-studded boots at every step they took toward Bab Eschmoun.

Queer how I, Thibaut Corday, was to play soothsayer. I, with the stupid confidence of thirty years and the ego of wearing the finest, longest and reddest beard in La Légion.

The detachment had toiled through a ragged landscape of heat-baked hills that had peppered us with torturing dust and sawed through our feet to the bone. I will never forget how the sun rolled down the horizon like a flaming chariot wheel, how we tramped through the blasting atmosphere, dripping sweat and oaths, and finally, at the top of a rise, old Papa Gautier lifted a gantlet and called the halt.

His staff drew rein, and our Lebel-butts thumped down on the scorched roadway. Only one in our number was not plastered with sweaty dirt, sunburned, slouchy, glaring like a ragamuffin from a Paris sewer. That was the colonel's wife. *Le bon Dieu* alone knows how some ladies can look fresh and clean and wind-blown after a train ride and a gallop through the mire, and this Nina was such a lady. *Sacré!*

For once, the men in the detachment were not staring with avid eyes at the colonel's wife. They slouched to the fore and glared down at the sweltering pan of desert below. There in the center of that sandy griddle squatted Bab Eschmoun, a huddle of burned white walls, lonely, deserted, quiet as a city of the dead. Silent? That abandoned outpost was deaf and dumb. No man had been there since the first detachment of the Legion had marched through and on southward to haggle a treaty that surrendered Tunis to France.

"Bones of Saint Emmanuel!" rasped Christianity Jensen, the little Dane, who stood with grounded knapsack at my elbow. "It is the end of the world, Corday, old *cochon*. And we are going to be stationed there!"

Now the sun had sunk to the horizon's rim, and a spate of stormy crimson light slanted across those deserted walls to wash them with somber color. A hot breeze conjured little spirals of dust and sent them whirling across the sand like the ghosts of departed dervishes. So soundless and uncanny was the aspect of the whole place that I tugged in my prize red whiskers and turned on the Dane with an oath.

"It looks," I muttered, "like a splendid place for a murder!"

Ventre bleu! That night Colonel Achille Gautier was found leaning in the doorway of his new headquarters. He leaned because his knees were sagging. Those sagging knees hadn't buckled, because the knife stabbed through his throat had entered the old wood of the doorsill, to nail him standing where he had died.

I SHALL not soon forget the details of that first horror. Mark that word "first." There were others to follow, you comprehend, until that garrison writhed in such a reign of terror as might whirl through the jabberwock dream of an absinthe drinker; until blood and hate, suspicion and fear chittered loud out of the moonlight, and men's nerves jangled, and every shadow gave promise of a deadly knife.

Your soldier of the Foreign Legion is a man who snaps fingers at death. But he likes to see it coming; likes to know from whence it comes. Had we known what lay in store for us, festering behind those sullen walls ahead, every man of us would have dropped his Lebel and fled back to Sidi-bel-Abbes. Had I guessed what lay waiting for me, I'd have led that precipitate flight.

But we in the detachment did not know. We were just a rabble of chance-picked Legionnaires led by our Papa Gautier with his most beautiful wife, by Captain Cellini and two young lieutenants. Maybe there would be trouble over this lady in our midst. Ladies invariably make trouble.

"March!" called Papa Gautier; and we shouldered our Lebels and picked up our *brodequins* and marched into Bab Eschmoun. The desert we crossed was a furnace floor and the heat welled around us like some smelted, invisible liquid fire. Although the sun was setting—a copper disk poised on the peak of a brassy cliff—the scorched air simmered. It was one hot frying pan of sand that surrounded that clump of walls.

One thing those ancient Carthage engineers had done: they had built an unapproachable stronghold. A lone squad mounting guard on those walls could see in all directions. Attackers would have to cross that open span of desert. No place to hide or creep. Only a ghost could enter Bab Eschmoun unseen.

But it looked like a haunt of ghosts, I can tell you. That was because the place was so old. You could tell by the way the wind had polished off the corners of the stones, by the stagnant smell of antiquity that crept from the cracks in the mortar. The place was of simple enough structure. Four walls rose steep to form a rectangle with a bastion at each tower. A broken-down gateway under an arch in the western wall, and a squat, square tower that rose from the center of the south wall like a chimney and boasted a tiny barred window in its outer face, made the only break in the prison-plain symmetry of the structure. One could glimpse in the shadows beyond the gate arch a few discouraged palm fronds limping skyward. That was a promise of oasis water. And beyond the palms a scribble of flat-roofed adobe buildings crowded the inclosure under the walls.

Aunt of the Devil! It was a simple enough arrangement, and perfect for the military. We debouched into the enclosure, and in six seconds every soldier was busy. Water to be drawn, guns stacked, wood sought, a guard mounted on the walls, four *Chauchat* rifles planted at each bastion, a drill field swept, all those thousand and two odd-jobs that are done by peasant yokels and sweat-drenched Legionnaires.

We were, you understand, supposed to turn that relic of the past into a presentable Legion outpost. This would be a task for Hercules. The dust on the open ground was ankle deep, mounds of wind-blown sand banked in the bastions. Great cobwebs masked the arched doorways of the adobe buildings backed against the walls, and gloomy bats flickered over our *képis* as we poked our rifles into the narrow entryways of the dark, empty huts and looked for snakes or chance prowlers.

AGAINST the northern wall shambled a long, barn-wide, one-storied house of plaster walls and thin windows that would serve, the colonel pointed out, as barracks for the soldiers. A row of low-roofed huts stood in line before this lovely barracks. The staff staked these out to see service as cook house, supply rooms and ammunition stores. A second long, low building hung under the east wall.

This would be used as a *caserne* where the penny-a-day Legion dogs could buy chocolate, wine and soap, and stage their boot-throwing and curse-slinging battles. And a second row of box-square adobe houses, across an alley from this *caserne*, would do for officers' quarters.

Thus the northeastern end of the stronghold was crowded with huts, and the rest of the enclosure, save for the clump of palms and covered well near the broken gate, was barren ground. There we proceeded to pitch the dog-tents.

A thick blue dust descended on the place. Shadows and heat hung along the walls. The tramp of studded boots echoed strangely as the advance guard marched through the ancient buildings. The guard came out with spider webs hanging on their shoulders.

"It was like walking into a graveyard," Christianity Jensen told me, when he returned to the encampment where I'd set up our tent and bundled our *pacquetages*. He pointed at the adobe buildings.

"Once I went into a tomb that hadn't been opened for many years. Inside, those huts have the same smell. I do not like this place, Corday. We are stirring up the past. Over near the date palms we found an old grave. A mound under a bowlder. There was an Arabic inscription. The good Captain Cellini—may the devil toast his bones!—said it was the tomb of a heathen dog, and spat at the bowlder. Do you know? Colonel Gautier and his wife were walking around, and she came over and told Cellini not to be unkind. She told us that was the grave of a Moslem priest who had tried to found a monastery here. That vile Captain Cellini blushed red. He cursed us when she and Papa Gautier walked away. But I think he was angry because the woman criticized him for spitting. That captain—I have a feeling he would like that lady for himself, yes?"

"And so would every other man in the detachment," I snarled. "And as for this ancient stronghold, you are right. It is a tomb. I do not like the echoes, my friend. Let us hope there is an Arab attack, perhaps, and we hear the sound of good honest gunnery before long."

Thus I talked with my stout little *copain*, while the Legion dogs around us reared their lines of tents on that age-old parade field. I was engaged in trying to sneak a smoke in my pipe and avoid the eye of one Jules Parbonne—the foulest sergeant ever to boss a squad—when a corporal appeared to tell me the colonel had chosen me for orderly, and I was to report to his headquarters.

NOW I remember this thing well. I remember it only too well. I dream about it sometimes, when the drinks of the day have been bad or the roast ill-cooked at dinner. I dream about it and wake from my sleep with a cry and much sweat on my face.

The good Papa Gautier had taken for his headquarters the adobe house last in that line of huts that faced the *caserne* building under the eastern wall. The colonel and his wife had already installed themselves in this house. It was a place of two rooms, square, low-roofed, a single door leading from the front room into that alley which divided the row of huts from the *caserne*. Because the post commander must be settled first, the men had cleaned out the place, set up tables and cots, pinned maps, arranged luggage. Mme. Gautier had officiated. Good housewife.

Now our company had been encamped for perhaps an hour. The sun had westered but for a straying, final beam that drifted into the stronghold and made promise of torrid to-morrow. The tents of the men were dark, save where camp fires blossomed in the gloom and tossed wavy shadows. I could hear the thud of boots patrolling the high walls. We were settled for night and a grimly hard workday to follow. Out beyond the walls the silence of centuries poured up out of the sand.

I left the cluster of dog-tents and bent my steps for the colonel's headquarters. Lamplight made a pale yellow patch of the window in that house. The adobe buildings beyond it were huddled in gray dark. A fat Bavarian guardsman strolled past me, whistling softly through dirty teeth. I remember how the sweat was creeping down his pudding face, and I remember the song he tried to whistle: "The Helmet of Father Bugeaud."

When he sighted me he stopped his piping. "Who goes?" he growled, peering. "You, eh? What do you want in this corner of the post, Corday? Did you not hear the orders? The men were commanded to stay by their tents, though God knows they've men straggling all over the place."

"Where are the headquarters?" I snapped.

"The staff is in tents down that alley where the *caserne* is to be," he growled. "Papa Gautier occupies that building where the light shines. If you want his beautiful wife," he sneered, "she has gone to bed. I heard her tell her husband she was tired just a few moments ago, and I saw her go into that back room when I passed the door on my previous round. I presume," he went on with an evil leer, "that is what you want. You might as well tell the Legionnaires and save them the trouble of trying to find out. Every one wants to know.

"'Is Colonel Gautier's wife in comfortable quarters?' that young Lieutenant Gers asks me. I overhear Captain Cellini say to Lieutenant Castelnau: 'No doubt Papa Gautier provides his wife a charming boudoir in that two-roomed hut!' Bah! Shades of Friedrich Wilhelm! The wife of the colonel seems the only object of interest in this hole of hell. If we are here for one year—"

"You foul gossiping dog of a scandal-seller," I snarled, "close your cave-like mouth." I should have liked to shut it for him, that pig of a German. I felt sorry for that young wife of the colonel, *c'est ça!* It would be too bad for the girl, locked up in this end-of-the-world outpost with a gang of gutter-sweepings.

The Bavarian grinned. "Oh-ho. It would seem our famous red-beard champion defends the cause of womanhood—"

"Be damned!" I gave him, promising myself I would punch loose this guard's teeth the first time I found him drunk in the *caserne*. "No more from you, or I report you for defaulting duty and watch you squirm through police drill for a week. I am to be the colonel's orderly, you fat son of a Rhineland swine."

"Pass, then," he grunted, swinging his Lebel. "The colonel stands in his doorway. You can see him from here."

YES, I could see good Papa Gautier leaning in the doorway of his newly-occupied headquarters. The foul German guard stumped off on his patrol, and I hurried toward the headquarters hut. The ground I covered was deserted. The sun was down and I crossed a deep pool of shadow. Far on the wall overhead I could catch the voice of the mobile guard: *"Rien à signaller?"* And the answer of the stationary sentinel: *"Rien!"* The echoes trailed away. All's well!

All's well! But all was not well, that is so! I began to realize it as I neared the figure of Papa Gautier leaning there in his doorway. The darkness had settled now, deep and blue-black save where the lamplight streamed past that leaning figure and cast his shadow, grotesque, across the dirt before that little house.

Sacré! I saw that shadow and I saw that motionless figure and the prickles began to play down the nape of my neck. Aunt of the Devil! the man leaned so strangely. A queer shine illuminated the glasses on his nose so that they gleamed in the dusk like watery moons. Those spectacles stared a fixed stare at me as I approached. And their wearer clutched his omnipresent book so stiffly under an armpit; leaned wearily against the rotted wood of that palely-lighted doorway, and stared at nothing and held tight that book.

I saw the knees were sagging oddly; and something was dripping from the leaves of that book. Was the good Papa Gautier drunk, I wondered? Of course. And he had spilled wine all over his precious volume. But *non!*

By heaven! That wine was running from his mouth—a narrow thread of wine running from the corners of his mouth. *Sacré!* I was scarce a pace away from him then, and I stopped still in my tracks. I went sick. My fine red beard stiffened as my jaw froze. My Lebel tumbled out of my fingers. For I had sighted the glint of a knife-hilt, and that knife-hilt jutted from the colonel's neck.

I squalled. Men came running, shouting, spilling out of shadows from everywhere. A pale, slim shape appeared in the lamp-lit room behind the leaning colonel, slid past him where he leaned, voiced a stricken small cry and tumbled in a heap at my feet.

CHAPTER II.

THE KNIFE AND THE PANTHER.

I **N THE** Foreign Legion of France, you comprehend, a violation of the smallest rule is regarded as serious crime. Talk back to a drill sergeant who has just pronounced you a son of a camel, and you go to the guard house. Let that same Legionnaire appear in dirty tunic and he rushes to police duty once again. A failure to stand up at roll call or be prompt at a summons means weeks of severe punishment. Desertion in peace time sends a Legionnaire to the chain gang at Oujda for a couple of years. Let him strike an officer, and that Legionnaire goes into the *Battalion d'Afrique,* the terrible penal corps. Let an officer be murdered—

Uncle of Satan! If the assassination of Papa Gautier did not send our garrison sky high in one grand uproar! To an army where failure to salute a ranking commander is grand offense, this murder was the sin against the universe. The unthinkable! That a post commander should be murdered in the very doorway of his garrison headquarters! *Sacré bleu!* In *La Légion Étrangère* that was the crime of all crimes.

If you think our first night in Bab Eschmoun was not a wild one you are wrong. That place was one storm. In half a minute every man in the outpost knew what had happened; such a jostling and whispering and running about, while non-coms cursed to bring order and the staff officers bawled furious commands—such a furore I had never before witnessed.

Captain Gepetto Cellini had sprung out of shadows, automatic in fist, swart face purple with excitement. "I am in command, now. Line up, you dogs. God above! But somebody is going to suffer for this. Mutiny, perhaps? Then the first of you jackals to lift a gun dies in his tracks. We will find who has slain Colonel Gautier, and that man will suffer, never fear. Back, dogs! Line up! Attention! I am in command, now. I—"

There was Anatole Gers, shirtless, yellow hair tossing, swinging a pistol through the crowding men, shouting, shoving them back from that fateful door. I recall a brief impression that the young officer's face was white as rice and that the excitement of the moment had colored mauve a slim scar that lanced along the left side of his jaw.

Queer that I could see anything about me, for my stomach was knotting under my belt and I was bent in terror over the recumbent figure of Nina Gautier. But she had only fainted. And it was young Lieutenant Castelnau, fat and fully accoutered, who sped to the fore and snatched the shock-stricken lady up from the dirt.

"Name of heaven! Name of heaven! Name of heaven!" Castelnau chattered the words in shrill repetition. And he looked queer carrying that girl. Limp she was, and wrapped in some manner of clinging lingerie, peach-colored, that dragged in the dust and confused the lieutenant's boots.

I remember how peaceful her face had become, lolling against Castelnau's shoulder, eyes closed, long lashes motionless, her hair a golden shower against the ivory pallor of her cheek. I remember how Castelnau staggered into the headquarters hut with his burden, and as he passed the gesturing and frantic Corsican captain, that captain bawled at him:

"Quick, Lieutenant Castelnau. She will be all right alone in her room. I want you back at my side immediately."

Meantime the desperate non-coms had grabbed torch-flares. Lights flowered in the shouting gloom. Darkness and dust, lambent spots of flame, mad shadows flickering against twisty, slanting, unfamiliar shadowy walls. Every one pointing. Every one cursing. Every one spouting questions.

"Who did it?"

"When was he stabbed?"

"Did you find him?"

Noise and darkness and red light swirling like a crazy kaleidoscope against that spectral background of a stronghold built on the works of Carthage. And the center, the vortex of this raving excitement, just leaned there in the doorway. Leaned as if he was tired, and stared blankly at the noise and lights, and clutched that dripping book, and made no move.

"YOU found him, you red-bearded ape!" Lieutenant Gers had a fist on my wrist; spun me to face him. "Stop standing open-mouthed. You found him, *oui?*"

"He was dead already, and stiff!" I yelled. "That knife in his neck—"

"Get the colonel out of that doorway!" Captain Cellini's pitted face squalled. "Draw the knife from his throat. We will find the cursed fiend who owned that weapon, and it will be a sorry hour for him. Quick! Is this a Legion company or a band of jackals? Move, I tell you! You, *m'sieur le lieutenant!* Help him, you red-whiskered jackass! Get down the colonel. Blood of the devil, if some one won't suffer for this!"

We got down the colonel. It was no nice job, that is so. Our poor Papa Gautier was not so pleasant to carry as his living wife had been, *non!* The blond young Lieutenant Gers stooped his giant's shoulders and looked very ill as he drew the knife that had killed our commander. Without a word he passed the weapon to Captain Cellini.

I saw the Corsican go deadly pale. I saw him stare. Then every man of us near enough to see was staring, too. How we stared! Listen! The light from the torch-flares fell on that knife and blazed on its metal handle. *Mort de diable!* The handle of that knife was lettered with a queer inscription, but that wasn't what made us stare like fools turned to stone. It was not! We stared, because that knife was solid gold.

GENERAL CESAR PAZAINE was a Provençal Frenchman with the body of a gorilla, the face of a grouchy bulldog, a reputation for savage fearlessness and sagacity, a habit of scowling and grinning at the same time, and a name that struck fear and smart salutes wherever it went. Legionnaires and officers alike watched the step when this general who wore so well his nickname of Panthère—The Panther—made one of his unexpected appearances.

Graduate of the École Militaire, veteran of the Indo-China wars and the Dahomey campaign, founder of a secret service that had smashed the power of the rebellious Aissaoua in Morocco and tricked the deadly Touareg, this Panther Pazaine of Legion General Headquarters had become a tradition. The soldiers of La Légion had a saying. "Trouble will be followed by the Panther, and then there will be trouble, indeed."

Rebellious Berber tribesmen would find themselves confronted by this bold French general who would, as like as not, reveal an intimate knowledge of their secret plotting and a promise to wring their necks if they carried out that plotting. Gun smugglers would come up against Pazaine and die. Soldiers scheming a mutiny in a Saharan outpost would be suddenly confronted by one General Pazaine, appearing like a ghost from the north. Fractious troops would be put under his command and turned into companies of lambs. Traitorous officers would be exposed by this genial Panther and walk in dishonor before the firing squad.

IT was General Pazaine, with a cordon of regimental officers, who galloped through the gate of Bab Eschmoun three days after the slaying of Colonel Gautier. It was General Pazaine who took command of the investigation, turned the outpost into a police round-up that would rival the workings of Scotland Yard in London. Panther Pazaine, of the Foreign Legion. When I saw him ride through that gate with his thunderous frown and his back like a ramrod in the saddle, I knew one thing. I knew I was very glad I was not the man who had murdered poor Papa Gautier.

But the French law works along this idea, in contrast to Yankee and British justice. The Americans and English say every man is innocent until proved guilty. The French claim every man guilty until proved innocent.

Panther Pazaine was not the general to alter this plan. He was not. He had not been in Bab Eschmoun five minutes before every Legionnaire of the garrison stood at parade on the drill field, and Lieutenants Gers and Castelnau, and Captain Cellini stood there, too. I shall not soon forget the happenings of that morning and the workings of the following days.

General Pazaine wheeled his horse to face the line of Legionnaires, stood in his stirrups and bawled from a dark face.

"Every dog of you is guilty of this beastly crime," he shouted. "Not a man of you is innocent until I find the one who did it! Not a single person who stood within these walls when the murder was committed will be allowed to leave until I find that assassin. Captain Cellini, Lieutenant Gers, Lieutenant Castelnau, the wife of Colonel Gautier who lies grieving in the house where he was slain, the men who mounted guard at that time—all are under suspicion.

"I am not the one to mince matters, *mes braves*. I shall go over every inch of this place, follow every clew, interrogate to the last question. Any man seen attempting to leave the outpost will be shot on sight by my staff who will guard the walls. The dispatch rider sent by Captain Cellini with the report of the murder is the only person who has left Bab Eschmoun since the killing. He will be held under suspicion in Bizerta until I find the guilty man."

His sharp blue eyes traveled down the rank of Legionnaires. A savage smile thinned his lips. "I am commanding here from now on. Before I question each of you separately, I will question all of you in public. Should one of you detect a falsehood or be able to controvert a given statement, speak out. But beware! I am the Law. Any man of you withholding knowledge that would expose the murderer will be considered party to the crime and die with the guilty. *Alors*—"

That was Panther Pazaine. An uneasy tremor moved down the line of Legionnaires. Already his own men tramped the walls overhead. Another gesture, and his adjutant had procured a camp table; set it up before the general. General Pazaine dismounted with an agile leap.

"ATTENTION!" The Legion line snapped to stand like tin soldiers.

"Captain Cellini, your report said you had certain matters of evidence preserved in a kit bag. Had you used your wits you would have left the murdered man in the position when found and not removed such evidence. No doubt the articles are plastered with the fingerprints of half the men in the post, thus eliminating that method of detection. However, bring me these articles. Also summon the widow of Colonel Gautier."

Another stir animated the line of men. Mme. Gautier had been seen by none of us since the night of the murder. Rumor—there had been ten million rumors—had it she was ill, had confined herself to that back room of the adobe headquarters hut and seen nobody. We waited, taut, as Captain Gepetto Cellini stamped off toward the buildings under the east wall. I looked at the men on either side of me. They were pale.

"Look at Lieutenant Castelnau," Christianity Jensen whispered from the corner of his mouth. "That one is as white as snow."

Oui. I peeked from the corner of my eye, and the fat little officer last in line was colorless of face. I saw him watching the door of the adobe hut whence the Corsican had vanished. Then Captain Cellini reappeared, and the Legion line stirred again. The captain had a bundle in his fist, and behind him came the colonel's widow.

Aunt of the Devil, there was one pathetic sight. I hated General Pazaine for dragging her thus into the eye of that line of desperadoes, for she walked with slow reluctance and her head was lowered. How the girl must have suffered during those three days of confinement with her husband lying murdered on a cot before her door; lost, widowed, solitary in a strange outpost at world's end, surrounded by strange men and ugly whisperings!

The Legionnaires stared and General Pazaine stared; and as the girl drew near we stared the harder. Do you know what she had been doing to wear out those three solitary days? She had made herself a dress of mourning. My throat twisted when I saw that. Why, the unfortunate girl had fashioned herself a gown of deepest black, and her sorrow lay hidden behind a flowing veil of black lace that fell to her shoulders and shrouded her golden head and masked the beauty of her eyes.

Can you imagine such a shocking picture? That grim-walled, age-old fortress looming about us in the blatant African sunshine. That dour-faced General Pazaine holding rigid a rank of ruffian Legionnaires across the dun-hued floor of the parade field. And solitary in our midst a tall, bowed, slender figure in flowing black lace—the very spirit of sorrow and death.

I think even that doughty old Panther Pazaine was taken by surprise. But Captain Cellini dropped the bag of nice murder-exhibits on the camp table, and the girl stood silently before him, her white, thin hands twisting at the veil that shrouded her face. Panther Pazaine was once more a captain of police investigating murder.

"I regret this necessity, Mme. Gautier," the general conceded. "But, as head of the investigation committee appointed by General Head-quarters in Algiers, I am commanded to a task unpleasant for all of us. This is my method of taking first steps to find the assassin who killed Colonel Gautier. I want to see all suspects together for the first time. Would you be kind enough to remove the veil?"

I shall never forget how white her face looked as she drew aside that masking black shroud of lace. Like marble her cheeks and the finely-sculped arch of white throat. But lips red as fever, and eyes that shone like lightning, deep-set with sorrow.

"Any possible thing I can do," she said in a voice that seemed to come low, like an echo from a sunken well, "to assist in the capture of the fiend who slew my husband—that I will gladly do. Gladly! And now, because the sun is so hot—"

I remember how the general gestured; how once more she hid sunny hair, jewel eyes and marble cheeks behind the shrouding black; how bravely she declined the proffered camp chair.

I remember how a fury burned in my mouth. Those gossiping wives in Algiers who had called her faithless—tainted her as half Arab. Those evil-hinting Legion dogs who talked! I cursed them roundly in my beard and shed oaths at the assassin who could murder her husband and throw her thus—pitifully before the stares of the Foreign Legion. It was no pleasant business for a woman, that is so.

But the morning's investigation went on. I recall the affair as if it happened but yesterday. The details of that first inquest, were indelibly etched on my mind; and I recount them faithfully because of their import on the sinister and astounding events that were, later, to uncoil.

CHAPTER III.

"ALL ARE GUILTY!"

G ENERAL PAZAINE started by drawing a sheaf of documents from his tunic, glowering at the men who were guilty until proved innocent, and reading harshly: "Report of Captain Gepetto Cellini to Regimental Headquarters: 'Some time between the hours of nine and eleven, the evening of the thirteenth day of the present month, Colonel Achille Gautier was found murdered in his headquarters of the outpost of Bab Eschmoun. Assailant or assailants undetermined.'" General Pazaine read and scowled and grinned.

"Captain Cellini, this is the report you sent by dispatch rider to Bizerta? And that dispatch rider is the only Legionnaire of the company you have permitted to quit Bab Eschmoun?"

"*Oui,* General Pazaine." The Corsican wiped a nervous hand across his mouth. "Directly after the finding of the body I took command and issued orders that no man was to leave the post. It would be impossible for a man to leave the outpost unseen. I also placed the staff mounts under guard."

"One of this number, then, must be the slayer of Colonel Gautier." The general shafted a piercing gaze down the line of men. Every Legionnaire in that line shifted uneasily. It was stifling, standing at attention there in that fierce sunshine of morning, but Panther Pazaine had an eye to chill one's spine to the marrow. I thought to myself that some one among us must have a spine like an icicle. Ananias himself would have faltered in an attempt to lie to this Legion general.

He called the roll of the detachment in a voice like a roar. "Now," he snarled, "I have obtained the record of every dog of you in the detachment. A fine lot of criminals, I must say. Half of you, it would seem, have done time in the *Battalion d'Afrique.* Nice training. The other half have flown into our Legion ranks to escape a justice that would have served you well. You, Pierre Perousse"—he pointed at a thin-faced Gascon standing at the end of the line—"it would seem the Paris police want you for a nice stabbing on the Seine water front, eh?"

His accusing finger bored at the next Legionnaire. "You, Émile Gulick. Why did you leave your native land in such a hurry? Did you, perhaps, shoot down a woman in Hamburg? Your face grows pale. *Bien.* A killer, too."

The general's finger moved again. "You, Wenceslao Pizarro. A little bird told me you escaped from that pretty Spanish prison in Utrera, where you had gone because of a bomb-throwing in Seville. Another assassin." General Pazaine laughed grimly. "It appears that Colonel Gautier was commanding the nicest crowd of cutthroats in our army. Murderers and defaulters, eh? So. One of you may have escaped his deserts the first time. This time he will not escape.

"But there is one point. Is it possible, Captain Cellini, that the slayer of Colonel Gautier could have been some prowler, an Arab, perhaps, who was hiding in this place at the time of your entry?"

"It is possible, *mon général.* But Colonel Gautier sent in an advance guard, which I myself commanded. We searched through the adobe buildings. We found no evidence of prowlers. No foot tracks. Nothing. There was no one here. There was nothing but blank walls. The place has been unoccupied for years."

"You make your point well, Captain Cellini. No Arab would come near Bab Eschmoun. I know that for certainty. They hold the place haunted, and their priests decree that they must stay away. *Bien.* Then one of you forty men who stand before me betrayed the honor of the Legion and murdered his commanding officer."

General Pazaine wheeled suddenly on Mme. Gautier. "Behind every murder lies a motive," he snapped sternly. "Mme. Gautier, you knew your husband better than any one of us. Do you know of any quarrel he could have had with one of these men? Did Colonel Gautier ever tell you of any trouble? Can you tell me of anything that might establish a motive for his killing?"

HER voice whispered out of that deep black veil, but every man of us heard what she said. We were listening, I tell you. We listened with ears stiff as tin to every word spoken during that fateful inquisition.

"No," she whispered. "Colonel Gautier was a gentleman. I believe the men under him were as fond of him as he was of them."

"You married him in the city of Marseilles two years ago, I believe? *Oui.* So then. You were dancing in a café at the time? Please answer promptly, *madame.* I regret these questions, but I must go deeply into the background of all concerned in this miserable affair. You were a dancer, *oui?* You say you were. And previously to that you had been an actress, that is so? Yes. Good. Now then." The general spoke slow incisive words. "I am informed that Captain Cellini was at one time a barytone with the Florence Opera. Did you know *him* at that time?"

An angry exclamation snorted from the pitted face of the Corsican officer. The widow of Colonel Gautier stiffened.

"What can such a foolish query mean?" she demanded coldly. "Cannot you treat a widowed lady with something like respect, General Pazaine? Your questioning need not be offensive. Of course I did not know Captain Cellini. I never saw him or any of these men or officers until my husband brought me to Sidi-bel-Abbes. Why do you subject me to this harassment?"

General Pazaine bowed stiffly. "I am sorry, Mme. Gautier. My only wish and duty is to see justice done in the cause of your husband. I repeat, I look first for a motive. Please permit a personal question.

You loved your husband—" He waved an apologetic gesture. "I mean, you and Colonel Gautier had never—eh—thought of a—a separation?"

"I loved him dearly," she answered softly. "Dearly...."

"Then," the general said quietly, "you will help me solve this case. *Alors.* The report says your husband was found in the doorway of the headquarters house chosen by him. You were with him at the time?"

"We had been established in our new quarters only an hour or so. Colonel Gautier had been busy about the stronghold. We were both very fatigued. It was darkening. Perhaps half after nine by the clock. I was unpacking our luggage in the back room of the house. I told my husband I was retiring. He told me he would have an orderly soon. I went to bed and left him reading. Colonel Gautier was always reading."

General Pazaine fumbled at the bag on the table. "Colonel Gautier was found with this book under his arm." The general extended the worn volume. That volume with the dark stain across its cover. "This is his book, Mme. Gautier? The book he was reading?"

"It is. Colonel Gautier had a most extensive library."

"A scholar," General Pazaine observed. "The title of this book is a strange one. *Carthago Delenda Est.* I take it the colonel was informing himself on the historical background of this land. This book apparently deals with early Carthage. I see a reference to Queen Dido on the fly leaf. Unfortunately I read but little Latin. The book is in Latin. Do you read Latin, Mme. Gautier?"

"No!" Her voice showed irritation. "What can such a query have to do with this proceeding? I am tired, General Pazaine. Why must you ask these questions?"

Why, indeed? I tell you, the men about me and I, myself, wondered what the general was driving at. But I noticed one thing. *Sacré!* While the general appeared to question the girl, he kept the corner of an eye on the line of Legionnaires. Not a gesture or a foot-shift in that line escaped that eye. That eye was a point of ice.

"ENOUGH of the book, then," General Pazaine countered, tossing the macabre volume on the table. "So. Your husband was reading. You had gone to bed. To sleep, *oui?* You were sleeping, then. What followed?"

The pale white hands fluttered against the black veil. Like white butterflies.

"I heard an outcry," she stammered softly. "I sprang up. I was asleep in the back room of the house, you comprehend. I fled into the front room. The colonel stood in the doorway. It seemed as if he had just finished his reading; gone to stand there for a breath of fresh air. The night was stifling. I could hear some one crying out. I ran to the colonel. He—he was dead—stabbed—murdered. I—I fainted." The black-veiled figure swayed. General Pazaine studied his knuckles.

"Colonel Gautier was stabbed where he stood, I believe. So. I believe he had just finished his reading; had gone, as you suggest, to stand for a breath of air. Some one approached him. Some one with a knife hidden under a coat, perhaps. Nobody is around. It is dark. The murderer does his work. He drove the knife deep, skillfully. But then, Mme. Gautier, the report says the officers took charge. The body of Colonel Gautier was wrapped in blankets and left for examination. *Alors.* Three days have elapsed. You have spent those days confined in the back room of the headquarters house?"

"That is so. It was a terrible shock to me. I am alone—among strangers. I am ill. I shut myself in my room with my things. But I—I could not stay quietly, or I should have gone mad." Her voice broke. "I worked. I wished to revere and honor my husband. In my luggage I carried all that I owned, for we were to stay here a year. I was making black lace shawls. The wives of army officers are poor, as *m'sieur le général* knows. I was making these shawls to take back with me when Colonel Gautier got leave. They would sell— But I must mourn my husband. I—I spent the three days sewing these veils."

Now, by heaven, I, Thibaut Corday, have heard some pathetic revelations in my life, but never as touching a speech as that of Mme. Gautier. *Sacré bleu!* The poor creature was being tortured. Did you ever hear a murder investigation? Did you ever hear the words of the widow in mourning, caught into the net of the diabolic affair? It is never pleasant. And this was the strangest inquisition in the world, this military investigation, way down in Bab Eschmoun. A court on the rim of the universe, nightmarish, improbable.

For General Pazaine had swung on Captain Cellini with a snarl. "Captain Cellini, you know these dogs of soldiers under you. Had any of the men in this company a quarrel with Colonel Gautier?"

And that beautiful Corsican martinet growled: "You know their records, General Pazaine. Dogs and vagabonds. Not one of them above a murder. The worst detachment I have ever commanded."

"Where," General Pazaine demanded, "were *you* when the murder took place?"

"The staff—the two lieutenants, our three orderlies and I—had set up tents under that east wall. We were not to assign permanent quarters until the next day. We had seen the men bivouacked on the ground where their tents remain now. It was dark. I had made a final inspection. I was sleeping in my tent when the murder was committed."

"Then you know when the murder was committed?"

Captain Cellini's pock-marked cheeks flushed red. "I do not, of course. I mean, the cry of the guard woke me from sleep. I dashed from my tent; stumbled in the darkness. When I reached headquarters it was to find the lieutenants and the guard already there. Colonel Gautier was dead in his doorway. I feared mutiny; took command at once."

General Pazaine fingered his jaw. "Captain Cellini, I wonder— Tell me. Do you read Latin? No! Now then. What officer was quartered in the tent next you? Lieutenant Gers? So. What is your story, Lieutenant Gers? Were you in your tent when the outcry started?"

"**I HAD** been there for half an hour, General Pazaine." The young St. Cyr graduate stepped forward and spoke glibly. "I heard the cry and dashed to headquarters. I saw at once what had happened. The Legionnaires were milling about, and Mme. Gautier lay in a faint in the doorway."

"Lieutenant Gers." It was Panther Pazaine speaking now; slow, brittle words. "Did you ever have cause to resent Colonel Gautier? Did you ever wish your commander out of the way? Did you—"

I swear the general's words had a startling effect on that young officer, Anatole Gers. He stepped back a pace. His hands knotted at his sides. He shot a harried glance at the men about him, and that lean scar on his jaw went livid.

"General Pazaine, if you mean—?"

"That is precisely what I mean, *mon lieutenant*. One year ago in the city of Algiers, while you and Colonel Gautier were on leave, the colonel challenged you to a duel. You chose rapiers. In this affair of honor, Colonel Gautier took satisfaction by marking your jaw. It would seem you were not the best of friends. So, then—what was the cause of this duel?"

The giant shoulders of young Gers squared angrily. His scarred jaw thrust doggedly as he spoke. "The affair had nothing whatever to do with this," he snarled. "Colonel Gautier and I were reconciled completely. He went so far, later, as to ask for my appointment in his company. We were good friends. Of his murder or its cause I know nothing. I was alone in my tent when it happened."

I guess the line of Legionnaires had not listened eager-eared to this foray of tongues. We waited stiff as stone for the unfortunate who would next come under Panther Pazaine's deadly eye.

It was Lieutenant Castelnau. General Pazaine demanded his particular story, and the fat little officer mopped his face.

"I was in my tent, also. I heard the cry of the guard. I ran from my tent. The men were at the door of the colonel's headquarters. There was wild uproar, *oui*. It was I who carried Mme. Gautier into the house—the men would have trampled her underfoot—"

"Were you sleeping when the guard cried out?"

"I was not. I had not yet retired. I was having a drink. Very good wine it was, too. *Sacré!* I know nothing whatever of this so dreadful affair. I cannot read Latin, *mon général.* Not a word of it. Nor had I any quarrel with Colonel Gautier. In fact, the good colonel was one of my father's best friends. My father was president of the Bank of Algeria. The colonel often visited our home when my revered parent was living and I was but a youth. I was fond of the colonel."

"You knew his wife?"

"My dear General Pazaine!" The fat Castelnau face changed color. "I have seen her on occasion, of course."

"We are getting somewhere," General Pazaine scowled, "when we find the undertones of this business. I trust you gentlemen will pardon my seemingly irrelevant questions. Naturally my queries to the men will be different. They would not know so intimately the—shall I say, personal—inside affairs of the post commander. Now, then, the men!"

And so it was for the men. That Panther Pazaine started at the end of the line where Legionnaire Pierre Perousse, the fox-faced one, stood squirming, and he fired questions like bullets.

Those Legion dogs had been standing at attention for an hour. The sun was like flame on their necks and their backs were breaking and their feet groaned aloud. They had enjoyed listening to the haggling of their officers, but they did not enjoy their turn, that is so. General Pazaine forked into their midden-hill pasts with a barbing prong. He prodded and questioned and harried.

"Where were *you*, you dog, when the alarm was cried?" But each one answered with the alibi. They were in their tents. They were mending their boots. They were standing guard on the wall.

TWO facts the needle-eyed general seemed to establish. First, that every man in the line was not above stabbing an officer or a grandmother to death. Second, that every man in the line might have sneaked off in the darkness, murdered Colonel Gautier, and slunk back to his tent without detection. Even the men mounting guard might have dropped from the walls and done the stabbing, beating back to their posts, unseen, before the alarm.

When the general came to the ugly Bavarian guard who had passed on patrol before the headquarters hut, he flung a barrage of questions that led the foul-tongued German a frantic word-dance. But, though he revealed the German's record as unsavory as the worst in the company, he could prove nothing more.

"Himmel!" the man squawked, lobster-faced. "I did not kill him. I am the guard, yes. I pass the headquarters and see him reading at table in that front room. Twenty minutes later I pass again. He is standing in the doorway. Is he dead or not? I do not know. I salute and go by. A Legionnaire does not stare at a colonel. Perhaps he is already dead. Perhaps not. I walk on. I meet one Legionnaire—that one with the red whiskers—who is on his way to headquarters. He says he goes to be the colonel's orderly. I let him pass, after pointing out the colonel on the doorstep of headquarters. He goes past me, and I walk away."

It was *my* turn then. General Pazaine stabbed at me with his eyes like points of ice, and I know I turned every color of the rainbow. Listen. Let me tell you something. If you ever want to feel like a murderer, let some detective accuse you of the crime. You may have a thousand alibis and may have been in China at the time of the killing, but you will blush and choke and, perhaps, go to the gallows because of a silly feeling of guilt. *Mon Dieu!* Not only did I feel like a criminal, but I looked like one.

"But certainly I did not kill him," I gasped. "I was setting up my tent all evening. Then the squad corporal came to tell me Colonel Gautier had summoned me for orderly duty. I was to report at headquarters on the instant."

General Pazaine offered me a sneer. "It takes a Soldier of the First Class all evening to set up his tent?"

"Not all, *mon général.* I was in the tent—waiting," I stammered.

"For what?" he roared. "You were sitting alone in your tent. You had not gone to bed. Why not? What Legionnaire would sit in a dog tent on a broiling hot night? What were you doing at the time the corporal came? Between the time the corporal left Colonel Gautier and this German guard passed him standing in the doorway, Colonel Gautier was slain. You say you lurked in your tent. You, too, were seen by nobody at that time. Why?" He slammed his little table. "Why were *you* hiding?"

Uncle of Satan, but I began to sweat. "I was taking a smoke in my pipe," I told him truthfully, feeling like a fool and a triple-tongued liar. "I did not want the sergeant to see me. Then the corporal came with the summons. I walked to the headquarters—" And I told him the exact details of my discovery of the slain officer.

The sun was at noon. General Pazaine was scarlet with anger and sunburn. He finished my toasting with an oath, and wrote at such length in his little notebook that I could almost feel the bullets of the firing squad skidding through my insides.

I think each ruffian in the line was feeling the same creeps. Only the one who had stabbed the post commander could have felt a trifle cheered. Certainly the finger of guilt seemed to point at everybody. Then it pointed into more confusion. The grim-faced general yanked a whistle from his tunic and shrilled a note. The shrill blast brought his adjutant sprinting from the direction of the fatal headquarters hut.

WE had forgotten this adjutant of General Pazaine's staff. He hurried forward, now, a wizened little Frenchman with a scarlet *fourragère* on his shoulder, a death's-head grin in his teeth and a sheaf of papers in his fist. A moment he conferred in whispers with General Pazaine; then the general swung about, frowning blackly.

"Mes braves," the Panther snarled. "While I interrogated you, my adjutant has gone over the grounds of Bab Eschmoun, and inspected the body of Colonel Gautier. His inspection of the colonel told us nothing we do not already know. His search among the adobe houses revealed nothing. But, on going through the equipment of the officers, he did find something of interest. Your pardon, gentlemen. This is a murder case. Formalities cannot be observed. I ordered my adjutant to open your luggage and inspect the kits of the men as well. In the kits of the men he found nothing. In the kits of Captain Cellini and Lieutenant Gers he found something of interest. Captain Cellini, I

have here what seems to be a love letter. It is addressed to one Nina. You were interrupted in the writing. I will return you your note. It has told me enough."

Stepping forward, he thrust a paper into the Corsican's hand. I tell you, that Captain Cellini's face was contorted. But his twisting mouth said nothing. Panther Pazaine was speaking again:

"Lieutenant Gers, it would seem you, too, had started a note. I find the paper with the name Nina scribbled several times across the top. Or perhaps you were only sitting and thinking, eh? Men write their subconscious thoughts in such a way.

"As for Lieutenant Castelnau, he was more clever. Monsieur the lieutenant, my adjutant found these in a canister in your tent." The general held out an open palm cluttered with strips of carbonized paper. "You burned your letter, it would appear, before delivering. However, I discover that some of the words on the burned paper may still be read. What was this letter, lieutenant? Why did you burn it?"

The fat Castelnau's voice was squeaky. "It is just a letter, General Pazaine. I—I burn all my letters."

"A careful gentleman," the general leered, grimly. "Do you burn them before sending them or after receiving them? Good, in either case. However, I discover the words Nina Gautier written across this charred paper. Three of you with letters to Nina Gautier." General Pazaine spun toward the girl. "Do you know of these?"

But she shook her head; stood quietly, the black shadow of a beautiful lady, shaming savage words and savage sunshine. A bitter laugh escaped the lips of General Pazaine.

"I HAD thought to discover the murderer this very morning and expose him before all of you," he rasped in a voice that had the quality of a saw on teakwood. "I am opposed by one with the mind of the snake. The killer of Colonel Gautier plotted well. Opportunity? Not one of you but had the opportunity. Motive? There are all the motives from hate of an officer to revenge, from plotted mutiny to the sort of love affair where a man kills a husband to get him out of the way.

"I speak plainly, *mes braves*. By now you realize that General Pazaine does not do things in the ordinary fashion. Officers and men I treat alike in this case. Motives? All of you may have a motive. Robbery is the only one unlikely. The robber does not stab his victim with a gold knife!"

His hand flickered into the bag on the table, came out closed around that long-handled weapon with the blade that flashed pure yellow in the sunlight.

"The murderer of Colonel Gautier was not after money," he declared sternly. "For he stabbed his victim with a weapon worth twice its weight in gold." General Pazaine glared at the knife. "There is an inscription on this blade. I believe it to be early Roman. It is such a weapon as only a man of wealth could procure—a valuable curio. When I have determined the owner of this knife, I shall trace the hand which held it last. The owner of that hand, *mes enfants*, will pay a price. One last word. Did any of you ever set eyes on this dagger before?"

Not a man of the Legion line stirred. Name of a name! What soldier of the Foreign Legion would be likely to set his penny-a-day eyes on a dagger of gold? Our officers, too, remained mute. In that unbroken torrid quiet, General Pazaine stiffened to attention. The eyes in his cast iron face flashed to match the blaze of the golden knife in his fist. His voice came through his teeth, sharp as that golden blade.

"One of your number is a liar. One of your number saw this knife before the moment of the murder—held it in hand—drove it with the strength of a demon killer into the throat of Colonel Gautier. Colonel Gautier was one of the finest officers in La Légion. I shall remain here until I find the murderer who slew him; stay here if it takes me forty years. I place the officers and men of this garrison—every occupant of this outpost at the time of the murder—under arrest!"

CHAPTER IV.

IMPRISONED WITH A MURDERER.

WELL, THERE was that incredible military inquest; and I remember thinking at the time that the famous fiction character detective, Sherlock Holmes, with all the dope in the world jabbed into his arm, could not have selected Colonel Gautier's murderer that morning.

The court of France considers all suspects guilty until proved innocent. By heaven, it certainly would have taken a court of wizards a lot of deliberation to prove anything at all about that detachment of Legionnaires, save that all looked guilty as sin! Guilty-looking? I assure you that row of sun-bitten, big-nosed, knife-hacked Legion faces would have made a Paris Sûreté rogues' gallery look like a hall of saints' portraits by comparison.

As for our three officers, they merely thickened the puzzle. I had to laugh in my throat when I thought of them; and I could imagine the things General Pazaine was thinking when he studied the problem. Obviously each of the three had been intrigued by the charms of poor Mme. Gautier. Captain Cellini, the Corsican, had written her a note decidedly unconventional. An ugly, saturnine character, that Corsican. A bitter eye and a bitter mouth. A southerner with the easily-exploded soul of those born in the Mediterranean cradle. Hot-blooded, sullen, vengeful. Gepetto Cellini looked the sort of man who might kill a beautiful woman's husband to get him out of the way, that is so.

There was Anatole Gers. No man among us had looked more guilty at the inquest than that big young French lieutenant. In love, himself, with the wife of his commanding officer. He, too, had penned her name. And there was the matter of his duel, unearthed by the wily Panther Pazaine. Lieutenant Gers had been challenged and defeated in an affair of honor by Colonel Gautier. What of that duel? Had the hulking lieutenant nursed a grudge against the man who had scarred his face? Had he, perhaps, hoped to destroy the husband of a woman he wished to win?

And then Lieutenant Castelnau—little and fat, with a dimpled face that could pale or flush at a word. Why had he tried to burn that letter? The colonel had known his family. His father had been president of the Bank of Algeria. That meant the fat little officer was rich; and who but a wealthy man would possess a knife of gold—a valuable antique, as General Pazaine had named the weapon? Love makes a man do terrible things....

"BY the bones of St. Stephen, this is a wild mystery!" Christianity Jensen swore that night, as we lay whispering and sleepless in our tent. "There is something in the air, Corday, old *cochon*. Something in the air that my nose does not like. Something that makes my hair want to raise. This ancient stronghold is a haunt for werewolves, I think. There are too many shadows around. We are not here an hour before our colonel is stabbed through the throat. Any one of us might have done the deed. It was dark. Mme. Gautier herself is under suspicion. Those three officers are in love with her, eh? Perhaps she is in love with one of them? Could she have killed poor Papa Gautier?"

"It is possible that is so," I agreed. "But you saw her face and heard her speak her devotion? *Non,* my little Dane. That woman is no assassin. And life in the army is poor. Papa Gautier had money once, but lost it. She was sewing veils to sell for a spending pittance, like those other army women in Algiers. Would she be likely to own a knife of gold? Would she be able to stab it deep?"

An oath escaped my companion. "That weapon is the puzzle. The men have been buzzing like flies, wondering about that knife. I would think it was some rich ghost from the outside who crept in and slew with this gold treasure. But no outsider could have mounted the walls unseen. Nor could any one have entered the guarded gate. And as for the strange book the colonel was reading—why did old Panther make such a point of that? What had that volume to do with the murder, I wonder? A book in Latin. What of that?"

What of that book? What of the knife? What of any of it?

"Le bon Dieu only knows," I told the little Dane. "I think our general has too many clews and too many possibilities on his hands. Name of a name! Forty years, Panther Pazaine said he would stay. And I think he will have to stay here that long—"

Forty years? Day after day lagged by, and each day was a forty years. The months piled up, taking centuries. At long last six calendar months wore past.

What months those six were! I have spent some hard days in the service of La Légion, but none to equal those that dragged along under General Pazaine's investigation. That fortress was nothing but a prison, and the men of the detachment were convicts.

As the days dragged on the Panther grew savage. Investigations? We had one every day. Inquisitions? There was one going on all the time. Legionnaires tramped in and out of Pazaine's headquarters hut. The general sat behind a table weighted with notebooks and questionnaires.

Woe to the Legionnaire whose memory was inaccurate or missing. "You cannot remember what you said to the colonel that afternoon, you dog? Lieutenant Castelnau reports that the colonel spoke to you about your kit, and you answered him. You fail to recall? Then try defaulter's drill for a week and see if your brain is refreshed."

Woe to the Legionnaire trapped in a lie. That would mean for him the "plute"—that nice little pastime of marching eight hours of the day with a sixty-pound sandbag nesting on the shoulders. And as the days dragged along and General Pazaine came no nearer to the solution of the murder puzzle, the discipline flowered into full vigor.

WE cleaned up Bab Eschmoun. We policed the walls and swept the open ground and washed out the adobe buildings. The Legionnaires moved into the building under the north wall. No barracks house was ever as spotless.

The Corsican captain and the two lieutenants occupied huts in that row facing the *caserne* and lived under a suspicion that must have infuriated them to madness. And Mme. Gautier lived in the little two-roomed house last in the line; remained in the house where the colonel was killed—a solitary, lone figure, recluse in her little back room.

I think if there was anything that got into the back teeth of the men, it was this picture of Mme. Gautier locked in the midst of this brain-racking prison encampment at world's end—alone and widowed and sorrowing. Always she wore her gown of mourning, her shroud of a veil. Briefly she might appear during the day, hurrying to the well near the gate, or bending quick steps toward General Pazaine's headquarters established in that house behind hers, or standing for a moment, usually at sunset, in the doorway where her husband had leaned in death, her veiled face turned toward the scarlet western sky.

We had wrapped Papa Gautier in the Tricolor and buried him at evening under the palm trees near the well. The bugles had blown in the twilight, and Mme. Gautier, standing near the fresh mound, had turned toward the line of Legionnaires. Her voice had come, somber, through the veil. "I will stay here a while with him," she had said.

There she would be in that grim door; black, shadowy, silent. Daytime transfigured by tragedy into Night. Othertime she ate and lived in seclusion. Her appearance would startle the men. Her bleak sorrowing, her mutely-accepted privation, wrought a queer effect on us. One among us had betrayed her. So we spoke of her in whispers, suddenly respectful, like clumsy men with a daughter of the church in their midst.

Talk. It was one of the things that kept us from going *cafard* during those maddening, drill-cursed, monotonous desert days. Evenings in barracks we discussed, argued, speculated, sprawled panting on our beds after a day of grueling military life under the iron fist of General Pazaine.

He was drilling us around those infernal old walls until we knew and hated every inch of Bab Eschmoun. We knew the interior of the stronghold's prison, too. That high, chimney-like tower on the south wall, with its lone barred window and promise of bread and water diet, was a constant threat to keep rigid discipline.

One climbed a steep stone staircase into the tower, sat alone behind a bolted stone door, with spiders and heat for company. One stared out of the airless window on to a lifeless desert below and a blazing sky above. Panther Pazaine was easily induced to commit a Legionnaire to that *salle de police*, so we Legionnaires drilled like automatic toys and spent our evenings in well-behaved gossiping.

Our constant source of converse was the murder; and we grew to hate the murderer as a personal enemy. He had restricted our personal liberty. He had brought the scourge of the Panther on our heads. Under suspicion, each man was suspicious of the other. A spirit as ugly as a tiger's tooth began to gnaw its way through the dull floor of the barracks room. Old grudges were remembered. There were secret fights in the dead of night. Petty thefts and snarling. Some blackguard hurled a boot one night and struck me a fiendish blow on the skull.

"*Sacré Dieu!*" I observed to the stout little Dane who shared my rations with me. "This outpost is planted with a dynamite that will not stand much more of this jolting. Six months, now, we've been locked up here. If we stay shut in this place much longer something terrible is bound to happen!"

Once again, I, Thibaut Corday, with the finest and longest red beard in La Légion, played soothsayer. For something terrible began to happen that very night. I was mounting guard on the wall near the gate and the new stars were out when it started. If I live to be ten thousand I shall never be able to forget that wild and frantic night when a demon struck, red-handed, through the darkness.

MOUNTING guard in Bab Eschmoun was a precise and strict task, for the sentries were not only commanded to watch the desert for a possible enemy, but to keep a sharp eye to see that no man within the stronghold ventured out. A stationary sentry was posted at each of the corner bastions, while a mobile guardsman patrolled the wall between. I was mobile guard that night, and I tramped wearily along the west wall over the gateway.

An hour the sun had been gone, and the sky was a sweep of indigo scattered with pale stars, and moonless. The outpost lay smothered under blankets of heat and darkness; I could scarcely discern the ground directly below and must march within forty paces of each bastion before I could make out the dull bayonet-gleam of the fixed sentry.

Sapristi! It was quiet. The measured tread of the patrols on the other three walls stole like echoes through the sceneless black; the clump of my own hobnailed boots was muffled in the silence of the night.

"Rien à signaller?" I would call when I arrived at a bastion.

"Rien," the fixed sentry would drone. Phantom voices in a place where phantoms would be. "All's well—"

Clump, clump, clump. I would face about and tramp for the other bastion, a long, slow stroll with only myself for company. As I passed over the gateway I covered half the distance of my beat. I would stop and rub a sore eye. It was hard to stay awake. I would peer through the darkness at nothing.

Now surely the good saints would never criticize me if I stopped to sneak a little smoke. Just a little smoke. Three puffs to keep me alert, provide companionship and ease the soul. Lord help me if an officer below should chance to see, but a match-flare would not pierce that darkness for fifteen feet, and there are ways of lighting matches under one's coat.

I think it was my tenth tramp over the gate when I halted to reach for my pipe. But my hand never got to the pocket. Suddenly I was tight-nerved, rigid, down on one knee. Some one was at the gate below. No, two men!

My feet were silent—they thought I had passed. I hunched lower. Sibilant whispering drifted up from that well of black.

"He's gone on. Now, then, for God's sake what do you want of me, calling me out for this devilish rendezvous at such an hour? Speak fast. If the infernal Pazaine should hear of this he would be on our necks with his vile inquisition again. What do you want of me?"

Whose voice was that? I could not tell. Holding breath, I flattened myself atop that wall, every nerve in my body tingling, my ears out like fans. I drove my eyesight through the darkness with every effort of will and could distinguish nothing but blurred shadows. Two men standing together, pressed against the wall.

"Quick, then," whispered the second. "Six months we have been shut up in this devil's cesspool. The fools at headquarters may keep us here a year. General Pazaine has bungled the affair. But I have made some searchings of my own. In secret. I—"

"Castelnau, you are a fat, driveling fool!"

I could not determine that first voice, but the second was established. Lieutenant Castelnau! I lay like a stone image with little electric wires sparking up and down my spine. Castelnau's voice whispered on, ignoring the interruption.

"The sooner one of us solves this thing, the sooner all of us escape this cursed suspicion. You look as guilty as anybody, remember that. If Pazaine ever knew of those other love letters you wrote—"

"How do you know of them, you fat dog?" came the snarl from the unknown.

"Don't get angry. We're all in this rotten boat together," Castelnau returned. "I saw you writing notes. To whom, but to her? A beggar with one eye could tell you are in love with her. Don't stop to argue. I wish to get you out of this, too. Quick! We must talk fast. I believe I have figured out this case. Listen, now. I lied at the inquest. I can read Latin. Was quite a scholar as a youth, you comprehend. Now I am certain the key to the murder lies hidden in that book. You have better access to Pazaine's quarters than I have. Get me that book! Pazaine believes it has something to do with the killing, but fails to follow it up. Will you try to get me that cursed book? Soon—"

"You believe the book that old Gautier held under an arm—"

"For certain. It had something to do with Carthage, eh? And this vile outpost marks an old Carthaginian fort. The Arabs built on the ruin. But most of the walls are the original. And that knife—"

The words drifted lower, heated, muffled. Then clear again. Castelnau's voice:

"So much the better if you think you can get it now. I promise you, if I can find anything it will clear you. And me. Who can tell? I believe I know the killer, my friend. If I could read that volume I could prove, I am certain. But we must be fast. In secret. If the assassin knew of this, the tracks, perhaps, could be erased. Go quietly, and for the love of heaven, believe me. Get that book—"

MY eyes were smarting with the effort to see, but I saw one of the shadows melt away in the darkness. Now the remaining shadow hung along the wall beneath me. A minute ticked away, taking a year. Another minute. Cold sweat bubbled out on my forehead. What should I do? I must move at once, or the sentry at the bastion would explode an alarm.

But now there was fresh movement on the part of the figure below. I got my eyes over the rim of the wall and stared down. A rain of perspiration watered my cheeks. Had I heard a sound like a blow? Impossible. The dark was thick as cotton, but no second shadow had appeared, I was certain. Still, it sounded as if the man beneath me had struck the wall with his fist.

Name of a thousand Satans! That shadow was weaving, twisting, agitated. A thin, wry gurgling coiled up from that shapeless figure. A weird gurgling that terminated in a wheezy squeaking cry. A cry? Ten hundred-weight of silence fell into my ears and the sweat froze icy on my face. Brittle with nightmare fright, I slithered over the stone, hung by my hands, dropped.

My boots crashed in the dirt. A match trembled violently in my palm. The wavering, pallid light cast a yellow gleam on the contorted features of Lieutenant Augustin Castelnau, a fat squatting hummock against the stone wall. The fat hummock grinned with its eyes squeezed shut; and a gold knife hilt supported its double chin to keep it lifted.

I bawled, my eyes on the stars. Alarm guns tore the darkness and quiet to shreds. Bab Eschmoun awoke.

CHAPTER V.

THE BEARD.

LANTERNS BLOSSOMED in the gloom. Slants of amber light shed a grotesque mob of shadow-men charging down the wall. Shirtless Legionnaires raced toward me, saw the hummock, stopped short with oaths.

"Bones of Saint Jean de Luz! It is Lieutenant Castelnau!"

"Stabbed to death! Murdered!"

"Holà! See the knife! A gold hilt!"

"*Sacré!* Who did it? When was he found? When did *he* get it?"

"Killed by a gold dagger! He must have been slain by the man who

The post commander nursed his
neck-nape with a pistol-muzzle.

stabbed Papa Gautier!"

"Another one! Aunt of the devil! Who found him?"

Shrill yells. Hoarse oaths. Milling feet. Faces strangely twisted, steaming sweat, swirling like carnival masks through the lambent, mad twilight cast by lanterns. And there, maestro of the carnival, hunched Castelnau grinning like a cat. He grinned at the sentry who bent to touch the knife buried beneath his chins, and he grinned at General Pazaine, who stormed into the uproar like an avenging, black-browed angel.

I did not grin. You know very well I did not. My mind was a bird's nest. A mighty ticklish position I was in, let me promise you. Only too well did I know what Panther Pazaine would say. As sentry I should have challenged those two men the moment I sighted them under the wall. I had failed to do so. Now one of them lay dead. And I had not seen the murderer, my eyes betrayed by the dark.

Parbleu! I tried to think in that bird's nest brain of mine, but the hot wind blew through my ears and scattered the straws. And cold, salty water ran into my eyes when General Pazaine fastened a clutch on my wooden wrist and jabbed his bulldog countenance into mine.

"You saw it, you red-whiskered weasel? Quick, then. You found the body; saw the murder? Speak fast and speak truth, or you will die by my hand. Who stabbed Lieutenant Castelnau?"

Greasy faces, tinted and damp, made a ring about me. Panther Pazaine's eyes dug into my head, his face was a Gorgon's skull, his chest rammed against my ribs.

"I did not see the stabbing," I squalled. "I was on the wall over the gate arch. It was darker than pitch. When I caught sight of two shadows below me—there were two men—"

"Fighting?"

"*Non!* They were whispering. Then one of the men went away—I could not tell which one it was or where he went. I only know this: I heard the name Castelnau spoken familiarly. The second man must have been an officer. He went away in the darkness. A moment later—Uncle of Satan!—I heard a strange sound from the figure who remained below. A sound like a hard blow, *mon général.* Like—like a fist striking flesh. I could not tell. But the shadow voiced an odd cry from its throat. I dropped from the wall. There was Lieutenant Castelnau—as you see him now."

Teeth gleamed in General Pazaine's tight mouth. Words sawed through.

"You were on the wall? You sighted two men in the dark beneath you? They whispered together? The name of Lieutenant Castelnau is mentioned. One of the men walks away. The other stays by the wall. A moment later he is stabbed to death. But you gave no challenge? And you saw no fight, caught sight of no assailant?"

"The dark was thick!" I blattered. "I saw nobody stab this officer, I swear. Perhaps the unknown man who spoke with him struck him dead as he departed. I could not see. But I did not hear the cry until a moment later. How could I tell? But there were strange words spoken by the two. Most of the whispering I failed to catch. But they spoke of the book—that Latin book found under Colonel Gautier's arm when he was dead. And of love letters! The lieutenant accused his companion of writing more love letters." I was sweating, thick-tongued, fighting out the words. "It must have been one of the other officers!"

"The book! Letters!" General Pazaine spun on his heel, shot a glance at the corpse against the wall. "And a gold-hilted dagger in his neck! Name of heaven, here is devil's own work." He whirled about, savage-voiced. "Captain Cellini! Gers!" he roared. The Legionnaires fell back, chattering. Every man from the barracks was there. But the Corsican captain and the big blond lieutenant were not. The voice of the Panther snapped like a whiplash. "Scatter, you Legion dogs! Quick!

Back to officers' quarters and summon those two officers of yours. If they are not there, search the post!"

THE murmur of crowding men rose to a bellow. They surged about me, yelling. And how they yelled! My story seemed to establish Cellini or Gers as the mysterious assassin, and the absence of those officers from this uproar gave evidence of guilt. Off we stampeded *en masse* toward the officers' quarters. And I? I was glad to be off in the shuffle. I had not enjoyed the way Pazaine's shark eyes flickered as I spouted my story; and it was a pleasure to leave responsibility and the moribund grin of Castelnau behind.

Therefore I banged across the parade ground with the men, my mind executing a series of acrobatics. One thing I knew. Lieutenant Castelnau had been on the verge of solving the puzzle of Papa Gautier's murder. Believing the key to that mystery lay in the colonel's strange book and considering General Pazaine a bungler, Castelnau had plotted to solve the crime by himself.

But the book about Carthage was held in the hands of the general. Whereupon Castelnau had asked a friend to join him in the plan—some friend with easier access to the general's headquarters. Name of a name! It was obvious that this "friend" entrusted with the task of pilfering the book was either Cellini or Gers. Which one? You may guess I would have given a thumb, right then, to know.

At any rate, that "friend" had left Castelnau, and departed. Had he sneaked back on his tracks to knife the unsuspecting lieutenant? Or had some one else, the original assassin perhaps, overheard the whispering, and, knowing Castelnau could betray his identity, done the stabbing?

But no! I was certain as death that the fat lieutenant had been *alone* at the last. *Parbleu!* He might have stabbed himself. My poor brains churned as I sprinted along with the turmoil.

Can you see that gang of Legionnaires, baying like bloodhounds, lanterns bobbing in their black fists, legging it across that night-hung drill ground?

Those soldiers of the Legion did not particularly care that one of their lieutenants had been assassinated. Not they. But every blackguard can be righteously aroused when somebody else commits crime, especially if evidence involves a superior officer. And what scoundrel does not enjoy a man-hunt? The murderers were after a murderer.

We (I was no murderer, you comprehend, but simply a stupid

soldier who had enjoyed the raising of a first-prize beard) floundered across the outpost, then, heading for the row of adobe houses. Now that corner of the beatific fort was darker than a whale hole. The only light awaiting our charge was a sickly shine in the window of Madame Gautier's little back room. I could picture the unfortunate widow roused and fearful at this midnight's bedlam.

The shouting Legionnaires poured around the darkened front of her little house and pounded for the huts occupied by Lieutenant Gers and Captain Cellini.

And on passing that dim-lit window of Madame Gautier's we got a shock. Midst all those raving hours in that improbable night, I recall best that vision of Nina Gautier standing in her window. Here was a picture of exotic beauty hung outstanding in a gibbery chamber of horrors. For the colonel's widow was there in her little window, an elbow on the sill and a dim spirit lamp in her white hand; paused motionless.

As if carved she stood there, head and shoulders and that small hand holding its tiny gleam framed by the square of sill; and my heart stopped pumping and my feet stopped dead when I saw the picture.

She did not look at the men; she did not move; her head was turned toward the west whence this tumult had come. The veil had dropped from her face, and the lamp-glow illumined her features so that the profile stood out in sharp relief, startled, white, like an alabaster carving, and her hair was a halo of pale beams. An artist might have posed her there, unreal, startling. Her loosened veil made a black drape, the dark of the room behind her made a velvet background for that perfect head. Like an alabaster profile, I say, poised in a frame against black velvet.

MEN'S minds do incredible things in moments of high tension. Mine made a flying gyration as my feet stopped dead and I halted to catch a fleeting glimpse of that painted vision in the darkness. The American poet, Poe, caught that very scene in his classic ode to Helen; and the words flashed through my head "Lo, in yon distant window-niche, how statue-like I see thee stand, the agate lamp within thy hand—Ah, Psyche, from those regions which are holy land—"

Then Nina Gautier was gone from her window, and it was no time for a third-witted soldier of the Foreign Legion to be remembering odes to Helens or masterpieces in poetry. My wild-eyed comrades had run on ahead, and I moved my boots to catch up with them. But they had already gained the doors of the officers' quarters. Captain Cellini and the big blond lieutenant were not there to be summoned.

I cannot quite remember how it happened, then. I know the non-coms shouted orders, and the Legionnaires scattered, so many jackrabbits in the hot excitement, ready to obey with alacrity the order to "find those two officers of yours."

That Panther Pazaine was a wily man-hunter and no stickler for rules when it came to attaining an end. The Corsican captain and the Gascon lieutenant had not been on the job when the alarm detonated, and the Panther wanted them found. The Legionnaires scattered through the gloom, lanterns making floating blobs of yellow in the dark and dust, boots thudding in the dirt.

I skirted the *caserne* and plunged along the rim of the supply huts with a knot of panting men; then fell behind in the aimless, excited shuffle. A sergeant with a swinging lantern rushed past me, and told me to get the devil back toward the gate.

Left foundered in the dark, I stumbled along by myself, anxious to join a flickering group of lights up ahead. The lights picked out the boles of the date palms that hovered about our well near the gateway; suddenly they clustered and remained motionless. It was, possibly, five seconds' sprint before I joined the men and saw fists holding lights aloft, bent and heaving shoulders, faces stooped.

Dancing along the outer fringe of this ring of men under the palm trees, I strove to see the object of scrutiny. *Diable!* A Legionnaire was on his knees beside a shadow. The Legionnaire was that criminal Pierre Perousse, and the men crowded him close, and he cursed and tugged to lift this shadow in his arms.

I scrabbled to the middle of things by that time, I promise you, and when I saw the shadow was a limp man's body I felt the hair stiffen tight on my scalp. The lanterns flagged, and the light dropped full on a tortured face.

By the bones of Saint Sebastopol! It was Captain Cellini. With a gleaming, yellow-hilted dagger deep in his chest. A crimson blot welled and fattened down the front of his tunic. The Legionnaires chorused a yell.

Then the lips in that pitted, rice-white face moved, and the men stifled quiet as the wall beyond the palms to hear the gaspy words. Legionnaire Perousse supported Captain Cellini in his arms, as the stricken officer struggled to utter speech.

"I saw him!" came that whistly, incredible gasp. "Just—a glimpse. *Pardieu!* Sprang at me from behind those palms! It—it was dark. But the face came close. Held an arm over one side of his face. Wore a—a cloak, I think. But—I fought back—saw the face. A—a man with a beard. Terrible eyes—and—a beard. *Mon Dieu!* Get him—get a man—with a beard. *With a beard!*"

A man with a beard! By the sainted name of Saint Julienne of Avignon! The words struck into my head like a driven bayonet. A man with a beard! Now there were only two men in that befouled and death-ridden Bab Eschmoun detachment who wore beards. Sideburns and mustachios and goatees there were in plenty. But there were, you see, only two in the detachment who owned beards. The big blond Lieutenant Anatole Gers wore a pale and feeble one. And I? *Mort de Diable!* I, let me assure you, wore the longest and reddest beard in the Foreign Legion of France!

CHAPTER VI.

"TO DIE AT SUNRISE."

NOW **HERE** was a situation to chill the spinal ganglia of an Egyptian mummy; and I was no Egyptian mummy. No. I was a Legionnaire with a prize-winning but suddenly unwanted set of whiskers. You can believe me when I say I did not want my beard at all. I wanted none of it. For the Corsican captain, Gepetto Cellini, lay stabbed to death by an assassin with a beard. Chance had blessed the men in Bab Eschmoun with a dearth of beards—in fact, there were only two. And mine was one of them.

It took what was left of my brain just half of one second to realize what would happen when the statement of the dying Cellini percolated through the heads of the Legionnaires. This third killing, this triple murder out of the night, had struck a tenor note of terror in the dark.

Somewhere in this outpost at world's end lurked a manslayer, a savage dacoit, a fiend who smote out of shadows to kill with a golden blade. Here was no wharfmongrel cutthroat such as Legionnaires could understand. This wielder of death was a creature of the night, a slayer with the strength to strike hilt-deep, inhuman.

Your professional soldier is a superstitious man. One knife of gold, perhaps two, would not be beyond the possible. But a killer who left behind three golden blades verged into the realm of the werewolves. It was easy enough to believe in the phantasm, in that kobold dark under the palms with the lantern-shine shedding weird shadows, and with mysterious death underfoot.

The crowding Legionnaires glared at one another; wiped hands across dewy faces. Voices squeaked out of throats.

"See, Pierre! *Mon Dieu!* Once more the killer leaves a gold knife behind!"

"The captain must have got it just before we arrived! Who—"

Pierre Perousse sprang to his feet. "You heard what the captain said, my friends? The slayer came from behind those palms! The slayer wore a cloak; held an arm to shield his face. But he wore a beard, this slayer. You heard the captain say that? The slayer wears a beard—" The voices squeaked high. "The killer wears a beard. A beard!"

Right then I got out of there. I got away from that crowd under the palm trees, and I ran. It occurred to me that suddenly I was about as scared as I had ever been in my life. My knees wanted to loosen, and if there was one thing in the world I never wanted to do, it was to dash off in those glooms unaccompanied.

"You must do it, you fool!" I heard my teeth clicking. "You've got to do it!"

What I had to do was simple, I had to find the other man in Bab Eschmoun who wore a beard. I had to find Lieutenant Anatole Gers.

Gers was the murderer. The young giant was the only other man within a thousand miles who boasted a beard. Where to find Gers? North, south, east, west—where to run? Already the men under the palms were yelling; their lanterns waving, frantic. Panther Pazaine's voice could be heard bawling near the distant gate. The night was shot with the new alarm. And to vindicate my own lovely beard I must find that huge lieutenant, somewhere in this swirling *brouhaha* of darkness, dust and shouts—waiting, no doubt, with a dagger of gold in his maul-big fist and the killer's glow in his eye.

RUNNING like a chicken with its head cut off, I scampered along that lane which made a corridor between the empty barracks and the row of supply huts, jabbing my bayonet and bouncing with raised scalp at every hollow echo.

Rounding the turn to race along the path fronting the *caserne*, I stumbled and sprawled in the darkness, slamming my jaw in the dirt. Snatching up my Lebel rifle, I galloped on. The east wall of the stronghold loomed gigantic, black above the *caserne* roof. I wallowed in half-blind darkness. The only light in that corner of the post was the dim, weak yellow ray that stole from the window of Madame Gautier's house at the other end of the lane.

I was mighty glad for that illumination, feeble as it was. The window was cut off from my view by the box-square hut that served General Pazaine for headquarters, but the pale yellow beams stole out to thin the black gloom and drop witch-light across my path.

On the other side of the outpost the men were yelling and hallooing. I wondered if they, too, were looking for Lieutenant Gers, I wondered if they were looking for me. I wondered why in the name of my patron saint I had grown such a prominent beard; and I hurried toward the yellow beams which struggled so faintly with the Stygian night.

Then my feet stopped under me; stood rooted in the dust. The light from Madame Gautier's window slipped around the sharp edge of a clay wall and stole timidly, I say, across my path. It picked out a patch of that lane, reached farther into smoky shadow, and touched something that gleamed. This something lay against the wall of General Pazaine's house—a shine of metal against a dark and shapeless hulk.

I saw that hulk huddled shapeless against the house, and the throat knotted in my neck. The hulk sighed, moved, groaned; unfolded and reached a talon-like fist into the pool of light.

Dropping my rifle I grabbed at that hand and dragged into light a soggy and terrible figure. This man had suffered some terrific battle. The tunic fluttered in rags on his back, the collar torn away; his shirt was a maculated, crimson mass of tatters. Face down he lay in the light where I had dragged him, a grotesque and awful find; and a yell of terror choked in my constricted throat when I saw the glint of gold fastened into his side.

"Saw him—" came the voice from that face pressed flat against the dust. "Attacked me—as I ran down from the bastion where—I'd gone to—to see about the alarm." The shoulders heaved as a cough rattled from the hidden face. "Came at me—out of—the dark. Stabbed me—in side. But I—I caught at the cloak. We fought. I grabbed him—grabbed him by his throat. We fought. But the knife was deep—I—*mon Dieu!* I seemed—seemed to have caught hold of a beard! I grabbed at a beard—"

A bubbling drummed in the stricken man's throat and dark liquid welled to melt in the sand. Good God! This man had just been murdered but a moment ago. The assassin had struck like a thunderbolt five minutes after I, along with that mob of soldiers, had charged up this lane bent on summoning Cellini and Gers for the murder of Castelnau. Meantime Cellini had been slain. And now, this one.

MY head reeled and my stomach turned behind my belt. Reaching sick hands, I fumbled at those heavy shoulders. Words were still fighting from that rattling throat.

"He—he stabbed me hard," the voice twisted out. "But I—gave him a—battle. Caught him—by his beard—" The throat drummed, and the heavy figure flattened, face down in the wet dust.

"Gers killed you," I shouted, tugging at the lead shoulders. "It was the lieutenant! He killed you. He is the only other man among us who wears a beard. He did it. Lieutenant Gers—"

"But of course he did not," came a voice from behind me. A voice like a file on iron. "Of course Lieutenant Gers is not the killer. Because the man who lies in your path—"

I sprang from my knees and whirled. There stood General Pazaine, eyes like points of fire in his savage face, a massive blue steel automatic swinging in his fist. A harsh laugh grated through his teeth.

"I have been standing here for the last minute," he snarled grimly. "So you, once again, found the murdered man, eh? Then turn him over, you dog, and look at his face!"

Now I obeyed the command, and the nerves froze down my spine. I had not, in the fright of the moment, owned wits enough to recognize that ragged figure sprawled face-down at my feet. But I recognized that victim when I saw his face, picked out in the straying light. And the teeth rattled like gambler's dice in my jaw. I stared down at the face of the blond lieutenant. My mouth fell open and squawked.

"Lieutenant Gers!"

"So I could see!" General Pazaine stepped at me, the gun in his fist levelled straight. "And at last, I believe, we have the man we want. The assassin who killed Colonel Gautier. The murderer who dropped from the wall to stab Castelnau, then faked a story to throw suspicion on the remaining officers of his detachment; the murderer who got away from the scene, murdered Captain Cellini as the captain hurried to answer the alarm, then sped back here in the confusion and dark to slay Lieutenant Gers. Fast work for a fiend. But not quite fast enough." General Pazaine slashed the words. "Not quite fast enough, my death-dealing, stab-in-the-back spawn of hell. *Non!* Because Captain Cellini lived to tell that he saw the *beard!* And, as I came quietly upon this little devil's scene, I overheard the victim speak the same accusing words. I heard the lieutenant. With his last breath he cried it. He failed to know that the man who pretended to find him with that dagger hung in his side—"

"You mean me?" I screeched. "I did not do this thing. Not I! This is madness you talk. You accuse me? That is not the truth, name of God!"

My brains were scattering. I must have yelled like a maniac, and I had good reason to do so. There were faces gathering in the gloom behind that mad general's shoulder. A row of faces that grinned teeth and squinted hard eyes and mumbled a thunder that wanted only to break in storm. While the face of Panther Pazaine struck terror to the pit of my soul. His eyes were polished stones and the veins bulged like threads on his savage forehead. That automatic in his fist was pointed at my heart.

Name of the blessed Paul! He believed I was the assassin!

"You are mad," I tried to shout. "Why do you blame me for these crimes? I found this man lying here, I tell you. I was hunting for the lieutenant— How could I have killed him? Not I!"

"Murderer!" Panther Pazaine thrust his gun into my sweating face. "The evidence of your guilt is on you like the hand of God! You are the only man in the detachment, the only man here with a beard—"

THE faces massed behind the general's shoulders began to squall. Fists waved. Grinning mouths yelled:

"That is the assassin!"

"Corday did it!"

"Corday is your murderer!"

"Kill the bearded fiend! Tear the devil to pieces!"

"We have you now, you whiskered shark!"

"Shoot him where he stands!"

"You lie!" I bawled. "How could I—?"

"The dying words of Captain Cellini and the dying words of Lieutenant Gers gave you away!" General Pazaine's voice cut like

molten bolts into my pounding brains. "And did I not hear Lieutenant Gers say just now with his dying breath that he had battled his
assailant; grabbed the assassin by a beard. *Your own beard is torn!*"

Name of heaven! Instinctively I shot a hand to my jaw; felt a ragged
gash on my chin.

"I fell down!" I shrieked truthfully. "Back there by the *caserne!* I fell
down just a minute ago—"

But the general's voice hammered on; incisive, metallic, damning
me down to the ground.

"Did you fall down, you foul dog? Or did this poor lieutenant, in
defending himself against your assault, tear fingers at your jaw? Look!"

Pazaine swooped like a hawk and caught at the closed fist that lay
in death-clutch on the murdered lieutenant's chest. Some one held
close a light, and the general's fingers unscrewed the iron fingers of
the dead. And there in that fist of death, Lieutenant Gers had held
evidence as damning as eyesight.

"He had, indeed, grabbed this murderer by the beard," General
Pazaine snarled thickly. "See. He had snatched loose the hair—"

The general held to light a few fine strands. Eyes bent close in
scrutiny. The men behind the officer closed in. I felt as if an iron band
had tightened like a vise about my skull. Those strands of hair from
the dead man's fist were *red.*

The automatic of General Pazaine came slamming against my ribs
as his voice thundered into my face. "Legionnaire Corday, I sentence
you to death for the murder of Colonel Achille Gautier, of Captain
Cellini, of Lieutenants Castelnau and Gers. I sentence you to face
the firing squad. At the sunrise of this very day, you die!"

CHAPTER VII.

DEATH TOWER.

AT **SUNRISE** I would die—and sunrise only four hours away.
Holy Saint Antoine! Never had I been in such a box of horrors.
It was sardonic. I, Thibaut Corday, was going to be riddled at sunrise
for a series of heinous crimes of which I was innocent as a newborn
infant in Iceland. But I was guilty. I was guilty because I wore a beard
that fell to my belt, a beard whose color was red. Accordingly I was

condemned to stand against a wall at sunrise and die.

Believe me, I came very near to dying long before sun-up. When Panther Pazaine clapped his automatic into my ribs and bawled the information that I was the assassin and going to get the death sentence, those Legionnaires behind him snarled and yowled like tigers. Fists shot skyward. Heads bobbed. Black mouths opened and screeched abuse. Bayonets flickered like knitting-needles.

"Stab the murderer here and now!"

"Give the red-whiskered fiend to us now, *mon général!* We will finish him!"

"Let me have a shot at the son of a camel!"

"A killer, was he? Let honest Frenchmen finish him, then!"

"Down with the assassin. Grab the fiend, *mes amis!* We have him where we want him!"

"Kill him!"

Wolves around a piece of meat, those former comrades of mine closed in. A lovely mob spirit—that sort of spirit which starts lynchings—flamed like fanned tinder through those Legionnaires. Murderers after a murderer, again. And those pious villains would have slashed me to ribbons if the monster automatic of General Pazaine had not shoved them back.

"Keep away, you dogs. The prisoner is mine! I am in command here! This thing will be handled in the manner of La Légion, not a gang riot. I will waive the court-martial, but there will be a firing squad. A firing squad will execute this *salopard* at dawn."

The unlovely countenance of Legionnaire Perousse jabbed, yelling, out of the weaving fringe of angry faces.

"I say we kill the fiend now, *mes amis!* Is this red-whiskered assassin man or demon? Would a man kill with golden blades? Demon, he is! Slay the devil—"

The infernal fools would have slain me then and there if the Provençal general had not threatened to shoot the first among them to move, if my little friend Christianity Jensen had not raised a friendly voice to combat the clamor, and if four armed non-coms had not shoved forward with fixed bayonets.

Caged in this picket fence of bayonet steel, I was marched with a briskness out of that alley of death, across the parade ground to that wall where the prison tower loomed high and ghostly against the stars. *Tramp, tramp, tramp* I was marched, while the sweat wiggled down my cheeks and the post commander nursed my neck-nape with a pistol muzzle and the Legion gang followed at the heels of my guard, hurling taunts and oaths and invective. Then, stripped to britches and boots, I started the climb.

"Circumstantial evidence!" I yelled, as they hustled me up those tower stairs. "That's all you have against me. How could I have killed the officers? I did not do it. You are insane, mad! I am innocent! You cannot condemn me! You have nothing but circumstantial evidence—"

GENERAL PAZAINE'S automatic muzzle rammed against my neck. I tumbled over a doorstep and sprawled to my knees. The *salle de police*. The little room at the top of the high, square tower. My eyes glared through a film of sweat at a little window striped by iron bars. The sky beyond was blue-black, spangled with pale stars.

I knelt on that dusty barren floor while General Pazaine motioned at the guards in the doorway. A corporal planted a lantern inside the door, the thick door closed, and I was closeted with the toughest general of the Legion.

"You will not shoot me!" I raged at him. "If you do, you kill an innocent man. And you let me die for crimes I never—"

General Pazaine's gun muzzle fixed its gleaming, deadly eye at my head. "You have four hours to live. At daybreak you will be shot."

"For killing those officers? But you cannot prove it!" I shouted. "Circumstantial evidence—"

"It is plain. You stabbed Colonel Gautier. He had sent for you as orderly. You obeyed the summons; found him standing in his door. The moment was opportune. The Bavarian Legionnaire on patrol had just gone by. In fact, you had talked with the Bavarian, and knew he was making for the end of his beat. You stabbed the colonel. Then you pretended to find him thus slain. Your plot was well laid. In the confusion and darkness, any soldier in the post might have done it.

"*Alors*, you covered your guilt that time. Six months go by. You stand guard on the wall to-night. You have overheard talk, or you wish revenge. Your motive I cannot guess, but I can see you drop from the wall to stab Castelnau who happens to pass below. Again you give the alarm, cast suspicion on your superior officers, make off in the confusion. But you are apprehended, by Captain Cellini who meets you alone as he runs to answer the alarm. You try to hide your face. There is a fight. You stab the Corsican. But he has seen your beard and he is not dead when found by the men. You—"

Circumstantial evidence! I knelt there on the floor of that tower prison and listened to General Pazaine, a gargoyle in the lambent lantern-glow, build a trap around me that could have convinced the most skeptical of judges. The sweat ran in rivers down my forehead. I wanted to yell and tell him I had been with the men when they found the dying Cellini. Then I remembered I had not been there with the crowd. I had fallen behind; stopped to stare at the vision of Madame Gautier in her window.

Again, I had dashed off crazily by myself, bent on finding Anatole Gers—the other man with a beard. How could I prove this action?

"You killed Captain Cellini," Pazaine's accusation thundered on, "and then you fled through the night. You stumbled into Lieutenant Gers. You killed him, then, but not after a fight. He battles with you even as he dies from that blade in his groin. He tries to choke you; tears loose part of your beard. A pretty thin alibi, when you try to say you fell down and cut your jaw. But those red wisps of hair clutched in his fist—"

YOU see how the general reasoned? *Sacré Dieu!* Let me tell you, it was almost sound reasoning. And his conclusion that I was the assassin because I was the only possible suspect, being the only Legionnaire in Bab Eschmoun with a beard, plus the damning evidence of red hair, left me nothing but sweat and shrill denial.

"I did not do it," I snarled, hoarse-voiced. "While you hold me here the real assassin goes free. I am not the man—"

General Pazaine's teeth gleamed. "Who, then, is the man?"

Name of heaven, how was I to know? I, being the last man with a beard. A red-haired beard, in the bargain. I could have torn those confounded whiskers of mine out by the roots. I beat a fist against the stone floor.

"I only know I am innocent," I whispered. "I am no killer. You forget those queer knives of gold with the inscription. How about the book? How about that volume Colonel Gautier was reading? Follow those clews. I tell you, I overheard Lieutenant Castelnau mention that book—"

An ugly laugh rasped from the teeth of Panther Pazaine. "What a splendid, scheming liar you are, you *salopard!* Trying to trick me, eh? But you have played all the treachery you are going to. Gold knives? How do I know where you got them? I should like to know, true enough, but I suspect you will never tell. As for the book! Ho-ho!

Clever of you! You remembered how I tried to find a clew in that volume, eh? So you wish to revive the suspicion? Bah! Four months ago I planned to send that volume to Algiers with my staff when they went north. I thought I should have the Latin translated. The day before the book was to be sent, it vanished. Ho-ho. I think, perhaps, *you* know where that useless volume about Carthage disappeared. So you stole it to make it seem of importance."

He laughed bitterly. "And I remained these months in this sink of hell because I thought I—a general of La Légion—had lost an important clew through carelessness, and I did not wish to admit the defeat. Pah! But whether you stole the book, then, or not, I do not care. I shall look for it no longer. I have my assassin. The evidence at hand is enough."

More than enough, I can promise you. I could have shrieked. I could have wept. Somewhere in Bab Eschmoun hid a Satan incarnate, a master-fiend, a dacoit. And I was going to face a firing squad in that demon's place. Three hours and a half would bring daylight. *Mon Dieu!*

"But I had thought," General Pazaine said slowly, sullenly, stooping to lift the lantern, but vigilant with his automatic, "I had thought to give you chance for confession. If you have anything to say—"

"I say I am never the murderer—"

"Alors. One cannot expect confessions from such as you." The general rapped at the door. The guard without shot the enormous bolts and the door swung open. Far below, at the foot of the tower stairs, shone points of light. I could catch the murmur of angry, milling men. No doubt every Legionnaire in the place would volunteer for duty on the firing squad.

"I will return," General Pazaine growled sternly, "at dawn."

The door crashed. Bolts slammed. I was left alone in the darkness; glaring in damp horror at a barred window that, some hundred feet above ground, looked out on a blue-black sky. When that sky should fade into pink....

DID you ever wait for dawn in a little stone room at the top of a high tower, and know that impending daybreak signalled your death? Not a comfortable feeling, for sunrise is inexorable. The stars grow pale, faint. The sky alters from cobalt to heliotrope. In awful fascination you paste your eyes on the east and wait.

I pasted my eyes on the east and waited. It was not a joyous experience. Like a caged tiger I paced my narrow tower cell, fighting a desire to panic; then swung away from the bolted door and sped to that little window that faced the desert to the south. There were three iron bars in that window. Fists on the outer two, my be-damned face pressed against the middle, I glared toward the corner at the eastern sky and cursed the coming day.

After cursing the day I cursed the Foreign Legion, the generals of the Foreign Legion, one general in particular, the Legionnaires, Bab Eschmoun, and myself with my thrice damned beard. Always I would end with cold sweat on my face, cursing at the unknown, the bearded demon who had wrought this diabolic slaughter that would end with my futile death before a wall.

All the gods were against me now. I could even understand the attitude of those who condemned me. *Ventre bleu!* Who else looked as guilty as I did? Every shred of evidence had been planted on me by a sneering fate. But the terrible part of it all was the fact that I—the last remaining suspect—was not the murderer.

How I thumbed my forehead and strove to think out the puzzle, battling to go over the details of the bloody night, grabbing at re-membered incidents which might prove, at least, an alibi for me. I tramped around my prison, and my brain ran around in my skull like a squirrel in a cage.

But I was blessed, now, with a scant two hours and a half before daybreak. I could think of nothing but the skyline. I could see the horizon start its long, low sweep of chrome yellow flame.

Do you know something? I never enjoy dawns any more. Most people hold sentiments for the sunrise and love to chatter of the dawn coming out of the sea or the jungle or something. Not I. I am glad I can sleep through the daybreak; the sight of dawn is an unpleasant reminder of my little wait in that tower cell at Bab Eschmoun when I had but two hours to solve a murder case, or die.

And I could not solve the murder case. Could I convince Panther Pazaine of my belief that the assassin was an underworld were-demon conjured from the sinister atmosphere of ancient Bab Eschmoun? I could not. General Pazaine would pick his firing squad and see me shot to sponge and write out a report for headquarters and win a medal for his fine work in apprehending the maniac killer.

Back and forth I tramped. Forth and back. Up to the massive bolted door. Back to the evil window for a glare at the horizon. Dawn was on the way, that was so. It seemed to come at me with express train speed. By Julian the Apostate! was I going to die? I marched, and I do not mind telling you I was wringing my hands.

That fool Pazaine was going to stand me in front of the firing squad and let the real slayer go free. Or was the whole thing a loathsome dream? Had I gone mad and out of feverish phantasy imagined all this nightmare about murders and gold knives and red whiskers and firing squads?

Unfortunately, *non!* I could bruise a fist against the door of my prison. By hanging my ear against the same door I could hear the excited clamoring of men at the foot of tower stairs. That was a real and terrifying noise. The wolf pack was waiting for the show.

WAITING for death is an excruciating, a horrible sensation. Especially if you wait in a prison from which there is no escape. Sixteen strong men could not have clubbed down that door. As for the tower window—

I dashed to the window for the millionth time, clutched the bars, rolled my eyes around toward the eastern horizon. God alone knows how it was, but I must have twisted at the iron bar in agitation. At any rate the iron in my left fist moved in the stone sill.

That iron bar was old. It had guarded that window since the day a band of Arabs repaired this death-house on the crumbling walls of a Carthaginian fort. It was ancient and tired out and useless. I battled that rusty shaft of metal with a fist. *Crack!* Gently it snapped at the base.

Mouthing oaths at the futility of the effort, I bent the bar outward; got my head through the aperture and hung my chin out of that high window. The eastward sky was graying, and I suppose my face was, too. What was the use? I could have kicked open all of those iron bars. But I could not, then, fly out of the window. The desert spread some hundred feet below, baked hard as a pavement.

Then something flared in the back of my squirrel-cage head like a little star shell. *Le bon Dieu* alone knows where it came from, but there was Hope, the tragic and awful emotion that motivates men throughout their lives and keeps them gasping for the last breath. Hope and an idea!

A matter of minutes and I would hear the clump of bootheels on the tower stairs. A matter of minutes and the death-watch would be climbing to get me. Suppose those Legionnaires should open the cell door, peer in, see nobody! Suppose I could hang myself out of that window—I could wriggle through, and push the bar back into place, hang by my hands. *Non!* They would catch sight of my hands! They would see the empty cell, but they would glimpse my fists on the bars! If I could only find a rope—

Already they were fed with superstition; half believed they had captured a demon…. If they glared into the cell, saw it empty, the bars in the window—

Sacré! If I had but a foot of rope. Rope? The guards had stripped me of belt and shirt! But if I had something in color to match the hue of those rusty bars, I could hang from the outside—the guard might dash away—leave the door open. A bit of rope—

Another little foolish bomb bumped in the back of my spinning head. What an idea! I was mad, you will say. I was taking a long, too impossible chance. Let me assure you when I saw the African sky going gray in the east that morning, it was time to take the world's most impossible of chances.

Suddenly I was chittering like an idiot, working fast with my hands. Do you know what I was doing? I was making a rope! Legionnaires do lots of household things. They wash and cook and braid. I braided. Do not laugh. I braided like the very devil, and I braided at that fine red beard of mine until it hung like a long silly pigtail off the tip of my rattling jaw.

PERHAPS I was crazy, but that tower of Bab Eschmoun was a place to go crazy in, *c'est ça!* And the sky was mauve and the dim walls of my cell had begun to formulate in the gloom, and I worked my fingers until the joints cried out. Now I had that pigtail dangling from my jaw; rushed to the bolted door. Below there was an ominous sound. Any moment the firing squad would start up those stone steps. The fools. The *salopards!* This accursed beard that was spelling my doom might give me a chance at escape.

Rushing back to the window, I bent at the broken iron bar, flung a leg over the stone sill. Tying myself in a granny knot, I doubled myself up, straddling the sill, hunched low, and tied the end of my madman's pigtail to that middle bar. Then I squeezed and scrabbled; squirmed out of that window. Squirmed out of it, I tell you, with my beard tied to the middle bar; hung on the outside by a fist and a beard, and bent the broken bar back into place (and God helped me do it, I swear!) Then, with both hands clutching the sill, my red braid looping like a foot of rope from chin-tip to iron grating, I swung on the outside of that devil's tower and waited.

Did you ever read the story of Arundel who slung a braid of her hair from a castle battlement? She let down her roped hair and a prince climbed it hand over hand. Or did you ever see circus performers hang by their beards? Uncle of Satan! Arundel was a character in fiction and circus performers are trained. But think of me, Thibaut Corday! I was a flesh and blood Legionnaire taking the maddest chance in the world to save the heart from being drilled out of my chest. *Mère de Dieu!* but what a crazy, impossible chance.

And the sky in the east was paling. A hot dusk invaded the horizon. Footsteps sounded a funeral tread on tower stairs.

Bolts clanked in a massive door. Old hinges groaned. My bleeding finger-tips gave way on the stone sill; loosed their hold. And I hung. Head yanked skyward, clenched jaw almost torn from its sockets, sweat of agony flooding from every pore, I hung by my beard from that tower window, and heard the door moan open.

Afterward—long, long afterward—I would have given a last five francs to have seen my firing squad as it stood on the threshold of that high, impregnable *salle de police* and saw it empty of contents. Blue shadows were caught in there. The window—with every bar in place—was silhouetted against a dawn-dusked sky. A shadowy window striped by three upright black stripes.

Perhaps one of those bars had a lumpy rusty ring tight at its base where it sunk in the stone sill. Perhaps those bars were widely enough separated so that a gaunt man, squeezing through where one was broken out, could worm over the sill and so plunge a hundred feet to his death.

But my firing squad knew that there had been no coil of rope left handy in that cell. My firing squad had expected to find a prisoner gibbering against a wall and shouting for mercy out of red whiskers. And the prisoner was nowhere to be seen in that narrow stone room. My firing squad was imaginative!

I would have given (long after) my last five francs to have seen the face of the man who bawled: "Blood of heaven! The assassin is gone! *Gone!*"

Or the face of the Legionnaire who yelled: "A demon! Friend of the devil! Satan has taken him away—"

Or the face of the good comrade who screeched: "Devil's work.

Let us get out of here!" to start the sound of bootheels stampeding down the tower stairs.

MY own face must have been worth seeing. Certainly I could feel it. The jaw was coming out of my skull as I literally lifted myself in midair to grab handholds on that stone sill. Heaven knows how I ever hoped to haul myself upward, get elbows on that sill, untie my pain-screaming beard, squeeze back into the tower and so on out of the unbolted door. Heaven forgive me for the oaths I vented as I struggled in the attempt. How I cursed! No Legionnaire in Bab Eschmoun could have heard me, I say. There was a racket going on in the outpost loud enough to drown thunder in the sunrise-painted sky.

I fastened fists on the two stout bars, all right, but I could not hoist my tortured spinal column. My head was a cave full of noises and bright lightning. My wrenched jaw fired up shooting stars. My feet vainly flailed the wall for a toe hold. Knees battered raw, elbows bleeding, I hung on the outside of that high tower, battling like a fiend to ease the strain on my sensitive rope beard.

Somehow I chinned myself on the sill and, clinging by a fist, worked with free hand to loosen the knotted tip of my tweaked and tortured pigtail. I worked my fingers and kicked my toes. I kicked hard. I kicked loose a shower of masonry. I kicked a small flagstone out of the face of the wall. Another flagstone fell.

My boots dug into the crumbling masonry. A dozen flagstones went to pieces under my hammering toes. By the bones of Sebastopol! Those broken flags fell *inward!* My boots hung into a jagged and yawning black hole!

Chunks of plaster loosened by my grinding heels fell into that astounding hole in the wall, and I heard them go bouncing. Tearing free my beard with a violent and excruciating effort, I got a handhold on the stone sill of the tower window. I swung my legs into that jagged black hole. Letting go with my fingers, I flung my body after my legs.

Powdered with plaster that went to mud in running sweat, I dropped into the corridor of a mysterious, tunnel-in-the-wall honeycomb, to lie gasping and groaning on a crumbly stairway, my eyes on a ragged aperture that framed overhead a patch of scarlet sunrise.

CHAPTER VIII.

THE ASSASSIN!

S OMETIMES I stumbled over cobblestone. There were places where I stubbed my forehead against low-hanging brickwork, waded through fallen plaster, rounded sharp turns and banged my face. My fingers fumbling along the walls caught at cobwebs thick as matting; my boots tread a carpet of furry dust. There would be steps, crumbling and treacherous, burrowing down. Always down.

Blind in the Stygian dark, I followed that secret passageway inside the tower wall until I knew I must be nearing the middle of the earth. The intense, windless air was stifling with heat and dust, frowsty with a dank odor of age. Sweat wiggled down my cheeks. My mouth was muddy. Feeling my way with feet and hands, I kept on.

It is no pleasant task, playing blind-man's buff in an unknown labyrinth of passages, when every step may plunge one into an abyss or bury one alive in falling plaster.

That stroll in the dark seemed to last for miles. That tunnel must have burrowed through every one of those ancient, time-old Bab Eschmoun walls. Exhaustion was dragging my heels when I staggered at long last into a vast and high-ceiled cavern, leaned spent and gasping against a stone column and stared at the faint, thin glimmer of a distant light.

A light? I glared. The distant beam winkered and I saw I stood in the place where the ghosts flee to hide from the dawn, the bottom hall of the Netherworld. That subterranean crypt had been built in those days of the giants, and the giants had carved on the walls. Huge and fantastic faces bulged down at me from their frames in enormous stone murals. Great pillars marched along the rim of the wall to support a ceiling lost in long, long shadows.

I was tiny in that vast, deep hall; tiny, choking and scared. One glance at the carvings walling that cave and I knew I had stepped back the centuries. I had walked back two thousand years. The thought appalled. *Diable!* I had walked back into Carthage!

Old? That crypt had been dug when the pyramids were young and fires flamed in the teeth of Baal, when Phœnician triremes and Roman galleys skimmed the sea, and Europe, north of the Alps, was howling wilderness. And there I stood, a half-naked, half-crazed Legionnaire with a red pigtail dangling from my chin, panting in the stagnant air of vanished centuries, glaring at a point of light that must surely be of to-day, and wondering if I was insane.

The other end of that crypt was so distant that the light traveled far to reach me; and I traveled far to reach it. Shuffling in the dust of an ancient floor built before the time of Julius Cæsar, I crept toward the puny gleam.

And then I was stopped. I was stopped by a deep, broad crevice that yawned across the floor of that vast vault like a chasm in the mountains. Gashed out of the floor of that auditorium-big grotto, the cleft was a sharp-walled trench dropping down and down to the very middle of the earth. Deep? The sound of water rushing down the cañon's bottom came as the echo of a vanished past. The wind sighing out of those eerie depths was the last of the breath that had soughed across the universe to roll spiral nebulæ into worlds.

Forty feet from rim to rim that chasm yawned; and when I saw the bridge which spanned those forty feet the sweat burst fresh on my face.

NEVER have I seen so insecure, so narrow a foot bridge. That arch of stones was scarce fifteen inches in width. A mere thread of brick-work, it was; for all the world a bridge of cobwebs spanning that subterranean divide.

The thought that some one had swayed across that thread-thin trestle of ancient masonry would have rattled your jaw. How my back teeth clattered when I saw that some one, indeed, had crossed it. My eyes were growing accustomed to the gloom; things assumed shape about me like objects in a slowly developing photograph.

Listen! The cavern ended on the other ledge of the mile-deep crevice. A broad shelf, there was, formed by cliff-rim and back wall. Reared on this ledge, a monster dream-creature in stone sneered across the bridge at me—a fabulous Gorgon mounted on a stone pedestal.

I knew what that stone altar and its mounted infamy had been. A sacrificial altar! Here priests had chanted the pagan liturgies to sanc-tify their crimes. Here smoky torch-fires had glowed in the teeth of stalwart captives from Rome and Egypt; gleamed on the grinning eyes of veterans from Punic wars. The fire-lit face of the stone mon-strosity had grinned down on orgies vile beyond description; pleased with the shriek of tortured Phœnician slave girls and the tom-tom of Dido's drums.

As a boy in academy I had heard of such things and had seen in a book a similar stone face. Eschmoun, most savage of Carthage gods! On his foul-worshipped altar the ritual blood had run; infants had burned.

Yet it was not the sight of this nightmare that raised stiff my hair. Nor was it the awful chasm dropping at my feet, or the skinny bridge span. What did lift my scalp was nothing more or less than the tiny point of light I had trailed into this vale of sin. At the base of the Gorgon's stone altar winkered a Legionnaire's lantern!

The lantern was not all that winkered, either. *Non,* it was not! A stale wind-breath sweeping out of the deep abyss suddenly wiggled the puny lantern-flame, and the tossing beams brought to sudden light a constellation of metallic glitterings.

The eyes bulged in my head. Gold! There on the slab at the Gorgon's feet rose a mound of gold-hilted knives! Not a little clutter of them, you comprehend. A mound of them, heaped like restaurant silverware waiting the dishpan. And what I had thought a shadow shed by the lantern proved suddenly a human figure stooped low on that incredible heap of blades. A figure in shrouding black cloak. A hooded figure that whipped pale hands at the piled treasure; the metal clinked softly; knife after knife dropped into a bulgy black sack.

Aunt of the Devil! Can you see that picture? Can you see me, tiny, shirtless, a pygmy under the ceiling of that vast cavern, my boots on the rim of a truly terrible chasm, idiotic with my mouth gaping and a red pigtail dandling from my chin, my eyes protruding like marbles as they picked out the scene that was staged at the other end of that feeble bridge?

Can you see the slanting blue shadows; the phantom glow animating that demoniac granite face; the winkering lantern; that vampire-like figure in a cloak, its back toward me, its hands wildly snatching those gold knives and snapping them into a thief's bag?

Sapristi! The Legionnaire's lantern! The gold blades! The specter in a black cloak! My eyes went big as bird's eggs. Even the book was there. It had looked like a black stone lying flat near the lantern.

God knows I wanted to run. Sweat was ice water dribbling down my naked spine. And God also knows the source whence arrived the courage to weld my hands into fists and move my craven boots out onto that spidery bridge. Balancing like a tight-rope walker and a thousand times as scared, I edged out on that horrid span. The rotten thread of masonry seemed to jiggle under my boots. The stonework swayed.

The shadowy figure at work beneath the grin of the fierce stone face suddenly dropped the last piece of treasure into the bag; swung sack to shoulder, and wheeled. I heard a wild scream! The hooded head ducked, twisted; the free hand grabbing at the cloth. But the hood fell awry across the face, half draping the head, and I saw! I saw an eye like a flaming furnace-coal, a contorted mouth, a scraggly-bearded cheek and jaw! That beard was red! That face I had never seen before! Yet I *had!* Where? No time to wonder—

The mouth screeched again; and I answered with a screech of my own as the cloaked unknown made a frog-like leap, and came at me on that doddering bridge. Stooped under the weight of the sack, the assassin came at me, half-crouched, grotesque, a spider on a thread. The spider squalled and shot a hand to the sack on its back. The hand flipped out of the sack, and a gold knife spun like a streak of storm-lightning past my yelling head.

FATE forbid such misfortune, but should I live to be five hundred I could never forget a detail of the awful game I played against an assassin's hand on that high and horrible bridge. There I balanced, teetering on a fifteen-inch foothold where one false step would plunge me into the world's deepest and darkest abyss. Balanced, I say, and at the same time ducked and dodged a string of knives that flashed at me like lightning bolts from the murderer's demon-fast hand.

What a terrible game! Hunched in a half crouch, the cassock blowing like a clinging weird shroud of black smoke, that assassin moved out on the frail bridge; came slowly at me like some creeping Jabberwock thing of doom, while one devilish fist snatched in and out of the mouth of the heavy-laden sack with automatic speed, the wrist snapped, the fingers flew open, and the unleashed knife came screaming at my face.

How that fiend could throw knives! Let me promise you, if the light had not been uncertain and the footing bad, the first knife would have plunged deep into my skull. My assailant was hampered, too, by carrying that load of blades. No matter. One, two, three, four—the knives whistled.

I twisted my body. Ducked my head. Wobbled and teetered and

dodged. I dared not turn to flee on that brick tight-rope. *Sacré Dieu!* I must watch death spin at me and try to lean out of the way. If you do not think I was close to two kinds of death you are wrong. I was close to three kinds of death. Those knives just skimmed my hair. My feet danced on that fearful thin strand of footing and I writhed like a snake to keep balance. And my heart had stopped beating for at least two minutes.

The spider-like assassin advanced on the thread. Knowing I could not turn to escape, that fiend was going to close in; gain position where a knife-throw would not miss. And that devil never stopped flinging those blades. Not for a second. They shot past my cheek, skimmed my shoulder, whipped through my hair. Once I dropped to my knee to duck a low one. Another shaved the lobe of my right ear.

I defied the laws of equilibrium, that is so. I danced and shrieked, writhed, bobbed back and forth, and hung on. The knives, missing me, soared to drop in blank space below. I never heard them strike bottom.

Now the assassin was scarcely twelve feet away, and I was trying to edge backward, teetering on that terrible bridge. Name of a name! As if dodging knives and keeping balance with flaying arms was not enough, the bridge wobbled underfoot. That span of thin masonry wobbled, I tell you. It shivered and rocked.

It had been flung across that underground cañon by engineers who may have slaved later on the Appian Way. The tramp of succeeding centuries had loosed its foundations. Time had eaten into the cement. The flagstone arch was infirm. It was never a bridge for this grisly contest. Any second it might fall to dust beneath my fear-frozen boots.

Parbleu! The assassin winged a knife that tore a gash in my shoulder. I lurched. The bridge tottered. There was a sound like ripping cloth. A crackling, crying sound.

I heard a soprano shriek. A rattly smash. Scream after scream and a haze of white dust and the rumble of breaking stone. Do you know what had happened? That bridge had often supported the weight of a fiend who had traveled its span with but one golden blade in the fist. But the rotten masonry could not hold the weight of that knife-crammed gold sack. The section beneath my assassin's feet had snapped, given way, broken through. The bag of gold knives had plummeted into the chasm. Minutes afterward, it seemed, I heard the splash. And there hung the murderer, clinging, kicking, shrieking, clawing to hold on the fragile and crumbling raw end of the break.

I LAUGHED. I opened my green face and laughed. The sound of my laugh was one of the most terrible things I have ever heard, and I kept it going as I crawled, belly-to-stone, out on that broken-in-half span. Dangerous? Name of Saint Francis, it was the most dangerous thing in the world, for that fragmentary rag of stonework arched above the black abyss on nothing but its one foundation and its own accord.

But I was not thinking of that. My only thought was to catch that assassin hanging in midair. I wanted to catch that assassin with the red beard as an exhibit for proof of my innocence. I laughed and cursed as I crawled toward the clinging spider. The eye saw me coming and the hands let go, but a rag of the black cloak held on. Do you know what I was thinking? I was wishing I had a piece of rope. A little length of rope with which I could take a turn around that hooded head so I could choke it. I could not use two hands. A rope—

Then, *sacré!* I was leaning over the jagged rim of the span, lying flat, with one hand twisted in the fiend's black mantle, and my chin-pigtail dangling. Rope? It seemed like a million years ago, but then I suddenly remembered. The hooded head hung loosely on its neck. Do demons faint? I do not know.

I could see a closed eye and an open, bearded mouth that wheezed. I was wheezing, too. But I maneuvered my chin and caught at my braid of beard and looped the braid around the assassin's neck. I took no chances. Not I. With my free hand I twisted at the braid which made a cord around that neck. I twisted and the cord tightened and the wheezing stopped. After a long, long time I freed the noose. A long time later I was hauling an inert, cloaked figure across a fifteen-inch wide span.

The lantern was over forty feet away when I reached that rim of the chasm to stand on God's own ground. But faint as was the light, I could see. The assassin lay sprawled at my feet, and the sweat from my face dropped on the inert, shrouded shoulders. By the lopsided hang of the face-down head I could understand that once more I had cheated a firing squad. I turned the body over with a boot-toe so the dim light could fall on the face.

And then I began to laugh. Never before was there such a laugh. Never since. The only sound I have ever heard to approximate it was the ghoulish laugh wrenched from the Legionnaires who had found my hole in the rotten tower wall and trailed me through to Gehenna. Those Legionnaires tried to laugh like I did. They tried to laugh as I did when they found me rocking there and they, too, saw the assassin's upturned face....

EPILOGUE.

OLD THIBAUT CORDAY voiced a high-pitched cackle; looked startled, and plugged shut his teeth with a pipe-stem. At once we listeners were plunged into quiet—a quiet relieved only by the breathing of the American Express lad, who suffered asthma, and the measured tramp of a *gendarme's* boots far up Boulevard Sadi Carnot.

I looked about me surprised. Instead of black Carthaginian cavern walls I saw the shuttered windows of a closed Algiers café, the long vacant reach of an empty avenue, deserted boulevard ramps. Lost away on the mist-veiled harbor beyond, a steamer siren wailed. The mournful cry brought old Corday to his feet.

"Mon Dieu! The Marseilles mail boat! Do you know I have talked all night long?" He knocked out his pipe on the table. "The sun will be up in an hour—I must go. Believe me, I hate to see dawns."

"You *can't* go!" I cried.

"Till you tell us how and why—" began the British consular agent.

"And who was the assassin," finished the lad from the American Express. "I can't draw a breath as it is, but I'll smother if you don't!"

"Ho-ho!" The veteran Legionnaire chuckled. "I had thought not to tell you, for I fear you will, none of you, believe. But then, is it so incredible? Lust for gold has spawned murder in more than one heart. It was lust for gold which lay behind the killings at Bab Eschmoun. *Parbleu!* that little book of Colonel Gautier's planted the evil. That old volume in Latin—*'Carthago Delenda Est'*—telling a history of ancient Carthage; it described the early building of the stronghold, Eschmoun. Long after the shouting was over and the bugles blew *Aux Drapeaux,* the smart authorities at Headquarters translated the volume and exposed the subject matter.

"The chapter on Eschmoun depicted a fortress honeycombed with secret passages built over a crypt where Carthaginian priests dealt 'sacred' slaughter with sanctified knives of gold. The kind and scholarly Papa Gautier, reading the book for amusement, did not take the volume seriously. But some one who had learned to translate Latin, some one who had come across that chapter on Eschmoun (and any of a hundred people could have seen the book) had taken it for fact. That person had marched into Bab Eschmoun bent on finding a secret passage leading to those knives of gold. And had found it!"

Old Thibaut Corday mopped his leathern face with a cuff. "Tunnels?" he growled. "That place was an anthill, as later excavations proved. There was a stone trap in the flagstone floor of the very hut Colonel Gautier chose for headquarters. And you recall the grove of palms near the well? A tunnel opened there, its mouth hidden in a clump of trees. And a flagstone lifted from the floor of the barracks hut revealed another entry into that underground hive.

"Pardieu! We were not ten minutes in Bab Eschmoun before one of those trap doors was found. The tunnel led into the crypt exactly as the book had suggested. And there on an altar lay a mound of golden blades exactly where the ancients had left them. A treasure ripe for the stealing! A fortune! Murder blossomed in the finder's heart. Finders keepers, you understand, and it would take murder to make certain the keeping.

"Now life in the Foreign Legion is accursed by monotony and a poverty the most abject. A Legionnaire earns but a penny a day. Even the pay of a colonel is niggardly. The finder of that fortune in gold goes mad! Here is a way of escape. Paris, fine wine, luxury, life—all glitter in the sheen of those fabled blades. Our treasure finder snatches up a knife; rushes back up the tunnel with brain afire. Colonel Gautier is the only other person who can have read about this crypt. He must die. Too, if the colonel is murdered, the detachment may be recalled and the fortune may be spirited from the crypt and stolen from Bab Eschmoun then and there! Listen! The finder of that treasure is also a skilled knife-thrower. Flung or driven, the knife goes deep in the colonel's throat; nails him standing where he dies on his doorstep.

"**BUT** Captain Cellini holds the whip hand until Headquarters sends Panther Pazaine. The Panther holds the detachment in Bab Eschmoun. The murderer must make more plans, and does. I tell you, this killer has a brain to make Satan mighty envious! Delay in Bab Eschmoun fits into a new scheme. Pazaine unreels red tape, tangles the clews and allows his best clew to be stolen from his quarters while he busily unearths lots of what-not—for example, those three foolish love letters penned to Madame Gautier, the colonel's charming wife. Love letters? Bah! What Frenchman is not always thinking he is in love with somebody's wife and writing indiscreet notes which he never sends? Love was not the motive behind those Bab Eschmoun murders. *Non!* It was not.

"Meantime the days lag and the murderer plots with a deadly, incredible genius. There must be another killing and the guilt must fall on an unsuspecting, susceptible fool who will satisfy a Legion firing squad. Soul of a pig! But that fool is Thibaut Corday. I, with a long red beard that fits so nicely into the plan. How better to daub one with guilt? And Castelnau, who guesses too much and whispers to Cellini in a rendezvous under the wall where I mount guard, forces the fiend's game. When the Corsican captain leaves the fat lieutenant alone under the dark wall, the die is cast. So is a gold knife. The killer, hiding near, throws from shadow. Thus a man is stabbed almost under my nose and I see no assassin's hand."

Old Thibaut Corday slammed the table, and his voice came savage. "You see, then? Traveling by underground tunnels, the killer races from one end of the outpost to the other without detection. After slaying Castelnau, the murderer wishes to be seen, and thereupon appears in the middle of the confusion and alarm. Establishes an alibi, you comprehend. Then races underground to the tunnel-mouth hidden in the palm grove, springs from darkness to stab Captain Cellini who is rushing to answer the alarm.

"Name of God! It is part of the plot that Cellini must see his killer wearing a weird cloak; must live long enough to make known the fact that the assassin boasts a *bearded face!* Lieutenant Gers, too, in order to make doubly convincing the evidence. The killer catches Gers at another corner of the outpost.

"Gers gives battle. He will die telling the story that will implicate *me* with my prize red beard. The killer plays a master stroke and plants a few strands of red hair in the dying man's numb fingers. How the killer must have laughed when I was condemned to die that very dawn. Ho-ho!"

THE old veteran shook a knotted fist. "But Satan does not always win, my friends. Sometimes *le bon Dieu* interferes when the Devil goes too far. *Le bon Dieu* let me kick that hole in the decayed tower wall; allowed me to find the killer exulting and grabbing up the treasure. That fiend thought a road to Paris and riches lay wide open; thought the time had come to pack up for the get-away. But *le bon Dieu—*"

The young British consular agent jumped, exasperated, from his chair. *"Le bon Dieu* will knock you dead, Corday," he laughed, "if you don't tell us who—"

"Who the murderer was?" Old Thibaut Corday stroked his beard. "Who could it have been, *mes amis?"* he chuckled mirthlessly. "Who in that detachment from Sidi could have managed to pick up Latin, read the colonel's book, walked first off into one of those adobe houses and sighted a trapdoor, discovered a crypt, the treasure—and flung a knife into the poor old commandant? Who could have owned such a gold-lusting soul, such an inherited talent for villainy? *Alors!* Who could have shorn the long hair from *one side* of the head? Who could have had such hair and known how to dye it red and sew it into a beard? Who could have done this under cover—cut short the hair on one side of the head, you comprehend, but leaving enough hair on the *other* side so that it looked normal, hidden under her mourning. And it grew again—looked as beautiful as at first, when that head was posed like an alabaster profile framed in a dim-lit window, while we stricken Legionnaires ran past."

We yelled. The British consular attaché, the lad from the American Express and I—we yelled in chorus. "You don't mean—"

"Of course!" A dour laugh rasped from the cinnamon bush and old Thibaut Corday wagged his head. "The woman who had danced in Marseilles. She had once been in a carnival. A sideshow knife-thrower, a mistress of Apaches. And, you comprehend, she was half Arab, after all, as the gossiping wives had said. Bad blood to course through the heart. A heart? Pah! The fair Nina never owned one. But she did own fine long hair and she knew she could cut part of it off, hide the fact under a black veil, and wait six months till it grew in again. In the meantime she was clever with a needle to sew, and she knew how to dye. They said she dyed the hair with red wine. But I? I say she dyed it red with blood.

"And how I laughed when I saw that false beard come loose on the dead face of Madame Gautier. Never before was there such a laugh, my friends." Old Thibaut Corday shook his head. "And never since."

THE MUTINEER

IT WAS A MAD AND MERRY SCENE BEING ENACTED IN THAT LITTLE THEATER IN BISKRA WHEN THE ATTACK CAME.

CHAPTER I.

RIOT IN BISKRA.

"**L OVE,**" **SAID** old Thibaut Corday dryly; and turned his palms upward in a gesture of resignation. "You ask me, a Frenchman, if I believe in love. You ask me, an old man, what is love. *Sacré nom de Dieu!* I have not the faintest idea. But I know one thing. Love and madness are twin brothers.

"And I know something else. Love and hate are mighty close relations and look so much alike that it is sometimes difficult to tell the one from the other. The reactions, they are the same. Panting and grimaces and low voice and a gnashing of teeth."

The ancient Legion veteran leaned back in his chair with a chuckle and twined a gnarled finger in the cinnamon-hued beard that forty years of soldiering had been unable to fade. His eyes, like little blue stones, twinkled at me, and he wried his face into a grin. "Look here, *mon zig,* did I ever tell you what happened to that wild man, that giant of muscles and bones, that hard-fighting, hard-cursing *copain* of mine—that American devil we called Yankee Bill the Elephant?"

"Not yet," I said.

Old Thibaut Corday laughed softly in his whiskers. "There was one Legionnaire who was the good soldier. Strong? There is an old Arab cannon down in the Fort of Abedeyllan el Akbar in Bou Saada; and I have seen him lift this cannon in his arms as if it were a babe. March? He could outwalk any camel on the desert. Drill? He was perfection when it came to the manual of arms. He saluted his officers and never spent a day in the police jail. He was a four-bottle man. He loved the army and the army loved him.

"In eight years he had won himself eight citations. Officers pointed him out as the best soldier in the company; sergeants tried to get him in their commands. He was recommended for advancement, but would

The unbelievable scimitar lashed
through the moonlight.

take no stripes. He said he wanted to be a good soldier; wanted to stay in the line. He was a splendid army man. His officers rewarded his excellent conduct by getting him enrolled with the signal corps, which entitled him to remain a common Legionnaire, but booked him a little higher in pay.

"The outposts down on the desert were using the heliograph, you comprehend. Big mirrors that flash code signals in the sun. *Alors,* Yankee Bill won an easy berth in the signal corps, higher pay, medals, smiles from General Headquarters. And *then* what happened? You mean to say I never told you?"

"Not yet," I repeated.

Old Thibaut Corday chuckled in his cinnamon beard. "Listen, and I will tell you. For, by the bones of the Little Corporal! something happened to that Yankee Bill the Elephant. Something that has to do with those foolish twins, Love and Insanity. Something that has to do with those sisters under the skin, Love and Hate. Something that made one terrific crash in North Africa, and echoes in New York this very day!"

Old Thibaut Corday purred a laugh, waved a hand.

Hold your hat (the old veteran continued). You're going down to Biskra on the rim of the Sahara in the country of the Beni M'zab. A storm is gathering there; a veritable hurricane of Arab knives and Touareg guns, a blizzard of bullets and a rain of blood. The Legion-naires in the Biskra outpost do not know this. There is no barometer to tell them that one depraved holy man, one Habib ben Habib, is

sneaking around the desert inciting the Blue Veiled Silent Ones, the Forgotten of God, to war.

It is Thursday of a splendid night with springtide sweetening the air and a round white moon spreading soft shadow-carpets under the date palms, and the Arab muezzin retiring prayerfully from the silvered minaret of the big mosque on the square. It is the sort of gentle evening that only spring and North Africa can arrange; and the Legion garrison, dressed in its smartest, has gone up to the Casino de Biskra to hear an opera company from Algiers sing "Faust."

A gala occasion for a desert outpost, believe me. Every Legionnaire of the garrison who can get off duty and steal five *francs* is crowded in the stalls of the theater. Officers, their wives and the ladies who are not their wives sit glittering in the gallery boxes. You know how it is in a European theater. The low class mob—the soldiers—on the ground floor, the pit. The officers and ladies in evening gowns, what Americans call "high hat," in the gallery.

So Yankee Bill the Elephant and I and the rest of the Legion dogs are jammed in the pit, the high and mighty are up above us in the gallery, "Faust" is going full blast on the stage. You know "Faust." The opera is about an old fool who sells his soul to *Mephisto*, the Devil, a fat basso with black whiskers and red tights. After a lot of music the soprano dies. *Voilà!* It is a pretty dilapidated little traveling opera company capering behind the footlights of our Biskra casino that night. But there is nothing at all dilapidated about Mlle. Félice Froissart who comes, at the third curtain, sweeping grandly into the front box with her father, old Colonel Froissart.

Now Colonel Froissart is the post commandant at Biskra, and looks more like the Devil than the rummy on the stage, and has a worse reputation for temper and discipline. A tough Corsican of an officer with a mean scowl fastened on his bulldog face—one hellion of a commander. But his daughter! Sacred stove, this newcomer to Biskra is a beauty.

I have never seen a Frenchwoman with a hundredth of her looks. Tall and proud with a face of pure ivory, the high forehead of aristocracy and hauteur, the grace of breeding. She was wearing a white satin gown, most alluring on a figure like Ninon de Lenclos, the famous beauty, never had, and her raven hair was piled atop her head to give her face the profile of a goddess and the dim light of the theater found a blue in her eyes that would have battled the brushes of Da Vinci.

You do not often see a beautiful girl in a flea-bitten desert outpost's theater, and the arrival of that lovely colonel's daughter in the front box created a little stir in the house. I should have said a mighty big stir. The ladies in the gallery whispered behind their fans, the officers craned their necks, the soldiers raised their eyes to stare. And Yankee Bill the Elephant jumped up from his bench as if he'd been kicked, and stood at attention on his feet.

THE audience had hushed quiet, for the soprano was dying on the stage in front of a paper building and the Legionnaires packed in a salad jam in the pit had wanted to see her die. The big Yankee standing up in the first row looked as if he were dying, too. His *képi* shoved on the back of his rumpled black head, his eyes as big as electric lights in his face, he clutched dramatically at his heart and stared at the gallery as if he saw the train from heaven coming around a bend in the sky. Somebody in the back of the house yelled, "Down in front!" but Yankee Bill the Elephant did not sit down. You bet he didn't.

"Corday!" his voice sawed from his teeth in a whisper you could hear on the roof. "Who is that girl just came in with old man Froissart? Where did she come from? When did she come to Biskra?"

Well, wasn't that something? You're not supposed to talk out loud at an opera; nor are Legionnaires in the pit supposed to glare wild-eyed at the gods up above. Papa Froissart and his daughter had been sitting there as stiff and proper as stars in heaven; and Yankee Bill's whisper had the muted quality of a fog horn; and I saw the commandant scowl like a furnace while his daughter gave a haughty stare that would have frosted a cake.

"Sacred stove, you fool!" I nudged my giant *copain*, "that is the commandant's own daughter. She is not for you. High in Paris society, and she arrived but this afternoon, coming here for her health. And if you would value yours you had better quit staring like a lunkhead—"

Staring? A jubilant grin split the Yankee's face in half. "Why I *love* her!" he exploded. On my word of honor he was pointing a finger straight at that goddess in the officer's box above him. The declaration burst from his teeth with as stunning a repercussion as the American Declaration of Independence must have burst in England. *"I love that girl!"*

Sweat bubbled on my face. I was dragging at the Yankee's coat tails, and I couldn't budge the fool. A bumblebee buzz went up from the delighted soldiers behind us. The soprano on the stage began to expire at the top of her voice; and old Colonel Froissart leaned out of his chair and lanced a most blasting frown at the pit. Impossible for his daughter not to have heard. I saw a slow flush fire in her throat as she gave the audience a withering glare; then she sighted Yankee Bill, looked at him for an instant and turned her nose at the ceiling in disdain.

"You fool," I yorked at my companion, "sit *down!* You're in the guardhouse now for this. That's the colonel's daughter! She *heard* you—"

By Saint Jean de Luz! the Yankee's face was lit up like a torch. He was mad! The little punctilios of the social world are most rigidly observed by the French, and most rigidly of all in an outpost garrison of the army. I tell you, Yankee Bill had slipped a cog in his brain or he never would have done what he did right then.

"I DON'T think she *did* hear me!" he boomed. "Don't pretend, *mademoiselle*. A man like me doesn't make offers of love every day. What's happened between you and me is something wonderful! I didn't dream I'd ever found you. I mean *you!*"

And with that outburst the big Legionnaire snatched the *képi* from his ragged head and scaled it straight up through the smoke and square into that young lady's lap! Wow! A soldier, a low private of the French Foreign Legion had stopped an opera performance and thrown his hat into the lap of a colonel's daughter in front of the whole garrison. What a Romeo and Juliet that was!

The whole Casino de Biskra let out a yell that rattled the windows. The colonel's daughter whirled to her feet, white with fury, and she had that soldier's *képi* in her fist, and her eyes were blazing like blue daggers. "Who is the ruffian?" she screamed, and her fist sailed out and the hat came gunning down from the box like a boomerang and took Yankee Bill the Elephant smack in his grinning teeth.

How that casino hollered then. Officers and ladies in the gallery were bouncing around like jumping jacks. The soldiers in the pit roared with joy. Benches went over. The show stopped and the curtain on the stage fell halfway down. Yankee Bill staggered backward with his hand clapped to his mouth, and Colonel Froissart had one fat leg over the edge of the box, his voice bellowing thunderclaps of Jehovan fury.

"He dared insult my daughter! Arrest the dog! Arrest the *salopard!* Arrest the dog!"

"Get the Legionnaire!" the underofficers were howling. "Get that American!"—"Stop him! Hold him! Corporal of the Guard! Corporal of the Guard!"—"Dares affront an officer's daughter, does he?"—"The man's drunk!"—"Stop that man or I'll fire!"

Boots made a cavalry crash on the stairs, swords flashed in the cigarette smoke, the ladies in the gallery screamed, a gun bumped somewhere and a chandelier jarred from the ceiling and fell into the orchestra pit with a spouting crash. With that the pit was plunged in a half dark, the stalls were scrambled with bellowing officers and cheering, jeering men, bedlam of oaths and catcalls: "Get the Yankee! Get that American *salopard!*" and opera night in Biskra went to pieces with a bang.

In the rumpus I was knocked flat as asphalt by a sergeant's fist. A Spahi stepped on my face; and I came up in the middle of the brawl with a nose bleed and a fine head spin. I could not see what had become of that mad First Class Legionnaire, promoted signal corps expert, Yankee Bill the Elephant. I had a vague glimpse of the seat of his pants vanishing up over the footlights of the stage; thought I saw him go tearing off through the paper scenery. I don't know.

My main impression was one of Colonel Froissart sitting astride the gallery rail, capering like an idiot on a hobby horse, black in the face and rocking his fat hips and waving his sword and yowling: "Stop that Yankee cur! Bring me that dog! Two years in the stone quarries

I'll give him. This is mutiny—mutiny!"

I caught a momentary glimpse of his daughter standing with white hands pressed to cheeks that flamed with rage and mortification, a haircomb hanging in woeful disarray over one lovely eyebrow, her eyes as furious as little points of vitriol. "He insulted me. *He insulted me!*"

It was one gorgeous riot and pandemonium, I promise you; and smack into the middle of it all came the piercing blast of a bugle-call screaming an alarm.

CHAPTER II.

"TO ARMS!"

"**A**UX **ARMES!** Aux armes!"—"To your posts, men!"— "The Arabs! The Arabs attack at the western gate!"

Here was a surprise party. I told you the Biskra garrison had owned no barometer to tell them this storm was on the horizon. The oasis town is encompassed by a feeble mud wall. One minute the mounted guards had looked and seen nothing save shadows and sand, peaceful under the desert stars. Next minute every shadow had started to move, sweep forward yelling, rifles spurted hot flame, mehari camels came racing under a billow of ghostly cloaks, wheeling fast around the wall with the town as a paralyzed hub.

Those were the Touareg riders, the savage Forgotten of God, most feared of desert warriors. At the same signal every blessed Moslem in the town had drawn his knife to smite the town from the inside. The Touareg poured in through shattered gates. Biskra blew up before the Legion had even smelled the powder.

No moment for that little comedy in the opera house to stand around and argue social etiquette. *Jamais de la vie!* The town was roaring like a blast furnace by the time we got to the doors of that casino, and our frantic officers rushed us in a tangled, screaming mob to the barracks and firing steps. Negro Tirailleurs, Spahi cavalrymen, Legionnaires ran through the streets like mice in a box trying to get to their posts.

Every rooftop of every Arab house was rattling like a cornpopper. There was a blockhouse at the east gate, and by the sound of gunfire it was a red-hot corner. A vast pall of black smoke boiled up to the stars along the west wall where the Legion dogs were fighting; the west gate was a red hole in the dark; the Touareg were rushing through in mobs, and it was every man for himself.

Dead men were already littering the crooked streets between the casino and the Legion barracks. Balls of white smoke nested in the date palms and Lebel rifles made a red lacework through the dark. I remember running like a fool in a mob of squalling officers and men; and finding myself in the heart of battle much too soon for comfort.

The western wall was a holocaust. Legionnaires and Arabs hung, sprawled, dangled and fought hand to hand on the parapets. Bayonets knitted and flashed in fogs of smoke. Sabers and scimitars clanged in every dusky shadow.

The barracks were making a bonfire along one end of the drill field, and in the wild flame-light Legionnaires and Touareg riflemen hurled themselves at each other and shocked atop piles of dead. *Sacré Dieu,* it was a charming springtide scene.

I yanked a rifle from a corpse's fingers and found myself kneeling in a blue line, pouring hot lead at a gray line that moved forward with the slow, booming, unstoppable crush of surf. Crash! Crash! Volley after volley, and that gray tide came on; boiled up over the wall and came on. The Legionnaires couldn't hold ten minutes against that ocean of Saharan fiends. *Non!* The Legionnaires on the west edge of Biskra held for an hour. Then a captain with his hands pressed to the pit of his stomach came sprinting through bullets and fire and smoke and told us to fall back.

WE fell back into the middle of town, hop, skip and jump through the maze of bazaars and streets where the smoke writhed in fat twists from every window and Arab rats on the rooftops lay on their bellies and sniped at unlucky Christians down on the curb. In the dark and din with the bullets whistling through the air from every direction the streets of that town were unfamiliar as the lanes of heaven and dangerous as the walks of hell.

I remember finding myself in the middle of a squad of comrades, retreating up Rue Saint where the statue of Cardinal Lavigerie stands as a monument to piety and peace on the public square. The monument to piety and peace was now the center of a most unholy conflict with a bunch of Arab dogs kiyiying around the cardinal's marble skirts and throwing knives into each white face that rounded the corner.

The Legionnaires with me began to topple. The rest of us fixed bayonets and charged the embattled statue. A Spahi on a roan horse galloped around a corner squalling something I didn't hear. My bayonet was stuck, and by the time I yanked it loose it was only to fling around and find myself without comrades in the middle of that raving street, surrounded by a swarm of hooded cobras who chopped at me with curved knives.

There I was, ragged and panting and lonely on that slippery curb, hemmed in by wolverines; and there across the street was a little blue door standing ajar under a balcony—a door with the hand of Fatima painted over the knob. The hand of Fatima painted on a door is supposed to make it lucky. I fought through the mêlée, spraying bullets like a garden sprinkler; made for that door like a rabbit going home. *Fichtre!* Just as I put my hand on the knob the door flew inward and two figures came flying out in a gust of cinders and wood-smoke, and almost knocked me kicking in the dust.

The first figure was a tall lieutenant of the Legion with one arm in a bloodied sling, his face seared blue as a girl's writing paper and every button torn from his tunic. Rushing from the door, he knocked me aside, and so was the recipient of a dagger that had been meant for me. The knife flashed down from an upper window, zok! and caught that officer hilt-deep in the chest. He clawed at his chin, spun about-face twice, and dropped in the gutter with a crash.

So the girl who had been running behind him stumbled on his legs with a cry, and fell to the cobbles and tore her white gown to the knee. Name of a name! I got to her at a bound; then her arms were around my neck and a terror-whitened face, pressed against my shoulder, filled my boots with ice, and my heart stood still.

"Save me!" the faint voice cried. "Oh, please. I'm lost. Run!" Turn me into a pepper mill! It was the daughter of Colonel Froissart!

BISKRA was a nightmare; and the girl and I ran. I do not know how we got through that blattering *cul-de-sac,* up one lane, down another, through alleys where guns barked and Moslems yowled, over walls and across roofs and past Limbo. I was too stunned to know anything. Once I'd been warming a bench in a theater and this girl had been a stately star in heaven with her father, the commandant. A crazy Yankee Legionnaire had broken up the show by firing his hat into her beautiful lap, next second the town had been struck by a hurricane; now the daughter of a colonel was clinging to my arm and

I was marooned with her in the exact center of hell. Guns were slamming on every hand; marauding Arab gangs were racing after us; I did not know where to turn.

"Where is your father, the colonel?" I screamed at her as we fled. "Where are the officers?"

Beneath the cloud of her loosened black hair her face was ivory lit by eyes like stars. "I do not know. Officers—father—took the women to the blockhouse at the east gate. But they feared the blockhouse would fall; sent the women elsewhere to hide. Father sent me with Lieutenant Gironde. We were to hide in that house back there—with a Moslem who was father's friend. We got there to find the Moslem already slain—the house in flames—"

I did not know where we were or where the east gate was. All I knew is a vast noise came traveling up the smoking alley behind us, and looking over my shoulder I saw a batch of devils bearing down on us with a speed that curled my singed beard. Savage brown faces under bobbing turbans. Fists waving bright knives. How those fiends screamed when they sighted the girl.

I stood long enough to get a couple of them in my gun-sights; walloped a salvo to hold them back; then tightened my arm about the girl's slim waist and told her to run as she had never run before. Thank God she held up like a veteran. If she had fainted in that alley we would have been murdered most immediately.

I got her up over a trellis and around the corner of a pink wall and we raced through a dark grove of date palms. The town was crashing and wailing around our ears as we fled across a cobblestone square where a dead Touareg lay like a bundle of soiled laundry. By the looks of the rubbish strewn around the Legionnaires had retreated across the square. And that Arab mob was on our heels. And we had come smack up against the portals of a shadowy building that loomed like a quiet back-eddy in the wake of a tempest.

"In there!" I squalled, pointing out a door under an archway. "Nobody here. Come on!" There was no place else to take that girl. I slammed a kick, and the wooden door whipped open, and I ran her to a dark flight of steps that led into a tower. The screams of our pursuers faded out on those cool stairs; and we rushed up the steps, gasping.

The stairs kept corkscrewing up and up, and we might have been ascending to the moon. Let me tell you, we were. We got to the top of the stairs, skipped through a narrow door and stumbled out on an open balcony high above the town, the rooftops of Biskra crackling and smoking far below and the big white springtime moon smiling right over our heads.

I could have kicked myself for a fool.

I crouched down and fingered my Lebel and looked at the colonel's daughter and was sick. That balcony faced the east and it was shaped like a crescent and ten feet wide. It was a seventy foot drop to the cobbles below and if the Arab dogs climbed the tower we were trapped like birds in a nest. Do you know where I had led that girl? Bones of the Little Corporal! I got a shock when I realized it. We were in the minaret of the big Moslem mosque. Up there in the prayer tower which was the precise soul of Islam!

CHAPTER III.

YANKEE BILL THE DEVIL.

A **CHANTING** like the din of a forest fire sailed up from the town spread below that minaret; and I looked at that beautiful girl beside me and the sweat wept out of my forehead. If those Arab dogs caught her—

"Courage, *mademoiselle*," I croaked at her. "We are safe—"

"My father!" she whispered, huddling down against the stone rail of that prayer nest. Her satin gown was torn, her cheeks smeared and her hair down about her shoulders; but her face was wonderful in the moonlight, and Helen of Troy would have been a hussy by comparison, even then.

"The commandant will be all right," I chattered, petting her hand foolishly. "By the sound of gunfire, the garrison has retired to the blockhouse. The Arabs cannot take the place in a week. You will be safe up here. The Moslems will never think to look for us here and it will not be long till sunrise—"

Sunrise! I could have pinched my tongue out for that remark. At sunrise the Arab priests would be climbing this minaret to sing their prayers. "At dawn I will try to go for help," I lied hurriedly. "Don't cry—"

"For myself I am not afraid," that lady returned. "Do you know this—this is the first really thrilling adventure I've ever had. Like a story." Her blue eyes shone like candles, and her words made my mouth hang open.

"I overheard father's staff officers say that a regiment of Spahis is to march through the mountains in the east at dawn. So close. But they pass beyond a ridge on their way to Algiers and will never see us. There is no way of sending for help because we're simply surrounded by Touaregs. Isn't it like—like a novel? Oh, if there was only some way to send for aid—"

Like a novel! Thrilling! And the town below us howling like a slaughter pen and somewhere down there an Arab mob baying blood anthems as they hunted us. I stared at the girl, pop-eyed. Lucky for her she didn't know just how thrilling her situation was.

"Be brave," I encouraged her. "Nobody saw us enter this cursed mosque—"

"Wrong again, my comrade," was the reply.

But that basso voice never came from the girl. *Sapristi!* It spoke right out of the moonlight and flung me around on my heel like a kick in the spine. I guess my eyes popped then. Popped at that monster conjured on the tower stairs while my back had been turned. A monster gargoyle, standing there on the threshold of the minaret balcony. The face smudged with grime, fiendish with a tiger's grin, Satanic with a bushing black beard. The eyes glowing like electric bulbs. A pointed, red witch's hat on its head. A scarlet cloak blowing on the shoulders. Muscle-slabbed legs encased in crimson silk tights; and mammoth, floppy red leather boots on the feet.

The wind blew out of my collapsed chest. On my word of honor, I was staring at the Devil from "Faust"! The demon *Mephisto* of the opera! But worse. For in its massive fist this terror brandished a gigantic Arabian scimitar; a sickle-shaped chopping blade twelve inches in width; a monstrous five foot cleaver that gleamed in the dusk like a silver slice pared from the moon above.

NO wonder the girl stepped backwards with a scream. I guess I screamed on my own accord. I yanked a piccolo shriek out of my windpipe, and flung my Lebel to my shoulder. But the terrific apparition was quicker. Moreover, it was not a dream. The unbelievable scimitar lashed through the moonlight; came down *zaff!* like a ton of lightning. The rifle flew from my torn fingers; went spinning over the stone rail of the balcony.

A bludgeon of knuckles smote me in the mouth. Roman candles sparked before my eyes, and I floated five kilometers through darkness and hit in a corner.

A giant bunch of iron fingers trapped my wrists; my sash was ripped from my waist; before I could get off a prayer to my patron saint my hands were fastened behind my back. You will never guess what happened in the minaret above the embattled town, then. You will not!

I was hoisting my weak frame into a sitting posture, my head spinning like a roulette wheel and all prepared for decapitation, when my ears heard a voice that flattened me to the stone again.

"Félice," said the grinning red demon, "I've come for you."

The demon grabbed its black beard. The whiskers were snatched away. A jubilant guffaw burst from the beardless, battered face under the red witch's hat. Meet a big American Legionnaire. It was, you comprehend, Yankee Bill the Elephant.

Sapristi! I had completely forgotten this comrade of the barracks of mine, and maybe you think I did not yell when I saw him in this fantastic masquerade. Besides loosening all my front teeth he had neatly bound my hands behind my back with my blue *cummerbund;* and I yelled like a fool when I recognized Yankee Bill in that outlandish opera costume.

Colonel Froissart's daughter cried out, too. She had been standing against the rail of the minaret prayer-box, one hand at her throat. When Yankee Bill pulled off that set of false whiskers and bowed with a wide grin, the colonel's daughter went wild-eyed with amazement.

"You!" she panted.

The giant swept off the witch's hat with a courtly gesture. "To have and to hold, my dear. You see, Félice," he was grinning from ear to ear, "clothes don't make the man; what's in a uniform, and all that sort of thing. Papa Froissart got sore at me just because I ain't wearin' epaulets an' gold braid. The Arabs would butcher me if I had on a soldier suit. You didn't like me because I didn't wear fancy evening clothes. But in a devil's rig maybe I can come to terms."

A rattle of gunfire sounding like riveting hammers on iron girders drifted up from the streets below the minaret on a smell of powder. The battle cry of the Beni M'zab, the screams of the attacking Touareg cameleers, the pop, crack, fizz and shuffle of exploding rifles, *chaut-chaut* guns and pounding boots surged up to that minaret from every quarter of the town spread below. Mingled with the radiant spring moonlight, those battle echoes were unreal as an opium eater's fancy. Not half as unreal, however, as that giant American appearing on the minaret balcony in those tights and togs.

"Yankee Bill," I cawed. "What in the name of—"

I WRENCHED at my knotted wrists, blurting and sweating. The big American bathed me with a merry and tolerant grin; moved his fantastic red boots to the middle of the balcony, planted them wide apart, folded his hands on the hilt of the horrendous scimitar, leaned his chin on his knuckles and lounged at ease for all the world like an executioner lounging on his ax.

"Don't worry, Corday old pig," he chuckled. "I know you. Sorry I had to larrup you, comrade, but you almost gave me a powder burn. Just sit tight where I put you; don't move an' keep your face closed. I'll see you get out of this easy. Meantime, it's the lady I'm calling on."

He tilted that witch's hat to a coy angle on his black scalp, and fixed on the colonel's daughter a cool grin. His blue eyes were brilliant with the quintessence of delightful insanity. He was as nonchalant as a man lighting a cigarette in an advertisement—one would have thought this a pretty little Mardi Gras byplay; and I caterwauled at him like a sick tabby.

"You've got to get us out of this," I howled. "The Arabs. They're after us. They're after the girl—"

He laughed. Laughed and jerked a thumb over his thick shoulder. "I know, old grasshopper. The whole tribe is at the foot of the stairs, right now. That's why I got to talk fast with Félice, here. Can't hold those wolves down there too long. Saw you two hiking for this mosque, an' I joined the chase." A grin of merriment bisected his face.

"Them Arabs think I'm the Devil from Gehenna, get it? When Papa Froissart got sore at me back there at the opera—two years in the stone quarries, can you beat it?—I had to light out quick; go on pump. I was just goin' out the back way when I heard the alarm. Saw this rubbish lyin' in a dressing room, and hopped into it. Some make-up, eh? Arabs think I'm Old Evil Eye, himself, come to bless their revolt. This rig works like a charm. I just told that bunch to stay below in the mosque an' stay quiet or I'd whisk 'em all to hell. They're scairt stiff of me. But I got to work fast. Those babes are out for blood, an' won't hold back for long. Quick, now. It's up to Félice—"

She stepped swiftly forward, moving from shadow into moonlight, a marble naiad brought to life in a rage. One silken knee shimmered through the rent in her gown, and her cheeks flamed pink as she stooped to pin the rent with a quick hand. Then she gave her black hair a toss and looked up at the grinning Yankee giant with eyes that shone dazzling fury.

"Up to me, you dog? What is this absurd folly? How dare you stare at me so? How—how dare you address me by my familiar name? Let me warn you, you shall pay for your base conduct, and your effrontery at the opera, too, when you get me out of this. Now get me down those steps and lead your Arab ruffians away, you hear? You're going to take me and this poor soldier you've assaulted back to Colonel Froissart; and there's a regiment of Spahis going to pass through the mountains in the east—"

"The Spahis won't come to your rescue," Yankee Bill wagged his head. "They won't see us. An' there's no need to shout, Félice. The Arabs know you're up here in their minaret. I told 'em I'd bring you down an' take you off with me. You see," he grinned, "I told 'em my wife was up here. They think I'm Satan, an' they wouldn't dare touch Satan's wife. Catch on?"

An anthem of savage yells drifted up through the tower and hung little icicles in the moonlight on the balcony. But the girl didn't seem to hear. Fists clenched at her sides, she faced Yankee Bill and gave him a withering stare. "A hateful scheme, I assure you," she told him. "Then quick with it, and get us out of this wretched tower. And please remember that to common dogs such as you I am always *Mademoiselle* Froissart!"

A bland grin spread on the American's face and he scratched his big chin lazily on the back of his knuckles, spread his legs wider apart and stood at ease as if he had all the time in the world. "But you'll be *Mrs.* to me," he told her, "because I gave them Arabs my word that I'd bring my wife down from this balcony; an' I'm going to keep my promise. Didn't I tell you back at the opera I loved you? Why? Because I could see in your eye you loved me, too, Félice. Why," the Yankee chuckled, leaning on that scimitar and crossing two fingers and holding them in front of the girl's white face, "why, we're just like that, you and me. Or I'd never have told those Arab hyenas it was my wife I was comin' for up here."

CHAPTER IV.

THE SLAP.

WASN'T THAT girl mad then? Wow! She struck the Yankee's fingers down with a slap, and scathed him with all the scorn of all the scorning women in history put together. "Ineffable boor! You low Legion dog, you. You dare—dare stand there and suggest, even suggest to me that I—"

"He only fools," I screeched from my corner. "In this danger he but tries to calm us with a jest. Yankee Bill," I wheedled at him, "in the name of Heaven, stop this flummery and get us out of here. Those Moslem dogs—" I choked. I was hysterical. Any minute those Arab fiends might take it into their heads to come raving up to the balcony, and Yankee Bill stood there teasing the girl as if time and tide were going to wait for everybody.

"But I'm not fooling," he protested. "Félice and me—"

"Dog!" she screamed. "You detestable scoundrel, you. Do you realize you are imperiling my life, not to say insulting the daughter of your colonel? Do you comprehend that I am the daughter of Colonel Froissart, and—"

"And charming in spite of the inheritance," the giant in the opera costume countered. "I don't hold that against you. When we're married—"

"Married!" the girl gasped. *Oui,* and so did I!

"And have a bunch of kids," the amazing American went on.

"Kids!" You should have heard the girl scream that.

"Sure," agreed Yankee Bill, wrinkling his nose in a gamin smile. "I'd like about ten. Hey, Corday? Put 'em all in the Legion. Now listen, girl, we'd better get started. Out of here, I mean. When we get to Algiers old Corday will be best man."

On my sacred soul, I began to believe that the Elephant meant every word he said. Standing on that muezzin's balcony, grinning as he lounged on that frightful scimitar, the noise of battle reeking down the sky, he talked of marriage and offspring to the daughter of the Legion commandant. Mad? Oh, he was mad, all right. And the daughter of the colonel was mad, also.

You should have seen her in that tarnished satin gown; seen the fire in her eyes as she stood there in the moonlight brushing furious fingers through her blowing hair and bathing that Yankee with punishment and derision. "You dare!" she whispered, in a voice like scalding water. "You *voyou*, you Apache, you ruffian. To the daughter of your colonel you dare voice such abuse. You dreadful—commoner!

"That you could for one second believe the daughter of a colonel, that any French lady of standing would so much as consider an alliance with a pauperized, nameless, nobody soldier in the ranks of the low! Ha ha! I laugh!" (A laugh that froze the boiling water to ice as it came from her clenched white teeth.) "I laugh at you, you cur. What a rancid jest. My father—the proudest family of Avignon. And who, might one pray, was your father, you despicable clown?"

YANKEE BILL never batted an eyelash under that scorching. You bet he didn't. "My father," he interrupted calmly, "was a good scout, girl. He was in the baked bean business in Akron, Ohio, see?"

"Baked beans! Ha! And what might your proud accomplishment in life have been; what splendid bid to aristocracy occupied your mind before—"

"Before I joined this lousy French army I was a pitcher. Baseball, understand? Boston Braves. Some team, too. Good men in the game in them days, girl. Iron Man McGinnity and Homerun Baker and—"

"*Mère de Dieu!*" the disdain of the girl's voice would have shriveled an oak tree. "Wretched fool, you need not give me the names of your gutter-rat friends!"

"They weren't gutter-rats!" Yankee Bill snapped out. "Those boys were aristocrats second to nobody."

"So you abandoned these sterling gentlemen to become a Third Class Legionnaire at a penny a day."

An air-shaking burst of gunfire lit the dark sky, and above the sharp echo the Yankee's voice crackled hot retort. "I ain't a third class soldier, girl, and don't ever forget it. Your old man knows my record. I'm the best heliograph signalman in this rotten army!"

"I'm not *interested* in what you are."

"But, by the Lord, you're going to be. I joined the Legion because I was framed on a gambling deal to throw ball games; me, that loved baseball—framed by a bunch of drawing room muckers with family trees in Boston as long as any French boulevard poodle ever had!

There's your aristocrats, see? Milk-fed pups raised on cushions, an' always turn out to be coyotes. Social background. That's the sort of garbage you want. Well, I want *you!* I don't care about your father, even if he is a fathead who bought his commission in the army. I don't hold him against you, no more should you hold 'family class' against me.

"Sure I'm just a bum Legionnaire. A bum Legionnaire who goes out an' dies for your country an' gives some fat colonel all the credit. I do the fightin'. Yes, I mean me. You'll never get a chance again to marry a *real* man, and Lord knows why I'm giving you the chance. Don't ask me why. I don't like you any better than you like me, but we were just made for each other, get it? You'll promise to marry me right now, or you'll never get off this balcony on *my* shoulder!"

What a speech that was! It came out of the Yankee's muscle-slabbed chest like a salvo from a cannon, and it sent Colonel Froissart's daughter pacing up and down through the moonbeams simply magnificent with rage. She laced that Yankee with a voice like a whip and she heaped his colossus frame with low, brittle, panting, scalding words that smote like pointed darts and ended: "Lowborn cur! Take advantage of a defenseless woman. Just like your cheap kind. Marry you, indeed. A thousand deaths I would rather die. But I shall see you dead for this, my American. Yes! Killed for being the deserter and scoundrel you are. Killed for being a truckling mutineer—"

The Yankee laughed, then. Laughed until tears rolled down his face. "Sure, I'm a mutineer. A mutineer against stupid social rules and monkeys like your father who'd throw a man in prison because he thinks a declaration of love is an insult. I'm a mutineer against the tribe of high-hats who won't give an honest fellow a chance. Yah! You and your old man took advantage of me back there at the opera, didn't you? Two years in the stone quarry? Ha! You ran the works, then. Now *I'm* running the works."

"Swine! Guttersnipe! Brawling common soldier! Boor!"

"Nonsense. I'm an honest, hardworkin' man who's not afraid to own up when he's in love with somebody he can see loves him. A good soldier, who can fight and isn't scared to die, and ain't afraid to break a fool rule—"

SPRINGTIME madness? Sacred stove! it was the balcony of an insane asylum. They were both screaming like children now, face to face, the girl getting whiter, the Yankee getting redder; voices going louder and louder and filling the moonlight on that cursed Moslem balcony with talk of children and baked beans, desertion and marriage and firing squads and social etiquette and mutiny and that game called baseball.

I sat tied in my corner as sweat-wet and silly as Little Jack Horner in some fabulous Mother Goose. The colonel's daughter with her torn satin gown, her fury-whitened face, her blazing eyes and tossing hair. The giant American in those poppycock red tights and flopping boots. The drumroll of gunnery on the late night wind and the baying of Moslem cutthroats in the street. By Saint Jean de Luz's Living Little Finger, there was never such a scene in Mother Goose or Don Juan or any other story. Romeo and Juliet never held a candle to the scene on that minaret balcony in Biskra.

The girl screaming: "Insufferable coward, I hate you, hate you, hate you!"

The Yankee thundering: "You're a little fool. You love me and won't admit it."

The girl screaming: "Rather than marry such as you I would die ten thousand times!"

The Yankee bellowing: "Then you are nothing but a spoiled ninny from a Paris drawing room, and you haven't got the stuff I thought you had!"

"I shall laugh when I see you die. Laugh when they shoot you as a mutineer!"

"I never thought I'd meet such a thick-skulled little fool—"

There was only one way this sort of antic could end—*smack!* Do you guess what that was? That was a slap in a thousand. The girl's raging hand swept out and took that big Legionnaire a stinging crack that left a little hand of fire printed on his cheek. *Sacré Dieu!* Yankee Bill the Elephant turned the color of a brick; threw out a palm as big as an elephant's ear, and *smack!* returned that slap; and the girl staggered back with a hand printed on her face, too. That wild Yankee Legionnaire had signed his death warrant then, if he'd never signed it before. Nothing short of a miracle would save him from court martial and firing squad for that.

And the thing that happened on the heels of those slaps was no miracle. No, it was not! A wild and terrible baying sound rushing up the tower stairway. Lusting yells and the clink of knives and the smash of pounding feet. *"Yah!"* was the cry. *"Yah! Yah! Yah Allaaah!"*

The girl ran to the rail, her face in her hands. I sat in my corner with my tongue hanging out, too frightened to stir a joint. Yankee Bill's crimson cloak made a swirling red cloud in the moonbeams as he spun around, scimitar in his fists. And then came the most stunning smack of all—a finger-snap, and the top step of the stairway to the balcony was wedged with a yowling, grinning, cursing, heaving jell of wicked brown faces, bobbing turbans, glittering eyes and clashing teeth and ringing knives.

Those weren't faces, there. They were devil-photographs, catching Satan in all his most malevolent expressions. I have never seen a wickeder bunch of demons. They scared the moon out of sight down the sky and brought to the minaret a ghostly, greenish dusk.

They pointed crooked fingers and squalled like tigers, and a bugaboo, hunchbacked spider in human form came pushing out of their midst to confront Yankee Bill the Elephant. This spider had a shriveled brown face and eyes like skinned grapes set in purple craters under a shrunken brow. The green turban of a holy man nicely hatted this Prince of Venom; and in one hairy fist he waved a needle-thin knife that gleamed in the dusk like a curse.

CHAPTER V.

THE SCIMITAR'S EDGE.

"**GO BACK!**" howled Yankee Bill. *Sapristi!* didn't he howl. He clutched that death-edged crescent in his fists, and glared at the spider that stood in the cobwebs of dusk spun on the balcony stair. "Go back, Habib ben Habib, lest my lightning smite thy brainless head from thy throat as the sickle shears the lemon from the bush!"

The Arabic threat scissored from the American's teeth, and brought a laugh trickling out of the Moslem leader's mouth. "Sons of Islam!" The spider shrieked and pointed at Yankee Bill. "Look, the jackal has fooled you. See the false beard at his feet! The man is naught but a *feringi*. Attack him, my brothers. Get the white girl!"

The desert-spawned demons saw the fake whiskers lying where the Yankee had thrown them, and squalled to Allah. The spider shot his fist at the sky. The needle made a flash in the gloom, *zing!* It whistled from the Arab's hand and shot through Yankee Bill's witch hat like an arrow and vanished out into the air. With a screech, the hunchback followed the needle, hurling himself at Yankee Bill's chest. The pack on the top step broke with a yowl; launched a hollering charge.

I told you that prayer balcony was shaped like a crescent, facing the east. The minaret was like the mast of a ship and that prayer-box was like a big crow's nest hanging seventy feet above the street. Colonel Froissart's daughter and I crouched at one end of the balcony and those mad Arabs poured from the door at the other end like rats coming up out of a hole, and between the rats and us was nothing except Yankee Bill with the world's biggest scimitar in his hands.

"Keep back!" he screamed at us. "Hold her in the corner, Corday. Keep her head down; I'll handle these butchers—"

His voice was drowned by the screams of the butchers; and I saw his scimitar leap up from the floor in a terrible swipe. The blade flashed *zap!* and the spidery holy man went tumbling in a scarlet shower. The lemon was sheared from the bush, let me tell you. A roar tore out of the Yankee's teeth and he whisked that giant knife to cut those leaping Arabs down in a row. They fell back shrieking oaths. They didn't want to get near that scimitar. But Yankee Bill had slain their leader, and those dogs were mighty mad. They had glimpsed the girl, too; and they wanted that girl. The mob on the stairs was pushing upward in a frenzy, and the first-comers charged once again.

"Come on!" the American screamed at them. "Come on, dogs, and die!" They danced at him, and he drove them back with a charge of his own. Swinging his mammoth blade, he charged. Swinging that blade until it made a wheel of light above his head. Cut, slash, parry and zaff.

Blood flew in the dusk. A ghastly uproar boiled up from the minaret. Shrieks and the clash of knives. Screams for Allah and screams for breath. The howls of the devils in the tower as they tried to get up the stairs. The shrieks of the devils on the balcony as they tried to get Yankee Bill. The screams of Yankee Bill, and the screams of the girl who had her arms around my neck, and my own screams.

I CROUCHED in a bath of ice and I screamed at the girl to untie my wrists. She was all right, that lady. She did not faint, and that balcony was a picture of hell to shred the nerves of an Amazon. Her fingers tore at the bindings on my hands, but she couldn't loose those knots the Yankee had tied. I could hear her breathing in pathetic little spasms.

She knew that big mutineer was done for. So did I. Sooner or later one of those knife-waving devils would dance in and stab him down. Against that mob he didn't have the chance of a lottery ticket in the National. The Arabs knew it, and rushed like inspired wolves. The only one who did not seem to know it was Yankee Bill.

Sacred stove! how that Yankee was fighting. Laughing wild shouts, whipping his terrible steel edged paddle, he faced those squalling Arabs and dared them to come by five hundreds. If the stairway had not been narrow they would have come in one drowning flood; but they tangled and shrieked and fell over each other, and the chopping scimitar hacked them backwards and piled them up on the top step like cordwood.

I raved. I fought at my bonds and the girl fought at my bonds and Yankee Bill fought in a clawing, shrieking kaleidoscope of cloth and hands and knives and legs back and across the balcony's end. The Arabs whirled about him, striking at him with daggers, cleavers and axes. Crimson rivulets began to ripple down his face. A gash opened at one corner of his mouth. His fists bled at the knuckles. His red cape flew in ribbons. Teeth clenched, trumpet yells blaring from his lungs, he thrashed his mammoth scimitar and never gave an inch.

The sun rolled up out of the east to see the pogrom. A hot ball of glowing sulphur wheeling along the horizon. The sky paled from sick blue to chrome. A blasting heat settled on the minaret. The balcony rocked with din. And when that sun lit the sky, the Yankee rocked the balcony with the loudest shout of all.

"Sunrise!"

I will never forget how that blast burst from his mouth; how the eyes in his head blazed like polished obsidian; how he fought *then!* That glowing sunshine seemed to strengthen the muscles of his arms. The scimitar flashed like a livid white flame. In the sunshine he twirled that dreadful mace until the blade was white fire, red fire, blue fire.

Have you ever seen a drum major juggle a baton? Child's play compared to that Yankee and his scimitar. What a blade. It dipped and blazed and dripped. It flashed and rang. He twirled it over his head, held it poised a second in the sun, flung it high and swung it high, tossed it skyward and caught it and piled those Arabs up like crushed strawberries and dared them to come by the million. The

Norwegian thunder god, Thor, never wig-wagged his lightning the way Yankee Bill the Elephant wagged his scimitar. Down it would crash—red! Up it would whistle—silver!

I tell you, the flash of sunshine on that blade would have blinded the eyes of an acetylene-welder. I know. A dagger had sizzled from a Moslem's fist, missed the Yankee and bounced on the stone rail behind the girl; and she had snatched the knife and slashed free my hands. I jumped to my feet, and the blaze of that big blade struck me in the eyes so I could not see to dodge the club that smashed me in the face.

Jehovah had punched me! I flopped down as useless as a mummy. That pelt in the face did something to my legs. I couldn't move them. I wanted to move them, I promise you. For just as I went down, Yankee Bill went down, too. A stiletto, skimming up those Arab-jammed stairs, had slammed into Yankee Bill's collar bone. I heard the *thud;* saw his knees begin to buckle. Slowly he went down, like a chimney starting to topple. The colors of the rainbow fled across his razored face. On his knees he balanced, heaving, lunging, tired. Muscles bulged in red-spattered slabs on his arms and back. Vermilion soap bubbles blew from the hilt of the dagger that bent him low. The deadly wheel of the scimitar went slower and more slow.

A BLOOD-FREEZING shriek of triumph went up from the Arabs. Squalling, they rushed. Chin wedged on his chest, head bowing as if sleepy, the smitten giant strove to drive them off. A curved blade hacked his forearm, and the polish went from his eyes. Sheeted demons fell on him like wolves on a scrap. Robes billowing and knives sparking in the hot sun as the big blade foundered out of sight. In a howling goulash of Arab bodies the Yankee disappeared.

Me? I was wailing my lungs raw. The girl made a soft weight, clinging to me, soundless. Thank God she had fainted at last. She never saw those gargoyle Moslems come bounding across the balcony to get her.

It was time for Gabriel to blow his horn in the sky, and it was not pleasant to lie there and hear him blowing it. Gabriel's horn? Listen! Those wolves of the Beni M'zab had just reached my corner of the balcony when a trumpet blast went off like the crack of doom. Bugles! *Oui!* Brazen, blaring bugles piercing the din with brassy notes that stopped those Moslems in their tracks. A noose of fierce, brass music that coiled up to the minaret and dropped on the necks of those Arab fiends and held them in startled tableau.

A splintering crash of gunfire burst in the street below the mosque. Wild shrieks came sailing up the tower stairs. A rattle of pistols and the crash of iron-studded cavalry boots. It was Gabriel's horn, all right. It blasted straight up the minaret stairway and burst like a firework on that bloody balcony of prayers. Like a story? *Mère de Dieu,* I should say so. For presently I was standing in a group of French officers with sky-blue tunics and bright brass buttons and smoking pistols in their hands. Spahis! French cavalrymen! And I heard a faint cry: "Father!" and saw a frail, slim figure in white clasped in the arms of a fierce-faced Legion commandant who swore.

I sat down again because I could not help it. In the face of a miracle one cannot be expected to stand, even for superior officers. The balcony swam weirdly before my eyes. But the miracle had not happened yet. Attend.

CHAPTER VI.

THE MIRACLE.

"**YOU COULD** not kill this specimen," the Spahi captain growled, "if you blew it from the mouth of a Napoleon gun. Give me some more adhesive tape from that kit, lieutenant. By my bones, it will take all the bandage in Africa. So. As beautiful a piece of carving as I have ever seen. *Bien!*"

The Spahi captain looked pleased with his ministrations, wiped his hands on his tunic and sighed up from his knees. There was movement in the half-naked hulk that lay on the stained floor of the muezzin's balcony. A sigh struggled out of the bandaged chest. One white-taped arm stirred. The features on the scratched and bandaged face assumed a sort of smile. An eye opened. A very bright, very blue eye. The captain of Spahis touched the recumbent mass of bandaged muscles with the toe of his cavalry boot.

"See. What can knives do to such a man? He does not know when he is dead."

The officers in blue and brass moved closer. In the town the guns had ceased. Blatant sunshine, pouring hot and brilliant down on the minaret, stifled the balcony. For a moment there was only the sound of breathing and the sound of flies going to lunch on the tower stairs.

In the broiling silence Yankee Bill hunched his muscles and sat upright. His cobalt eyes traveled the ring of faces looking down at him. His slashed and scissored countenance split in a tremendous grin.

"Good morning, *messieurs*—"

"Tough," said the Spahi captain, "as a camel's foot."

"Glad you got here," grinned Yankee Bill the Elephant. "Say. It was close. Hello, there's Félice. Beautiful as ever. Sorry I slapped your face, Félice—"

"He is recovering," said the Spahi captain with a determined nod. "What did I tell you? The American will live."

Yankee Bill the Elephant laughed hoarsely. "What made you think I wouldn't, *mon capitaine?*"

"You will live, all right!" The snarl came from the thin lips of one Colonel Froissart of the French Foreign Legion. Colonel Froissart's face was purple as a cabbage and the little sparks of anger flew from his eyes. The saber, askew at his belt, clinked savagely as he strode forward to push a trembling fist in front of the Yankee's nose.

"Oh, you will live, my fine Yankee. *Oui!* Mutineer that you are! Deserter! Throw your little hat into my daughter's lap, will you? Try to kidnap the daughter of your commandant, eh? Slap her face, too, is that it? Oh, I heard all about it," Colonel Froissart screamed, "and I do not care a fig for what you have done. Maybe you think the fight you waged up here is going to let you off! Well, my *zig,* let me tell you Colonel Froissart is not one to do away with regulations!

"If you think you are going to get away with this you are sadly in error, my fine hero. You know what happens to Legionnaires who resist their officers and desert in war time. Ha! You will live, all right. You will live just long enough," the colonel shouted, "to march out in front of the firing squad and pay the penalty for mutiny and desertion. You will live just long enough to be *shot!*"

The harsh command crackled out in the sunshine and was echoed by a cry. It was a streak of white that went like a wind past my shoulder and blew through that cordon of officers. And there was the daughter of Colonel Froissart on her knees beside that battered and grinning Yankee bandit. *Oui!* and her marble face was glistening with tears and her arms were around that chuckling giant's plastered shoulder and she was mothering his black head against her breast.

"No, no!" she was crying, her blue eyes fierce as a tigress, or I am a pepper mill. "No, no. You cannot shoot him! You cannot," she sobbed, "because he is *mine!* And I love him. I love him!"

Along the eastern wall of Biskra where the Touareg lay like harvested mounds of springtime wheat the bugles were playing.

OLD Thibaut Corday, the ancient veteran of *La Légion Étrangère,* settled back in his chair with a gentle laugh. "I told you," he pointed out, grinning, "that nothing short of a miracle would save that astonishing American maniac who had mutinied, slapped, jeered, laughed at and broken all the rules. That was the miracle, my friend—and that is always the miracle. Love. Love, the twin brother of Madness. Love, that looks so much like Hate. You should have seen that pair in the church at Algiers. You should have seen me as best man. You had better make plans for a house and a marriage license," the old man chuckled, "when a woman slaps your face."

Sentiment was all right, and I could believe the psychology, too. But I wanted a little practicality in this romance.

"Look here, Corday," I protested. "It's all very fine to have it work out right in the end, but what I want to know is why did those French Spahis who were supposed to be marching beyond the mountain east of Biskra—why did they suddenly come rushing to help in the nick of time? You said they wouldn't be in sight of the outpost," I accused, "and you said there was absolutely no way of sending for help."

The ancient soldier wagged his heard. "*Pas de tout.* I said there was no way for a Legionnaire in that surrounded town to go for help. But I made very careful to remind you that Yankee Bill the Elephant had been enlisted with the heliograph, the signal corps.

"Uncle of old Satan! that is what came out later. Those lovely cavalrymen marching innocently to Algiers had seen a veritable sign in the sky to the west.

"A flash and a glitter in the dusk beyond the sunrise. But look! A code signal. A glimmering wink of light that blinks for help. Sacred Aunt! it is a flash such as might come from a heliograph mirror or a giant scimitar whipped on a high balcony to catch the shine of the dawn." Old Thibaut Corday dug into his faded tunic with a faded hand and extracted from his shirt a faded paper.

"I told you that American was a splendid Legionnaire," he chuckled. "Can you imagine, *non?* Battling those devils in that minaret, winning the heart of the girl who was his colonel's daughter, and topping this insanity by flashing a call for help with his five-foot blade? That was the something which made the loud crash in North

Africa.

"For the next six solid years the Legion talked of nothing else. Then take a look at this."

He handed me the faded paper. It proved to be a photograph. Soiled but discernible; undoubtedly the prideful picture of a father with triplets mobbing his arm and a mother surrounded by a small battalion of littler ones. Old Thibaut Corday parted his beard with a laugh.

"And there is the echo that is heard in New York this very day."

THEODORE ROSCOE

THE **EDITOR** of *Argosy* has called on me to mount the stage first person. I feel a little as I did the night I staggered up the gangway of my first real ship—a low-hung, black, gloomy oil tanker lying in at Constable Hook. A big sailor from Texas guarded the head of the gangway. His mouth was stuffed with cut plug, his shirt was stuffed with muscles. His crooked nose gleamed in the lamplight. He boasted a skeptical cockeye. He looked to me like Long John Silver, Cap'n Kidd and Jack the Ripper candied into one. His cock-eye watched my landsman's struggle to climb the gangway.

"Wal, naow," came his wicked drawl, "if here ain't another one of them rod-rammed college boys!"

No; I didn't feel so big. Not so big.

Later that Texan and I became friends. He showed me how to start a monkey's fist, paint without leaving "holidays," loaf when the bos' wasn't looking, and drink the Mexican *tequila* otherwise burned in lamps. The seaman's ticket I snared on that trip will never let the wanderlust expire.

This wanderlust is inherited. My grandfather spent his life in India. My mother was born in the Himalaya Mountains near Nepal and could speak Hindu before she spoke English. When she was twenty-four she journeyed alone—a white woman with a party of native hillmen—down the dangerous borders of Tibet. At the same age my father beat a trail into the Orient to teach in a business college at Lucknow. Later he rocked down the Straits of Malacca to Singapore, back up Malaya to India, met my mother in a mango grove near Delhi—and their youngest son, Theodore, was born in Rochester, New York, United States of America!

However, an early escape could be managed. Had started writing.

In fact, at the sorry age of seven I wrote, bound, printed and illustrated my first novel. It was called *The Adventures of the Devil and Jim, the Knight*. At ten years I assailed a more scholarly work: *The Sheriff of Red Rock Ranch*. My spelling was weak. I consulted my two older brothers on most of the words. The word "rock" had defeated me. They spelled it for me behind grins. The volume came out titled *The Sheriff of Red Roach Ranch*. It is still a family jest.

Have been writing and misspelling words ever since. This gave me the chance to be footloose. After the trip on the tanker, went to France. Unfortunately was too young to enlist, but saw enough battlefields and cemeteries and blind Frenchmen to realize something of the Grim Game. Spent some time in Paris and Marseilles. Back to take a run into Canada. Saw something of Texas. Over to Madeira and the Canary Islands. Traipsed across Spain a-ways, but didn't see a bullfight. Back to Paris. One day in Ireland. Down to Morocco. Along the Mediterranean for a look at Gibraltar and into Algeria to see *La Légion Etrangère*. Down to Biskra for awhile to see the Ouled Naïl and a stretch of the desert. Back to the States for a bar of soap. Off to the British West Indies and the Caribbean.

That's about the way it goes, with intervals in Rochester and New York to tell the tale. Like best to write about Mohammedans, Hindus and Frenchmen, and I hope to see Siam some day soon. Also like the sea. Having appeared in just thirteen fiction magazines, am getting superstitious. Am unmarried (beautiful lady readers please copy) and hovering under twenty-five. Sold my hundredth yarn the other day to *Argosy*. I hope that first hundred was the hardest. If my indulgent reader-friends in *Argosy* have enjoyed reading 'em as much as I've enjoyed writing them—why, *Allah yeseemliq!*

PULPMASTER:

THE THEODORE ROSCOE STORY

AUDREY PARENTE

FOREWORD BY THEODORE ROSCOE

THE ALLURE OF FRENCH FOREIGN LEGIONNAIRE
THIBAUT CORDAY'S ADVENTURES FLOWED
FROM THE PEN OF THEODORE ROSCOE. EXOTIC
TALES FROM A DUSKY OUTPOST UNFOLDED IN
GLOSSY-COVERED 10-CENT MAGAZINES, BEFORE
TELEVISION. HUNDREDS OF ROSCOE'S YARNS,
PUBLISHED ON CHEAP PULP PAPER UNRAVELED
MYSTERIES, IMMORTALIZED HOMETOWN
HEROES AND STIRRED THE IMAGINATION OF A
GENERATION. IN REAL LIFE, ROSCOE STOWED
ABOARD TRAMP STEAMERS AND MINGLED WITH
LOCALS IN FAR AWAY CORNERS. HIS INTRIGUING
STYLE LATER ECHOED IN NON-FICTION WORKS,
WHEN HE WAS AMONG THE FIRST TO VIEW
DECLASSIFIED LINCOLN ASSASSINATION
DOCUMENTS AND WHEN HE DOCUMENTED
HISTORIC AMERICAN MILITARY OPERATIONS.
JOURNALIST AUDREY PARENTE BECAME STEEPED
IN AMERICAN PULP HISTORY WHEN SHE LIVED
BLOCKS AWAY FROM ROSCOE IN ORMOND BEACH,
FLORIDA, WHERE SHE CHRONICLED HIS LIFE FOR
THIS BOOK.

6327913R00127

Printed in Great Britain
by Amazon.co.uk, Ltd.,
Marston Gate.